Mason's Missing

A Tuper Mystery

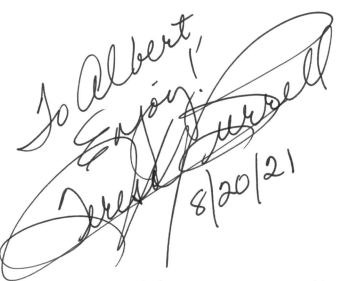

by Teresa Burrell

Silent Thunder Publishing

San Diego

MASON'S MISSING
A Tuper Mystery
Copyright 2017 by
Teresa Burrell

All rights reserved.
Cover Art by Madeline Settle
Edited by Marilee Wood

Library of Congress Number 2017913446
ISBN: 978-1-938680-23-6

Silent Thunder Publishing
San Diego

Dedication

To my brother, Phil Johnson, who always made me feel so special when I was a child. I'll never forget the little (and the big) things you did for me. I remember when you made us the monkey bar: the many weeks you spent whittling on the tree branch to make it smooth as glass so we wouldn't get slivers when we twirled on it; the many times you took a risk and shot prey out of season so our family could eat; and your teaching me to play cards and to observe the telltale signs of others while they played—all the important things in life.

This is for the many hours of joy and laughter you have brought our sisters and me over the years. You are loved more than you know.

And about that promise you made when I was five years old: to make me foreman of your junkyard when I grew up. Well, I'm grown up and still waiting.

You will always be my Tuper.

Acknowledgements

A special thanks to those who helped
make this book possible.

Bucky Crouch
Jerome Johnson
Phil Johnson
Clarice Preece
Alex Velasquez

My Amazing Beta Readers

Beth Sisel Agejew
Joy Almond
Vickie Barrier
Nancy Barth
Jill Parseghian
Rodger Peabody
Lily Qualls Morales
Colleen Scott
Nikki Tomlin
Brad Williams
Denise Zendel

OTHER BOOKS BY TERESA

THE ADVOCATE SERIES

CHAPTER ONE

The last time five-year-old Mason Jenkins was seen was when he dashed out of his kindergarten class at the end of the school day. It was the first day of class following winter break. As usual, most parents had parked and come to the school door to meet their children, but a few stayed with their cars, lined up along the street, waiting for the kids to come to them.

Ms. Stiles, their teacher, had just experienced her first day of teaching. She had replaced a teacher who had taken ill, and she was overwhelmed by the sheer responsibility of it all. She tried to keep the children all together, but instead of leading them outside, she made the rookie mistake of going to the back of the line. Several of the children spread like puppies in a new park, all going in different directions. One of them was Mason, who made his way toward a dark blue Toyota RAV4. A man in his early forties stood near it.

"Mason, Jamie, Cindy," Ms. Stiles yelled out to children who had broken out of line and run towards their parents' cars.

Mason turned and waved to the teacher and continued toward the car. The man picking him up waved as well and then opened the car door for Mason to get in.

Ms. Stiles went back to tending to the other children, and Mason and the man drove away.

CHAPTER TWO

A tall, rugged man with a thin face and a gray mustache sat at the bar in Nickels Gaming Parlour in Helena, Montana. Only when he turned to the left could you see the scar that ran down the right side of his cheek, starting at the corner of his eye and ending just under his chin. He was wearing a very old cowboy hat, a disheveled plaid shirt, jeans, a big silver belt buckle, and cowboy boots. A bottle of orange soda pop sat on the bar in front of him.

After perusing the crowd, an attractive blonde woman in her late thirties, dressed in a simple blue dress and a light jacket, began walking toward him.

"How do you do it?" the bartender, a long-time acquaintance of Tuper's, asked.

"Do what?" Tuper said.

"How do you get all those beautiful women?" He nodded toward the blonde woman. "You gotta be more than twice that woman's age."

"Don't even know who she is."

"I'm sure you'll find out," the bartender said, as the blonde strode up.

"Mr. Tuper?" the woman asked.

"Just Tuper."

"Denise Jenkins," she said, looking around the crowded bar. "Can we talk somewhere a little more private?"

Tuper looked at the bartender and raised one of the prominent eyebrows that sat over his deep-set eyes.

The bartender shook his head, paused, and then nodded toward the door off to his right. "You can use the office. And, Toop, no hanky panky."

"Humph," Tuper muttered.

Tuper stood up and moved toward the closed door, opened it, and went inside. Denise followed him. The office contained a small computer desk with a padded chair, a loveseat, and an overstuffed armchair. The walls were bare except for one large, black-velvet picture of dogs playing poker and smoking cigars. Tuper sat in the overstuffed chair and nodded toward the loveseat for Denise. She sat down. Tuper didn't speak; he waited for her to explain what she needed.

After a moment or two of awkward silence, she said, "A friend of a friend told me I might be able to find you here."

"You found me."

Denise rubbed her hands together in a nervous gesture. "My son is missing and I need you to find him."

"What do ya mean, missing?"

"He was abducted at school on Monday."

"How old is he?"

"He's five. He'll be six next month."

"Have there been any requests for ransom?"

"No."

"Has anyone contacted you?"

"No. I think his father took him, but I can't prove it. Randy swears he didn't, but I don't believe him."

"I take it you're not together."

"No, we've been separated for a while. I just got full custody of Mason. It's a temporary order, but I've been told that unless something drastic changes, it will become the permanent order. Randy was real angry about it."

"Tell me what happened."

"I dropped Mason off for his first day of school since before Christmas. He started kindergarten in September. Randy was supposed to pick him up, but he arrived about five minutes late. By then, Mason was already gone. The teacher told him that some man had picked him up in a dark blue RAV4. She guessed it to be about a 2000."

"Have you been to the police?"

"Of course. That's the first thing I did. They're looking for him, and the Amber Alert is still in effect, but I know they think he's dead by now. They said the first forty-eight hours were critical and it's already been three days."

"What do ya think I can do that the police can't?"

"My friend says you're the best, that if anyone can find him, you can."

"Wish you'd come sooner," Tuper mumbled.

Denise's eyes filled with tears. "Please help me."

"Don't know how much help I can be."

"I'll pay you. I don't have much, but I have a hundred dollars with me and a few hundred more in my checking account, and I'll get more. Please. I'll do whatever it takes to get what you need. I'll steal it if I have to."

Tuper brushed each side of his mustache with his thumb, two strokes on each side. He looked at Denise. After about ten seconds of silence, he said, "Got a picture of him?"

She took a deep breath and opened an envelope. She pulled half a dozen photos and handed the first one to Tuper. It depicted a young boy with curly, blond hair and hazel eyes. He was wearing khaki shorts, a blue knit shirt, and new sneakers and was holding a mint-green backpack. "This is Mason. The photo was taken Monday morning before he left for school. Those are the clothes he was wearing to school."

Tuper nodded but didn't speak.

She handed him a second one. "This is him a few months back."

Tuper nodded again but said nothing.

With the third and fourth photos, she said, "That's Randy, Mason's father. He's five-foot-eleven but claims to be six-foot. He has curly, light brown hair and eyes the same color as Mason's. He wears a cap most of the time to cover his quickly receding hairline." The photo showed a man standing next to a shiny tan car.

"Dodge Daytona?" Tuper asked.

"Yes, 1988."

"Is that what he drives now?"

"Yes."

"Tell me 'bout Mason's father."

"He's a jerk. That's why I'm divorcing him."

"We're all jerks. Could you be more specific?"

"He gets real angry and mean. Always threatening me."

"Threatening to hurt you?"

"Whenever he would get mad, he would threaten to take Mason away from me."

"Ever hit ya?"

"Just once. He got angry because I let Mason watch a Disney movie that gave him nightmares. His screams woke Randy up and he couldn't get back to sleep so he started drinking. Then he woke me up and we got into a big fight."

"Does he work?"

"Yes, for Big Johnson Tire. He's been there about a year."

"Ever been in trouble?"

"Not since he was a kid. He stole a car when he was a teenager, but it was more of a joy ride. He's thirty-eight now."

"Where's Randy now?"

"I don't know. He says he's looking for Mason."

"Ya don't believe him?"

"I think he ran off with him."

"Where's he living?"

"He was in Leisure Village Mobile Park on Herrin, but I don't think he's there now."

"I know the place." Tuper tried to remember which one of his past lady friends had lived there, but he couldn't think of who it was. Perhaps when he went there it would ring a bell. "What space number?"

"Number 34 on Riviera Drive. It's the street on the far left of the village."

"Lives alone?"

She hesitated. "Yes."

"What is it?"

"I think he might be having an affair. But I don't know for sure, just some things that I've noticed."

"Any idea who with?"

"None. I could be wrong."

"What else can you tell me about Mason?"

"I just need you to find him. I can't live without my son."

"I'll do what I can."

Denise opened her purse and removed five twenty-dollar bills from her wallet. She handed them to Tuper. "This is all I have on me. How much more do you need to start looking?"

"What kind of car are you driving?"

"A 2003 Chevy Aveo."

"Really? And it's still running?"

"Just barely."

"I charge what folks can afford." Tuper removed one twenty-dollar bill and handed the rest back to her. "I'm guessing that's about what you can afford."

"That can't be enough money."

"I don't do it for the money," Tuper said.

CHAPTER THREE

Tuper left Nickels right after Denise. He stepped into a beat-up, faded-red 1978 Toyota that looked like it was straight from a bad day at the junkyard. In addition to a dented and scratched body, the car's hatchback door was held closed by a rope that tied the handle to the bumper. A blond mutt stuck his head out the window as Tuper approached the car.

"Hi, Ringo," Tuper said, patting him on the head.

Ringo moved from the driver's seat to the passenger's seat, panting and wriggling around with excitement as Tuper stepped inside the car. Tuper rolled the passenger window down and drove off.

"We got a kid to find, Ringo. You up for it?"

Ringo wagged his tail and hung his head out the window, taking in the late afternoon air. He remained in that position for the ten-minute ride to Herrin Road, where Tuper turned right and then right again into the mobile home park. He stayed to the far left, turned right when he could go no further, and watched for number 34. He spotted the tan 1988 Dodge sitting in front of a mobile home about four spaces ahead. He wondered why Denise thought her ex-husband wouldn't be home, and why someone who worked at a tire shop had such bad tires.

Just as Tuper's car approached the unit, a man matching the description Denise had given him dashed out of the house carrying a plastic bag. Tuper glanced at the photo and was sure it was Mason's father.

Randy got into the car and backed out of the parking space, almost hitting Tuper's car. The man then turned in the direction Tuper had come from and headed toward the park's exit. Tuper made a U-turn and followed him out of the park, keeping his distance, partly so he wouldn't get caught, and partly because his car didn't have the speed of the Dodge.

The Dodge lost him on York Road. Tuper knew the driver could've turned off at any number of streets, but when he reached North Sanders Street, Tuper spotted him turning left at the intersection. Unfortunately, Tuper didn't make the light. When he was finally able to turn, there was too much distance and too many cars to see where the Dodge went. He drove along North Sanders hoping to see Randy's car. He was about to give up when he saw the Dodge parked in the Motherlode Sports Bar parking lot.

Tuper pulled into the lot and parked a few cars away from the Dodge. He rolled the window halfway up, told Ringo to stay, and stepped out of the car.

Once inside the Motherlode, it didn't take long to spot Randy Jenkins sitting at the bar. He had just ordered a beer. Tuper hung back to see if anyone joined him. Just as Tuper expected, Randy was approached by a brunette woman who was approximately thirty years old. As she dashed up to his barstool, Randy sat up straight and turned his head quickly toward her. Although he appeared to be surprised by her presence, he gave her a welcoming smile. Tuper couldn't hear what they were saying, but he observed Randy touching her lightly on the shoulder. After a minute or two, the brunette leaned in and kissed him on the cheek, smiled, and walked to a booth about twenty feet away where she sat down with two other women.

Tuper sauntered to the bar and claimed a seat about four stools away from Randy. From there he hoped to be able to hear Randy's conversation, and he could also keep an eye on the brunette. When the bartender approached him, he said, "Just water. I'm waitin' for someone."

By the time the waiter had brought Tuper his water, a man with light brown hair approached Randy and sat on the stool next to him. He had a similar build to Randy, but didn't have Randy's big, round hazel eyes.

"Everything okay?" Randy asked.

"Just fine," the man responded.

Randy handed him the plastic bag he had carried out of his mobile home earlier. "Everything you need is in there."

"What do you want me to do now?" the man asked.

"Just wait until you hear from me." Randy looked around. "You better go." As the man started to leave, Randy added, "And, Dusty, thanks. I appreciate this."

~~~

Tuper left his barstool and followed Dusty out of the bar, hoping he would lead him to his house so Tuper could find out the man's identity. He got outside just in time to see Dusty get into his vehicle, a dark blue 2000 Toyota RAV4, and pull out of his parking spot. Tuper backed up, and as he turned, he saw the license plate, but "2-74" was all he could get. He didn't bother to try and follow Dusty as he sped out of the parking lot and down the street. Instead, he drove back to Helena to Nickels Gaming Parlour.

CHAPTER FOUR

Tuper sat at the end of the bar in Nickels drinking an orange soda that Clarice, the bartender, had brought him. He could see who came and went from the bar. It was late on a Thursday night and the bar was about half full. Only two barstools were empty and the sounds of the slot machines rang out. The smell of beer and alcohol filled the room.

A young woman, about five feet tall with short, spiked, reddish-orange hair, capris, hiking boots, and a backpack, entered and glanced around, and then headed toward the back room. She passed a man sitting at a poker machine. A man in jeans and cowboy boots stood next to him urging him on. As the girl passed, the man standing reached out and grabbed her butt. She reacted so fast that Tuper would've missed it if he had blinked. She swung her right leg back like a mule kicking and her heavy boot landed on the front of his leg. He let out a yelp and reached for her, but she dipped down and to the left and kept moving. The man started after her, but his friend stopped him.

Most of the patrons didn't seem to notice, except when the man yelped, and just as quickly went back to feeding the money monsters.

Clarice, the bartender, was an attractive woman in her late fifties with naturally silver hair. She stood about five-foot-four with a thin, shapely body. She approached Tuper. "Can I get you anything else?"

"No. I'm 'bout to leave. Hey, you ain't seen Squirrely tonight, have you?"

"No, and if he was coming in, he'd have been here by now. He never comes in this late."

"Ringo's in the car. You got anything for him?"

"I'm sure I do."

He nodded toward the two men. "Might want to keep an eye on those two. The one standin' can't seem to keep his hands to his self."

Clarice looked at them. "Yeah, I had a little trouble with him a while ago. He's had way too much to drink. He's about to be cut off."

The young redhead reappeared from the back room. This time she stayed to the right side of the room, away from the "grabber."

"Ya know her?" Tuper asked, nodding toward the girl.

"Nope. I've never seen her before. She hardly looks old enough to be in here."

Tuper nodded in agreement.

"Let me get you Ringo's care package," Clarice said, and then walked around the bar to the kitchen.

Tuper stood up, taking a second to get his old bones working before moving toward the end of the bar, where he waited for Clarice. He was there long enough to see "the grabber" and his buddy escorted out by Stump, the bartender/bouncer.

"Here you go," Clarice said, handing a plastic bag to Tuper. "There's a couple of ribs in there. They're good and fresh. I put one in there for you too." She reached up, gave him a quick hug, and left.

As he approached his car, he saw the two men leaning against the wall of the bar about ten feet from the door. He kept moving, stepping off the sidewalk just as he reached them, since his car was parked directly in front of where they stood. Tuper's back was to the men so he listened carefully for any movement behind him. He heard the soberer of the two encouraging the grabber to leave, but with no success.

Ringo wagged his tail and wiggled around in the front seat as Tuper approached the passenger side of the car. Tuper petted him and scratched the top of his head and behind his ears. Then he opened the bag, took out a nice juicy beef rib, and handed it to Ringo.

He was just about to get himself a rib when he heard the grabber say, "What are you doing, old man?"

Tuper closed the bag and laid it down on the seat, reached around his back under his vest, and let his hand light upon his gun. He didn't respond. The man took a step toward him just as the young redhead exited the bar. The man turned away from Tuper and stepped in front of the girl. His buddy stepped up next to him, blocking her from leaving. She ducked and tried to get between the two men but the buddy caught hold of her backpack and pulled her back. She slipped out of it, but when she did, the grabber picked her up, dangled her about a foot off the concrete, pushed her backward against the brick wall, and pressed his body against her so she was suspended and had no leverage. She tried swinging her legs, but he had pinned her to the wall and she couldn't move. He tried kissing her on the lips, but she quickly rotated her head, so he moved down to her neck. She kept fighting and thrashing, but the only thing she could move was her head. She finally managed to get one arm loose and started hitting her assaulter, but the man's buddy dropped the backpack and grabbed her arm before she could have any impact.

"Put her down," Tuper said in a soft but demanding tone.

"Go away, old man," the grabber said.

The buddy's head turned toward Tuper. He glanced at Tuper and guffawed. He was still holding onto the girl's wrist when Tuper threw a left punch that landed on the side of his face. The man staggered a bit and then came at Tuper. Tuper hit him in the stomach with a powerful blow and then came down with a hammer blow to the back of his head. He fell to the ground.

The redhead started pounding her one loose fist against her attacker's head, but she couldn't get much leverage.

"I said, put her down." Tuper's soft voice had a chilling effect as he pulled out his gun and placed it against the back of the grabber's head. "Slowly," he ordered.

The man began to lower the girl to the ground, stepping back slightly to make room. As the girl reached the ground, she raised her knee and planted it in his crotch. He doubled up and his head hit the wall. Tuper tucked his gun inside his belt, grabbed him by the shoulder, and slammed him further into the wall. The grabber lay on the concrete, his foot catching on Tuper's bumper on his way down. His face was bleeding from the scrape against the bricks and what looked like a broken nose.

He yelped when the redhead cocked her foot and gave him a hard kick in the ribs. Then the girl looked up at Tuper and growled, "I didn't need your help, you know."

"He shouldn't have called me an old man."

Just then Clarice came out the front door with her purse and keys in hand. "What the heck, Tuper?" she said.

"They're both breathin'," Tuper said nonchalantly. "They was bothering this young lady."

"Do you want me to call the police?" Clarice asked.

"No," the redhead said a little too quickly.

"No need," Tuper said. "Just have Stump get rid of the garbage."

The groper's buddy wasn't moving. Clarice leaned down to check on him. "You're right. He's breathing." She straightened back up.

"You know him?" Tuper asked.

"No, but the bloodier one is named Terry something. He comes in once in a while. He's mostly trouble."

Clarice turned to the redhead. "What's your name?"

"Lana," she mumbled.

"Are you okay?" Clarice asked, gently touching her shoulder.

Lana pulled away. "I'm fine. It takes more than a dumb cowboy to rattle me." She made a spitting motion toward Terry.

Clarice went back into the bar.

Tuper walked over to where Terry's feet hung, one over the edge of the sidewalk and the other still caught on his bumper. Tuper pulled one of Terry's boots off, and Terry struggled a bit. When he yanked on the second one, Terry tried to kick, but he didn't seem to have much strength. Tuper yanked until it came loose.

"What are you doing?" Lana asked.

"Payment for denting my car."

Lana looked at the beat-up car and said, "Seriously?"

"He don't deserve to wear these boots. He ain't no cowboy. Real cowboys don't mess with women." Tuper opened his car door and tossed the boots in the back seat. When he did, Ringo jumped out and ran up to Lana. She crouched down, face to face with him, and vigorously petted and scratched him. Ringo wagged his tail with matching enthusiasm.

After a few minutes, Lana stood up, picked up her backpack, and walked away. "Thanks," she mumbled when she passed Tuper.

"Welcome," he said.

Ringo followed as Lana took several steps toward the street. She stopped and said, "Go back, doggie." He wagged his tail.

"Ringo," Tuper called. Ringo looked up at Tuper and then back at Lana. "Ringo," Tuper called again, and stepped toward him narrowing the gap between them. Ringo obeyed.

"Which way are you headed?" Tuper asked.

"I haven't decided yet."

"Do you have a place to stay?"

"I'm not staying with you," she said.

"Didn't ask you to."

Clarice, who had come back out of the bar, said, "Lana, do you have somewhere to stay?"

"I'll be fine," she said.

Clarice stepped up to her and looked her in the eyes. "You can't stay on the street. It's getting too cold. I don't have an extra bedroom, but you can sleep on the sofa. You can figure the rest out in the morning."

"You don't even know me," Lana said. "I could rob you blind."

"Are you going to?" Clarice said.

"No," she said sarcastically.

"Then let's go."

Lana took a step toward Clarice.

"Tuper," Clarice asked, "do you want to come by for a cup of tea?"

CHAPTER FIVE

Clarice and Lana drove to the mobile home park where Clarice lived with her sister, Mary Ann, and her dogs, Caspar and Izzy Bear. It was an older home but they had done a lot of work on it, including building a nice deck around the front and the left side. Potted plants had been set along the railing and a white, acrylic patio set adorned the front of the deck.

Tuper and Ringo pulled up just behind Clarice. He brought Ringo to the front door, where the dog drank from Caspar's water dish. The blond mutt decided to sit down and watch the group go inside.

The shag carpet was old and the sofa was worn, but the house was homey. The fireplace, though not lit, added to the coziness. Lana didn't seem to mind her surroundings. She immediately started petting Caspar and Izzy Bear. They hung around her like she was an animal whisperer.

Clarice pointed toward the end of the sofa. "You can put your backpack over there. The bathroom is right down the hall on your left. Would you like a cup of tea?"

Lana nodded.

"Caffeine or herbal?"

"Herbal, please."

Clarice and Tuper went to the right toward the kitchen/dinette area as Lana walked down the hall. Tuper took a seat at the small table. Clarice turned the teakettle on and set three teacups on the counter.

Lana returned and sat down across from Tuper who was on the phone.

"Sorry to hear that," Tuper said. "I'll come by the hospital tomorrow and see him." There was silence, and then he spoke again. "Thanks for calling, and let me know when he wakes up."

"What happened?" Clarice asked.

"A friend of mine, Pat Cox, is in the hospital. He fell off his roof."

"Oh no. Is he going to be okay?"

"He has a broken hip and he's still unconscious."

"He's the cop in Ulm, right?" Clarice asked.

"Right," Tuper said. "I have a partial license plate number. He was gonna check to see who owned the car." He sighed. "I'll have to find another way now."

"Are you some kind of private investigator or something?" Lana asked.

"Just helpin' someone out," Tuper said.

Clarice brought each of them their tea and a carton of real cream. She offered it to Lana, but she declined. Tuper poured a little in his cup and so did Clarice.

Lana wrinkled her nose.

"This is the way my mom always drank it," Clarice said. "I learned very young to put cream in my tea."

Lana shrugged. "I guess I'm a purist. I don't put cream in my tea, ketchup on my fries, or eat meat of any kind."

"Is that 'cuz your religion don't allow it?" Tuper asked.

"No. It's because I won't eat animals. I like them too much."

"I do too," Tuper said. "I like the way they taste."

In an attempt to change the subject, Clarice asked, "Did you grow up around here?"

"No. I was raised in Southern California."

"Like Los Angeles?" Clarice asked.

"About seventy miles from L.A., not in the city."

"What brought you to Helena, Montana?"

"My auntie was sick. I came to help her."

"Is she better now?"

Lana's face tightened. "She died a couple of months ago."

"I'm so sorry."

"Nothing you can do. We knew it was coming." She swallowed. "Mind if I warm up my tea?"

Before Clarice could volunteer to do it for her, Lana was on her feet and in the kitchen. She put the cup in the microwave for a minute and then filled it up with the hot water that remained in the kettle.

"So, what's your plan to run that license plate?" Clarice asked.

"I know another cop who can do it, but he always wants money."

Lana walked back and sat back down at the table. "I can help."

"You got money?" Tuper asked.

"No, but I can run the license plate."

"*You* can?"

"Do you have Internet?"

"Yes," Clarice said, "but my computer is really old and very slow."

"It's okay. I have my own," Lana said. She had her own Wi-Fi connection as well, but sometimes she preferred to use what was available. She retrieved her backpack and removed her laptop. "What's the Wi-Fi password?"

"I don't know it by heart. I'll go get it."

Lana set her laptop on the table and plugged it in. She turned to Tuper. "Are you sure this is to help someone?"

"Does it matter?"

She shrugged her shoulders. "Not really."

"You shrug a lot."

She paused. "That's because a lot of stuff doesn't really matter that much. What do you have for the plate number?"

"All I got was 2-74. It's a dark blue Toyota RAV4."

Lana wrote the info down on a pad of paper she had removed from her pack.

When Clarice returned, Lana entered the password and started clicking around. Clarice was in awe at how fast she could maneuver around cyberspace. Tuper had never used a computer and had no clue what she was doing. He could barely use his flip phone.

~~~

After about three minutes on the computer Lana said, "The car is from Cascade County."

Clarice smiled. "We already knew that. The first number on a license plate indicates the county that it was registered in."

"It's different in California." She read from a page she had Googled. "It says *California started the 1ABC234 license plate format in 1982 with 1ABC000. By 1993 they were in the 3's and now they're in the 7's.*" She looked up at two bored faces. "Sorry. Enough of that." She started clicking in a determined fashion.

Clarice and Tuper chatted, neither of them expecting results. When Lana's stomach growled, Clarice asked, "Lana, are you hungry?"

"I could eat," she said, not looking up from the computer screen.

"Me too," Tuper said.

"I know. You're always hungry." She patted Tuper on the hand. "I don't have a lot to choose from. I need to go shopping. Peanut butter and jelly okay?"

Lana nodded.

Clarice made five sandwiches, cut them in half, and returned to the table with paper plates for each of them. She passed out the plates and set the sandwiches in the middle. "Help yourself. There's two for each of you. If you want more, I'll make them."

She went back into the kitchen and poured them each a tall glass of milk.

Lana stopped for the first time since she had fired up her laptop. She ate the first sandwich like she hadn't eaten for days, chasing it with the milk. Then she slowed down and looked from Clarice to Tuper.

"Are you two together? Like a couple?"

"No," they both said at the same time.

Tuper smiled. "She should be so lucky."

Clarice laughed. "We've been friends for a very long time."

"Clarice helps me with my work sometimes."

"What do you do for work?" Lana asked.

"Depends," Tuper said.

"Depends on what?"

"My mood."

Lana finished her second sandwich and her glass of milk. Clarice had eaten half of a sandwich. She pointed to the other half and said, "I'm not going to eat that. Do you want it?"

Lana took it without hesitation.

"Do you want more?"

"No. I'm good." She returned to her search on the computer and before Clarice had cleaned up the plates and put the milk away, Lana said. "I got it."

"You found the owner?" Tuper asked.

"Yes, there's a dark blue 2000 Toyota RAV 4 with license plate number 2-740389 registered to Dustin Walker."

"That's it," Tuper said. "Randy called him Dusty."

"Want the address?" Lana asked.

"Yes."

Lana pushed the pad and pen toward Tuper and started to give him the information. Clarice reached over and wrote it down for him.

Tuper repeated the address and without taking the paper, he stood up and put his jacket on. He glanced at the clock on the wall and said, "I'd better get going if I want to catch Squirrely."

Lana picked up the scrap of paper with the address. "Don't you want the address?"

"Got it," he said, tapping his index finger to the side of his head.

Lana handed it to him anyway. He gave her a slight nod, folded the paper, and stuck it in his pocket. Lana kept looking at him.

"What is it?" Tuper asked.

"Anyone ever tell you that you look like the actor, Sam Elliott?"

"Yup. He's a lucky guy." He nodded his head at her and went out the door.

CHAPTER SIX

Tuper left Clarice's mobile home and drove to Humpty's, a small dive bar in East Helena, located on a side street next to a boat shop that had been closed for fifteen-plus years. The bar had an old sign that lit up but the "t" was burned out so it read *Hump_y's*. Only the locals went there, and not many of them. Tuper parked his car next to a 1994 Dodge pickup. Four other vehicles still remained in the lot.

Tuper stepped out of his car into the cold air, opened the back door, and removed the boots he had taken from the guy who had assaulted Lana earlier that evening.

Once inside, Tuper nodded to Sean, a large Irishman with red hair and a beer belly who stood behind the bar. He was in his early fifties and had inherited the bar from his father some ten years ago.

"Is Squirrely here?" Tuper asked.

"He's in the back," Sean said, glancing at the boots but not saying anything.

There were only two other patrons in the room. Both men looked to be in their late sixties. They sat at one end of the wooden bar drinking whiskey. The rest of the room held six small tables with chairs, two slot machines, and an old jukebox. As far as Tuper knew, it was the only working jukebox in town. It contained a mixture of really old country music and Irish tunes.

He could hear Patsy Cline singing "Crazy" as he approached the bar. The choice of music in the jukebox hadn't changed in thirty years, nor had most everything else in this bar: the same décor, same patrons, same smells. It was like a step back in time, but no one noticed.

"Are you in the game tonight?" Sean asked.

"No. Just here to see Squirrely."

Sean nodded toward a door about ten feet to his right. "Go on in."

Tuper entered, then closed the door behind him.

A man about five-foot-ten—who would have looked homeless if you were to see him on the street—was standing near a coffee pot. "Hey, Toop," he said. "I didn't know you were playin' tonight."

"I'm not. Just here to see you." Tuper handed Squirrely the boots he was carrying.

"What's this?"

"Thought you could use these."

"Nice." Squirrely walked to a round table; the front sole of one shoe flapped as he moved. The other shoe was wrapped in duct tape. "I ran out of tape so I couldn't fix the other one." He sat down and removed his worn-out tennis shoes, and the smell of dirty feet filled the room.

"Dang, Squirrely, you need to wash your feet, or bottle that stink and sell it to a dairy farm to cover up the smell of cow manure."

"Maybe next month," Squirrely said. He put the new boots on, stood up, took a few steps, and then sat back down. He stretched his legs out in front of him and admired the boots.

"Not too small, are they?" Tuper asked.

"Nope. With an extra pair of socks, they'll be perfect." He reached down, picked up the old pair of tennis shoes, and set them aside. When Tuper looked at him questioningly, Squirrely said, "With a little more tape, they'll make good summer shoes."

Tuper sat down at the table next to him. "I need your help."

"Sure, what is it?"

"I'm looking for a missing five-year-old boy." He removed a photo of Mason and handed it to Squirrely. "Have you heard any scuttlebutt on the streets?"

"Nope, but I'll ask around."

Tuper told him everything he knew about the case, including the information on the vehicle. "Maybe someone has seen the car. You still have contacts in Great Falls?"

"Yup."

Tuper stood to leave and Squirrely tested his new boots as he walked him to the door.

"You sure the boots are okay?"

"Yup. Just a tad wide for my skinny feet, but that can be fixed."

Tuper thought about the cowboy lying on the sidewalk and mumbled, "Shoulda taken his socks too."

CHAPTER SEVEN

The next morning, Tuper drove to the address in Great Falls on D Street that Lana had given him for Dustin Walker. It was a small tract home in an older neighborhood. When he knocked on the door, a woman in her late seventies or early eighties answered.

"Is Dustin Walker here?" Tuper asked.

"He's no longer with us. I'm his wife, Sally. Can I help you?"

"I'm so sorry, ma'am."

"He's in a better place now. He was very ill for such a long time. I'm just glad he's at peace."

"How long has he been gone, ma'am?"

"Eight months."

"I must have the wrong Dustin Walker, unless your husband was a much younger man than you. Did Dustin have a son or grandson named Dustin?"

"No. We only have one daughter and she doesn't have any children. We were never blessed with grandchildren."

Tuper stroked his mustache. "Do you or did your husband own a Toyota SUV?"

She chuckled. "No, we never owned a Toyota. Dustin was a Cadillac man. I still have his 1994 Cadillac in the garage." She paused and put her hand up to her head. "I just remembered. A couple of months ago, I received some mail from the city with a parking ticket. Hold on."

Mrs. Walker went inside and returned with an envelope. She opened it, pulled out the document, and said, "Yes, it's for a Toyota RAV4."

"What did you do about the ticket?"

"Nothing. I showed it to my daughter and she said to just ignore it. We never heard anything more. I was about to toss this away."

"Do you mind if I take that?"

She returned the ticket to the envelope, handed it to Tuper, and then asked, "Are you a cop?"

"No, ma'am. I'm just trying to help a friend find her five-year-old son."

"I'm so sorry about the little boy." She paused. "How do you expect this to help?"

"It appears this SUV was at the scene when the child was abducted. That's about all I know about the car."

"I don't understand. Why did the ticket come here?"

"I don't know, ma'am. We're trying to figure that out. I'll let you know if we do."

"I can't imagine how the ticket will help, but I hope it does."

"Thank you."

~~~

It was nearly ten-thirty in the morning when Tuper arrived at Clarice's home. She and Lana had just sat down for breakfast on the deck when Clarice saw Tuper park his car in the driveway. She went inside and dished up a plate of scrambled eggs and toast for him.

"Just in time for lunch, I see," Tuper said.

"How long have you been up?" Lana asked.

"Since about four. I'm not much for sleepin' in."

"Hi, Toop," Clarice said as she returned. She handed him the plate. "Do you want a cup of tea?"

"Nope. This'll do."

"Did you find the man with the RAV4?" Lana asked.

"Not exactly. I found Dustin Walker's house, but he's been dead for nearly a year. And he never owned a Toyota."

"Someone in his family, maybe?"

"Nope." He reached into his shirt pocket, took out the ticket, and handed it to Clarice.

"What's this?" she asked as she opened it.

"Whoever is driving that car got a ticket a while back. It was sent to Walker's address. His widow just ignored it."

Lana leaned over and tried to see what was on the ticket.

Tuper cleared his throat.

Lana looked up at Tuper. "How am I going to help you if I can't see what's on there?"

"Don't remember askin' for your help."

"I didn't ask for yours last night, but that didn't stop you."

Tuper gave her a blank stare.

"Look," Lana said, "I can check it out. It may not even help. Besides, I'm bored. I need something to do."

"Have you thought about gettin' a job?"

"No one wants to hire me. I have no skills that are legal." She paused for just a second. "Maybe you could hire me. What is it exactly that you do?"

"I'm unemployed," Tuper said.

"Then I guess I'll have to work for free for now." She stood up and went inside.

"Everything okay here with that one?" Tuper asked Clarice.

"She's been fine. Once she gets comfortable, she tends to talk a lot."

"About what?"

"All kinds of weird things. She has a lot of interesting but useless knowledge. Probably from all the time she spends on the Internet. She doesn't talk much about herself, but I get the feeling she's running from something."

"Most of us are."

Lana returned with her laptop and set it on the table. She reached for the ticket that Clarice had laid down beside her plate. "Let's see what we can find."

She started pecking at the keyboard. Her face became very intense as she focused on her work. She looked from the ticket to the screen, typing in information. "Bozeman," she said aloud, reading from the ticket as she typed. Then she entered the date and the number on the ticket. Approximately three minutes later she said, "The ticket was paid online with a credit card eighteen days after it was issued." She looked at the envelope. "Two days after this was postmarked."

"Could just be when the driver got around to paying it," Clarice said.

"Or it could be that someone knew Mrs. Walker got the ticket in the mail," Tuper said. "Mrs. Walker told me that she told her daughter about it. She didn't say if she told anyone else."

"You found that really fast," Clarice said to Lana.

"That was the easy part. Anyone could do that with the information I had. It's public record. The hard part is finding out who paid it."

"You can do that?" Clarice asked.

"Give me a few minutes and I should be able to get you the IP address from the computer where the payment was made."

"What's an IP address?" Tuper asked.

"IP stands for Internet Protocol, which are the rules that cover the activity on the Internet and facilitate actions on the World Wide Web. It's part of a grid that makes online communication possible by connecting one device to another."

Clarice and Tuper looked at her like she was speaking Greek.

"It's really just an address for any given computer—like a mailing address or a telephone number. If you don't know the address or the phone number, you can't connect, right?" Before anyone could answer, she went on to say, "The difference is that on the Internet you don't have to know the actual IP address because it is set up to find that connection when you put in other information you know, like an email address or a website name. That's the simplest way I can explain it."

"So, if you have the IP address, you know where they are?" Clarice asked.

"Not exactly," Lana explained. "It might tell us where their server is, unless they're using a VPN—a Virtual Private Network—but most home computers don't have that."

"So what good does it do to know the IP address?"

"Here's the way it works. Any program that wants to make a connection to something with IP standards will need to specify a port and then use either UDP or TCP standard. There are ports that are considered common ports, which are only 'allowed' to be used for certain things." Lana made air quotes when she said the word *allowed*. "For example: Port 80 is for HTTP, the unsecured portion of the World Wide Web, and 443 is for HTTPS, the secure portion of the web where you can buy from Amazon without fear of being intercepted. ICANN, which keeps track of domain names, also keeps a registered list of ports between the range of 1024 through 49151. The other ports, 49152 through 65535, are considered private ports, which can be used by anyone."

Tuper gave her a blank stare.

"It's like a door to that program. So if the user is in that program, the door would be open. And if someone knows the IP address and can get to the port, they can listen to what is happening between the program and the server. And depending on the firewall, it could be more work."

Tuper shook his head. "I ain't following. Can you find out who paid the bill or not?"

"Probably," Lana said. "Most people don't protect their computers like they should, but it could take a while."

"How long?"

"As long as it takes."

"How do you know all this stuff?"

"Practice." Lana gave a fake smile. "Are you going to let me help or what?"

Tuper stood up, removed his cowboy hat, and rubbed his hand through his hair. "I can't pay none."

"That's okay."

"Just this once," Tuper said.

CHAPTER EIGHT

When Tuper arrived, the 1988 Dodge was parked in front of the mobile home numbered 34 on Riviera Drive. He waited for almost two hours until Randy left and another five minutes to make sure he was gone before he put on his gloves, picked the lock, and went inside. It was a two-bedroom single-wide in poor shape. The sink held a couple of dirty coffee mugs, and a few clothes were strewn about the rooms. The furniture was tattered and several cupboard doors in the kitchen were attached with only one hinge.

As Tuper made his way to the back of the mobile home, he looked through drawers, most of which were empty. One drawer had some underwear and socks in it. Another had several t-shirts. The closet was bare except for a single tan overcoat hanging from a wire hanger.

The bathroom had two different-colored bath towels: a green one slung over the shower door and a brown one on a towel rack. A matching brown hand towel lay on the back of the toilet. On the top of the sink were a razor, a toothbrush, and a tube of Crest toothpaste. Tuper opened the medicine cabinet and found it empty. There was nothing under the sink except for a package of toilet paper. Before he left the room, he picked up the toothbrush and stuck it in his pocket.

The kitchen cupboards were as sparse as the rest of the house. They contained two mugs and a stack of paper plates. One drawer had a box of plastic forks in it. The others were all empty. Tuper found no paperwork of any kind except a couple of receipts lying on the counter next to a wrapper from McDonald's and some legal papers. Tuper picked up the legal documents, committed the case number to memory, and continued his search. The small wastebasket under the sink had additional fast-food wrappers, a couple of used paper plates, and two empty beer cans. The refrigerator contained the remaining four cans of Miller from the six-pack.

Within minutes, Tuper had finished his search. He looked out the living room window to make sure no one could see him, then opened the door and sauntered to his car.

~~~

Tuper drove to Big Johnson Tire where Denise said Randy was working. It was a small tire shop owned by Jerome Johnson, a blond, blue-eyed man in his early fifties. The shop was located in a large metal shed next to his home in East Helena. This was Jerome's day job. In the winter, he contracted with the city to plow the snow off the streets.

The only vehicles on the lot were a pickup, a 1969 Mustang, and a light green 1969 Ford Bronco that was being refurbished. There was no Dodge Daytona, so Tuper parked and went inside. When he found no one in the front, he walked to the service area. Racks of tires lined the east wall, and a table with tools was nearby. Jerome was in the back repairing a tire. The machine he was using was noisy and he apparently didn't hear Tuper enter as he didn't turn around.

"Romeo," Tuper called.

Jerome looked up, shut the machine off, and said, "Hey, Toop, nice to see you." He removed his gloves and took a few steps toward a table where a coffee pot was brewing. "Coffee?"

"No, thanks."

"That's right. You're not much of a coffee drinker. Sorry, I don't have any tea."

"No problem."

"Do you ever drink coffee?"

"Only when it's cold outside and that's all there is."

Jerome pulled two barstools out from behind the table. "Have a seat. What brings you out here? You need some tires?"

"Nope. Lookin' for a guy named Randy Jenkins. Heard he works for you."

"He used to. I had to fire him. He wasn't showing up for work. Know anyone who needs a job?"

"I'll ask around," Tuper said. "When did you fire him?"

"About a week ago. I felt bad. I know he was going through some personal stuff, but I couldn't depend on him."

"What stuff?"

"He said his wife left him and took his kid, but he missed a lot of work before that. There was always some excuse. And he wasn't all that good with the customers. He was all right at first, but the last few weeks he would get set off pretty easy. I couldn't put up with it anymore."

"Did you know his wife?"

"No, I never met her. I saw his kid a couple of times."

"When was the last time you saw the boy?"

"About a month ago." He paused. "No, less than that, maybe two or three weeks at the most. Randy brought his son with him when he came to get some new tires for his car. The kid is a cute little guy."

"I saw his Dodge. His tires were bad."

"It was for his other car, a RAV4."

"Dark blue?"

"Yes."

"Did he drive that often?"

"No." He shook his head. "That's the only time I ever saw it. He said his mom had been using it because her car broke down."

CHAPTER NINE

When Tuper called Denise, she offered to meet him at Canyon Ferry Mini Basket at the corner of Wylie Drive and Canyon Ferry Road. Tuper didn't know where she was living. She hadn't volunteered it and Tuper hadn't asked.

Tuper arrived a little early and pulled up to the pump at the Mini Basket. This was one of the cheapest places in town to get gas and his tank was low. He put twenty dollars' worth of gas in and then went inside and gave the cashier two ten-dollar bills. As he started back to his car, it began to sprinkle. He was inside his car before he got wet. He backed into a parking spot in front of the Mini Basket and waited for Denise.

She arrived only a few minutes late as a passenger in a black Kia. She stepped out of the car near the entrance to the Mini Basket and the car's driver put the car in gear and left. Denise looked around, but she didn't see Tuper at first. She wasn't carrying an umbrella and it was starting to rain harder. He reached for the steering wheel to honk his horn but then remembered it didn't work. He told Ringo to get in the back, and he stretched across the car and rolled the passenger window down.

"Denise," he called out.

She pulled the hood up on her sweatshirt and dashed toward him. She opened the door just as Tuper was laying a towel on the torn seat.

"Sorry, this is Ringo's car. He tore the seat up when he was a puppy." Ringo stuck his head right up by hers. "That's Ringo."

Tuper commanded Ringo to lie down and turned to Denise. "Do you want to just talk here in the car or do you want to go somewhere?"

"No, this is fine. My friend will be back in a few minutes." She pulled her hood back down. "Have you found Mason?"

"No, sorry. Just have a few questions."

"Okay."

"I did find your husband."

"Ex-husband, or soon-to-be."

Tuper nodded. "The car that was used to pick Mason up at school was a dark blue Toyota RAV4. Does that belong to Randy?"

"No, unless he got it recently. But I don't know how he could buy anything. He doesn't have any money."

"Did you know he lost his job at Big Johnson?"

"I heard."

"Have you seen Randy?"

"No. He's hiding out somewhere with Mason. I'm sure of it."

"He's living in the mobile park that you told me about. It isn't far from here; I've been there. Mason's not with him."

"Then he has him stashed somewhere. He must." Her voice cracked and she fought the tears.

Tuper knew what she was thinking. If some stranger had him, the boy was likely in danger or already dead.

"Do you have any idea where Randy might be hiding him? His mother's place, maybe?"

Denise frowned at Tuper and then took a deep breath. "His mother is dead. She's been gone for many years."

"Any other family?"

"No. He has no family. His father left him and his mother when he was a baby. He was an only child and so was his mother, so there is no extended family either."

"Did you ever see that RAV4 before? A friend of his, maybe?"

"No. I have no idea whose car it is."

"Does Randy have a friend named Dusty?"

She twitched ever so slightly, but Tuper saw it. "Not that I've ever heard of. Why?"

"I think he's the owner of the car, but so far I haven't been able to track him. The address the DMV has is incorrect."

"And you think this guy took Mason?" She seemed almost excited instead of concerned.

"It's likely."

"But that's good. If he's a friend of Randy's, he must be his accomplice and my baby is safe."

"I hope so," Tuper said.

"Have you heard from the kidnapper?"

"You mean Randy?"

"Or anyone?"

"No, no one," replied Denise. She threw her hands up. "It has to be Randy."

"I'm keepin' an eye on him. If he has Mason, I'll find him."

"I just miss my son."

Tuper hated to deal with the tears that he was pretty certain were coming, so he changed the subject. "Do you have your divorce papers?"

She glanced up at him. "Not on me."

Tuper thought he detected a slight change in her expression. Maybe it was just the blink of her eyes.

"I'd like to see them."

"What do you need those for? They're not going to tell us where Mason is."

"You never know, ma'am. Sometimes the most unlikely thing holds the clues."

"I'll get them for you, but I don't understand how they can help."

Denise's reluctance bothered Tuper and made him wonder if there was something in the papers she didn't want him to see.

"Divorces are messy. Lots of things go down that most people wouldn't do under normal circumstances. I won't judge you."

"It's not that." Her voice rose a little. "I just want you to find my son, not spend your time looking through a bunch of useless paperwork."

Tuper spoke more softly in direct contrast to her slightly edgy tone. "Is there something you're not tellin' me?"

"Why would you ask that?"

"I need to know everything if I'm going to be able to find Mason."

She didn't respond.

"You okay?"

"I'm fine. There's my ride." When she opened the door, the rain started to pour inside. She closed it quickly and turned to Tuper. "Please find my boy."

Tuper nodded. "I'll do my best, ma'am." She opened the door again, stepped out, and turned away just as Tuper said, "Hey, where are you stayin', in case I need to reach you?"

She kept going without responding. Tuper wasn't sure if she heard him or not, but he decided to follow her to find out. He didn't like it when he didn't trust his own clients, but he had found that most of them were keeping some kind of secret. That was often the reason they hired him.

CHAPTER TEN

"Welcome back," Lana said as she opened the door, still wearing a pair of flannel pajamas she had borrowed from Clarice.

Tuper wiped his wet feet on the mat, then removed his hat and shook it dry before he stepped in. He looked at her outfit. "You just get up?"

"A couple of hours ago."

"Dang, kid, you're gonna sleep your life away."

"It's just a little after noon. How long have you been awake?"

"Got up about 4:30 this morning. A little later than usual."

"That's the middle of the night. I was just barely getting to sleep. Why do you get up so early?"

"Someone has to get the roosters up." He looked around the room. "Where's Clarice?"

"She was called in to work early."

"Darn it," Tuper muttered.

"Do you need help with something? I can help. I take direction well."

Tuper shook his head and mumbled, "I doubt that."

"What is it you need? I bet I can do it."

"It's nothin'." Tuper turned toward the door.

"Come in," Lana said. "I'll make you some tea and I'll tell you what I found out about the ticket on the RAV4."

"Hot tea would be good." He walked to the table in the small kitchen and sat down.

Lana filled a teakettle with water and placed it on a burner to boil. Then she took a seat in front of her computer at the table next to Tuper.

"What do you got?" asked Tuper.

"I found the IP address for the payment of the ticket on the RAV4."

Tuper showed little response, although he was surprised. "Who paid it?"

"I don't know *who* paid it..."

Before she could explain, Tuper said, "Thought you just said you found it."

"I did. I have the address where the computer was located that was used to pay the ticket. I don't know who paid it because it could be anyone in that location. Actually, it's a house, so that's better. If it were an office building or something, it would be a lot harder. But maybe you can figure out the person now that you know where the computer is."

Tuper shook his head. "But I don't know that 'cuz you haven't told me."

"Oh yeah," Lana said. "I already gave it to you. It's the same house where the car is registered: Dustin Walker's house."

"Are you sure?"

"I'm sure. I took a chance that it was the same address and that's where I started my search. It wasn't easy to verify because I don't think they use the computer much. I needed them to have the Internet on in order to be certain. I started looking right after I found the Walker address. I kept watching it through the night but got nothing. A little while ago, I got lucky."

He held up his right hand, palm facing Lana, indicating she could stop talking. "Okay, I got it."

"What do we do next?"

"*We* don't do anything; *I'll* take it from here."

The kettle whistled, so Lana rose and quietly made Tuper and herself each a cup of tea. Tuper was enjoying the silence, which ended as soon as Lana set down their teacups.

"Are you going to go see Sally Walker again?" Lana asked.

"Not sure yet."

"Do you think she paid the ticket?"

"Not likely—unless she's snowin' me. She doesn't seem to be much into computers."

"So if she were going to pay it, she probably would've mailed it in."

"Right."

"Didn't you say her daughter lives there?" Without waiting for a response, she added, "Maybe the daughter did it."

"She could've taken care of it to keep her mother from worrying."

"Or maybe she did it to cover for someone else." Her voice rose with excitement. "She could be involved with the kidnapper."

"You're gettin' a little ahead of yourself, young lady."

"There's a little boy missing. The car that matched the description of the one that picked him up from school is connected to this house and to the boy's father. There has to be more to this whole car registration thing. Does the daughter have a car? Maybe the daughter is using her dad's information for her car for some reason. Have you checked her out? Is she a flake?"

Tuper sat there looking at Lana with his head tipped to one side as she continued.

"What's her name?" She put her hands on her keyboard. "Let me see what I can find out about her."

Tuper picked up his teacup and took a sip of tea before he said anything. "Don't know."

"Maybe I can find out. Do you have any more information on the Walkers?" She started typing as she spoke.

"Nope." He set his tea down and leaned forward.

"Wait here a second." Lana jumped up and went into the other room.

About three minutes later she returned wearing jeans and a flannel shirt. The jeans were hers; Clarice had lent her the shirt.

"I want to go with you," Lana said.

"Who said I was going anywhere?"

"I can tell. You're ready to move. You don't sit still long, do you?"

"And you don't stop talking much, do you?"

"I know I talk a lot, but mostly when I'm excited...or happy...or frustrated...or real comfortable with the company I'm with," she said with a grin as she shut down her computer.

"So pretty much all the time?"

"When I'm angry or scared I don't talk much." She put her laptop and power cord inside a black computer bag.

Tuper stood up and went to the door. Lana grabbed her coat and slipped it on. Then she picked up her purse and computer case and followed him.

"I know I can help you. You've seen what I can do and I can do a lot more than that. If you need something right then, I can look it up."

"Are you afraid of spiders?" Tuper asked as they walked to the car.

"No."

"Mice?"

"No."

"Snakes?"

"No. Why?"

"Just trying to figure out what scares you. You said you don't talk much when you're scared."

CHAPTER ELEVEN

Lana jabbered non-stop for the first half-hour on the drive from Helena to Great Falls, making Tuper wonder why he let her go along. She was an unusual young woman about whom he knew little. Even though she talked a lot, she didn't tell much about herself that was of any importance. He kind of admired her for that. She also seemed to have good deductive reasoning skills, as well as her knowledge of the computer, which he didn't understand at all. Every day he still fought with his "not-so-smart" phone.

"What all can you find on that contraption?" Tuper asked, pointing to her laptop still in the case.

"Most anything. Some things just take a little longer."

"Can you find court records?"

"Sure. Lots of those are public records. They're the easy ones. The rest take more effort, but it can be done. What do you need?"

"I have a case number for a divorce. Can you find it?"

Lana fired up her computer. "Is it yours?" Lana asked. "Were you married? Are you having trouble with an ex?"

He glanced at her and shook his head. "No. It's the parents on this case."

"That's even better. What's the number and their names?"

Tuper gave her the number he had memorized from the paperwork at Randy's home and the names of the parents. Lana began her search. For the next ten minutes, all Tuper could hear were road noise and the click of the computer keys. He had found something else that kept Lana quiet. "Guess I don't need no spiders," he murmured.

Lana didn't respond. She was so intent on her work that she didn't appear to have heard him. She seldom looked up except for the occasional glance in the side mirror.

"Are you sure of the number?" Lana said, breaking her silence.

"Yep, I'm sure."

"The number doesn't match the names. This divorce is for Trish and Daniel Peterson. The divorce was filed four years ago in Helena. You must have the number wrong."

"I didn't get the number wrong," Tuper said in his usual soft voice.

"Where did you get it?"

"Off the divorce papers at Randy's."

Lana's voice rose. "Did he show you the papers or did you snoop through his things?"

"It doesn't matter. I got the number."

"Did you write it down?"

"No. Didn't need to."

"Well, it's not correct. Why didn't you take a picture of it with your phone?"

"Don't know how."

Lana looked at him with furrowed eyebrows. "Let me see your phone."

Tuper removed it from his front pocket and handed it to her.

She opened the phone and punched a couple of keys. "It's pretty simple. I'll show you later, but you really should get a better phone if you want to get decent photos."

He reached his arm out with his palm up. She dropped the phone in his hand. "I'm good," he said. "Just find the divorce papers."

"There is no divorce filed in Montana for Denise and Randy or Randolph Jenkins. How long ago was the divorce filed?"

"Not sure. Within the last few months, I think."

"I've checked for any Jenkins couple in the last two years. I found a William and Sarah Jenkins." She paused. "Candace and Keith Jenkins." Another pause. "Steve and Marie Jenkins. That's it. No Denise. No Randy."

"See what you can find out about that first couple—the ones that matched the number."

"The Petersons, Trish and Daniel. What do you want to know?"

"Can you find out who they are? Where they're living now?"

"Probably. It'll take some time."

Tuper exited the Interstate and drove toward Mrs. Walker's house. Tuper noticed that Lana checked the side mirror again.

"You worried about my driving?"

"No, of course not."

"Then who are you lookin' for?"

"No one." She wrinkled her nose. "Are we almost there?"

"Not far."

Lana shut down her laptop and set it on the floor between the seat and the console.

"You're stayin' in the car."

"Why?" she asked. "I should go in with you. How am I going to learn if I don't watch the master?"

"You don't need to learn. This ain't on-the-job training."

"Come on. Haven't I been a big help to you so far?" She smiled at him. "And I can do a lot more."

"From your computer, not from there." He nodded toward the house as he pulled up to the sidewalk in front of the Walker residence.

"But maybe I can get on their computer and find out who sent the payment for the ticket. And if I can get in there, it'll be easier to get to stuff later."

"And how do you expect to do that? They aren't going to just invite us inside."

"Maybe they will."

"Just wait here."

Tuper approached the front door and rang the bell. Mrs. Walker answered.

"Remember me, ma'am? Name is Tuper. I was here yesterday askin' about the Toyota."

"Yes, of course. Did you find the little boy?"

"No, we haven't. And it seems the car you received the ticket for *was* involved in his abduction."

"Oh my!" She put her hand over her mouth for a second. Then she looked confused. "I don't understand. Why would my husband's name and our address be connected to that car?"

"We think someone stole your husband's identity. Have you seen anything else unusual—like your credit cards being used or your utility bills overcharged or anything?"

"No. My daughter takes care of all the bills and she would've told me if there was a problem."

Just then Lana walked up carrying her laptop. "Dad, I'm not getting a strong enough connection and I have to turn in my paper on child abuse prevention for my sociology class. I don't know what I'm going to do." She glanced at the time on her phone. "I only have seven minutes left. We can't get to a place with a computer and get this in on time." She looked at Tuper with wet eyes. She tightened her lips and blinked her eyes as if she were fighting the urge to cry. "Daddy, what am I going to do? I've been working on this paper for months and it's half of my grade. I need to get to another computer and there isn't time to get to a library and send it out."

Mrs. Walker put her hand on Lana's shoulder and patted. She didn't see Tuper as he scowled at Lana. "Dearie, I have a computer. Will that help?"

"Do you? I would be so grateful. I just can't afford to get a bad grade."

"Come on in."

Mrs. Walker stepped into the living room, followed by Lana and then Tuper. Lana smirked at Tuper as she stepped inside. Mrs. Walker walked to the den just to her left and pointed to the Dell desktop computer. "There it is."

Lana stepped past her and sat down at the desk.

Mrs. Walker asked, "Do you know how to turn it on?" But before she could get the question completely out, she heard the sound of the computer starting up.

There was no passcode on the computer so Lana was free to get right to work.

"This won't take long."

"Is this going to work?" Tuper asked.

She set her laptop on the desk and opened it up. "Yes, Dad." She held up her hand as if to stop him. "I just need to get the information off of my laptop and then send it in through the desktop." She glanced at the time again. "I only have a few more minutes."

"We better leave her alone so she can get it done," Mrs. Walker said, and led Tuper back to the living room.

"That's very kind of you, ma'am. She's a good kid and she's trying so hard in school."

"I understand. I'm glad I don't have to go to school in this day and age. I wouldn't make it with all the technology."

"Me neither," Tuper said.

Mrs. Walker extended her hand toward an overstuffed chair. "Have a seat."

Tuper sat down and she did the same in a chair near him. "Do I need to be concerned about the identity theft?"

"It may be that the man who did this just used it for his car for some reason, but I'd keep an eye on my credit cards if I were you."

"I'll have my daughter double-check." She sighed. "Is that why you came back here?"

"I thought you should know. I didn't have your number, but I'm not much for phone calls anyway. Since I was in the area I decided to stop. Also wanted to ask you if your daughter or someone might have paid the ticket because it was paid by someone."

"I'm pretty sure I didn't do it. I forget a lot more than I used to, but I think I would've remembered that." She started to stand up. "I can check my checkbook."

"Actually, ma'am, it wasn't paid by check. It was paid on the computer."

She chuckled. "Then I know I didn't do it, but I'll ask my daughter."

"That would be good."

Lana returned to the living room. "All done," she said. Lana glanced around the room and spotted a photo of a couple on the mantel. She meandered over to it. "Lovely photo. Is that your husband?"

"Yes, it is. That was taken on our fiftieth wedding anniversary. He passed away not long after that."

"I'm so sorry. He's very handsome." She pointed to a picture of a young woman in a cap and gown. "And who is this?"

"That's Nichole, our daughter, when she graduated from high school."

"She's beautiful." Lana walked back to the sofa. "Sorry, I'm always fascinated by family photos. They tell such a story of people's lives." She looked at Tuper. "Dad hates to have his picture taken, so we don't have many." Lana looked directly at the woman. "I don't know how to thank you, Mrs. Walker, for letting me use your computer. You're a life saver."

Tuper and Mrs. Walker stood up and stepped toward the door. "My pleasure, dearie."

"Dad, did you give her your number so she can call after she talks to her daughter?"

Mrs. Walker retrieved a pad and pen from a stand near the door. Lana reached out for it. As Lana wrote "Tuper" on the pad, he recited his number.

"I *know* your number, Dad," she said and smiled at him sheepishly.

~~~

Nothing more was said until they were in the car and moving.

"What's with this 'Dad' business? You think I'm old enough to be your father?"

"You're old enough to be my grandfather," she blurted. Then she smirked. "That's it. Next time I'll call you 'Pops.'"

"Ain't gonna be no 'next time.'"

"Oh, come on, Pops. I was a big help to you. And now we can really watch what goes on there."

"What did you do?" Tuper asked.

"I connected to her computer so it'll let me know whenever someone is on it and I can look to see what they're doing. I can also look around more and get into places I couldn't see before."

Tuper shook his head. He was amazed and a little afraid of what she could do. He had heard about people like this on the news, but had never met anyone who could do it. And before now, he didn't really believe that it could be done.

"That only took you a few minutes. Is it that easy?"

"Not for most people, but I'm no script kiddie."

"Is that some kind of cat?" Tuper asked, mostly to annoy her.

"What are you talking about?"

"You said you weren't a script kitty."

"Not a kitty, like a cat. A kiddie, like a child. It's a term for someone who wants to be a hacker or a cracker but doesn't have the technical skills. I'm good at what I do." That was all she seemed to want to say about the subject. "So, what's next? How do we find this little boy?" When Tuper didn't respond right away, she continued. "Do you think if we track the car, we'll be able to find him? And what about the divorce papers? What good would it do to find them? If you have the right case number, then it's not even their divorce."

"It's the right number," Tuper interjected.

"How can you be sure? You didn't write it down."

"Never do. I saw the number on the paper. It's right."

"You're a stubborn old goat, aren't you? Your name should be 'obstinate' or 'pig-headed' or something, instead of Pops."

"Don't call me Pops," he said, a little more sternly than he intended.

"What kind of a name is Tuper anyway? Is that your real name? What does it mean?"

He shook his head and muttered, "Your folks shoulda named you 'Agony.'"

CHAPTER TWELVE

Tuper and Lana sat in the car watching the house where Denise was staying. Denise arrived shortly thereafter. She was driving the car her friend had brought her in to meet Tuper earlier, but now she was alone. A green Chevy Aveo sat in the driveway.

"This is boring. Do you do this often?"

"Yup."

"Seems like we've been here for hours."

Tuper looked at his watch. "Only been thirty-three minutes."

"Tell me what this case is all about. Maybe it'll help pass the time."

"Already told you what you need to know."

Tuper knew it wasn't a good idea letting her come along, but he didn't want to take the time to drive her back to Clarice's. Besides, she begged to go. He didn't plan to stay too long, something he decided not to share with Lana. He just wanted to see if there was anything unusual going on at this house late at night. So far, nothing had occurred, but it was only a little after ten. He'd give it a few hours.

"All you told me was that there is a little boy missing and this is where his mother is staying. I know there was a car involved in the kidnapping that is registered to the dead husband of that sweet old lady we saw today. The ticket was paid by someone from her computer. Since it's not likely the old lady is involved, someone is using her computer. That means it's someone she knows."

"She doesn't know *you*, and you used her

computer."

"Good point, but someone also had access to her husband's information because they used it to register the car."

"Maybe it was someone like you?"

"You think it was *me*?"

"Not you, someone like you who does what you do. You know, a whatcha-call-it, a butcher, or a sneaker, or whatever you're called."

"I'm a computer systems engineer, but I think the word you're looking for is 'hacker.' Anyway, it's possible, but not likely. A lot of people can do some basic hacking, but most aren't that sophisticated. It's more likely just someone she knows—like Nichole, her daughter."

Tuper had to admit, although not to Lana, that she had good deductive skills. He was impressed with her lie about the school assignment and the way she got the daughter's name from Mrs. Walker.

Lana opened up her laptop and powered it up. "Let's see what we can find out about Nichole."

Tuper was grateful for the few minutes of silence that Lana's work afforded him. He was just starting to enjoy it when she spoke up.

"Nichole Marie Walker lives a couple miles from her mother. She's single but involved; no children. It looks like she was never married or if she was, she kept her last name. There are no aliases for her that I've found." She turned the laptop toward Tuper. "Here's what she looks like. That's her Facebook profile pic. Here are some more photos of her. See, there's her mother."

"Yeah, that's her, alright," Tuper said as he glanced at the photos, but continued to constantly check the house where Denise was.

"What else are you finding about her?"

"She has a boyfriend named Alan something. He doesn't appear to have a page."

"A what?"

"A Facebook page. He's not on Facebook. At least there's no Alan in her friend list."

Tuper shook his head. "Agony, you speak a whole different language."

"My name's not Agony."

"It fits."

Lana continued to scroll through Nichole's Facebook page. "Looks like she's been with Alan about a year. At least that's when she starts to talk about him on her page."

"Any photos of him?"

"Not that I've found yet," Lana said.

Lana got quiet for another minute and Tuper realized she was staring at him.

"What are you looking at?"

"Your scar. Where did you get it?"

"Met up with a bear and didn't have a gun."

"Wow. Tell me about it." Lana's voice showed excitement.

"Just did," Tuper said, and started the engine. "She's leaving."

Lana closed her laptop and kept her eyes on Denise's car. "Aren't you going to tell me how it happened?"

"Told you all you need to know."

Denise drove away quickly, made two turns, and then headed north on Valley Drive. She picked up speed and so did Tuper. He dropped back a little to avoid her spotting him, and a car sped past him and landed between him and Denise.

"Try to watch her car," he said to Lana.

"She's really moving. Can't you go any faster?"

Tuper passed the car in front of him. Denise

passed two more cars, made a rolling stop, started to make a left turn, but then straightened the car and crossed over Canyon Ferry Road. Tuper stopped at the stop sign and let the traffic go, creating a greater gap between them. Then he got caught behind an old pickup and he couldn't pass until two cars coming toward him were out of the way.

"Can you see her?" Lana asked.

"I think she turned left on Howard." He kept driving north and turned left when he reached Howard. He saw no taillights in front of him, but he knew someone had just driven on the road because there was residual dust in the air from the dirt road.

"We lost her," Lana said.

"I don't think so."

"Are you seeing something I'm not?"

"Nope, but I'm pretty sure I know where she's headed."

Tuper turned right on Wylie and drove toward Leisure Village Mobile Home Park.

"Where are we going?"

"To Randy's house. Denise's ex."

Once inside the park Tuper turned left but didn't go all the way to the end row where Randy lived. He turned right on the lane before it, circled around, and came up the other direction, stopping at the mobile home two doors down, which he had observed previously to be empty. Denise's car was parked in front of Randy's home next to the Dodge Daytona. A dim light shone from the living room area in Randy's house.

"Why would she be here if they're getting a divorce?" Lana asked.

"Not sure, but she thinks he has the kid," Tuper said.

"Do you think she's here to confront him?"

Tuper shrugged.

"Why would she do that? Wouldn't she call you?"

"I gave up a long time ago tryin' to figure out why women do what they do."

Lana ignored him. "I wish I could hear what they're saying."

She set her laptop on the floor, unbuckled her seatbelt, and opened her door.

"What are you doing?"

"I'm getting a closer look." Tuper objected, but she was already gone, gently closing the door behind her. He feared that if he attempted to stop her, it would cause too much commotion.

Lana snuck up to the mobile home and disappeared behind it. Less than five minutes later, she returned and got in the car.

"I think we can leave," Lana said.

"Were you able to see inside?"

"I'm afraid so," she said. "I climbed up the tree and I could see right into the bedroom window."

"So, what did you see?"

"She came here for a booty call," Lana said, wrinkling her nose. "It wasn't a pretty sight."

CHAPTER THIRTEEN

It was late and the clouds were threatening to drop a ton of snow before morning, so Tuper decided not to drive to his cabin in Clancy. His biggest concern was getting stuck there. Instead, he drove to a female friend's house and spent the night. Stacy always welcomed him even though she knew there were no wedding bells in their future. She had kept hope alive for the first five years or so but now, after fifteen years, she had given up and quit pestering him about it. He had finally convinced her that he had nothing to offer her with a commitment. She had a nice house and a good job. He had neither. His cabin was just a shack in the mountains. His work was sporadic and it often took him away from home, or so he told her. Sometimes he just needed his space.

He left Stacy's house around six, before she was awake. There wasn't much he could do this early, but he couldn't just sit around the house either. He drove up East Custer Avenue to the Residence Inn, near the airport. They served hot breakfast for their guests, and occasionally Tuper would partake of their generosity. He didn't do it too often for fear they would catch on to him. He hadn't been there in a couple of months, and sausage and eggs sounded tasty this morning.

When Tuper did go there to eat, he would generally go two or three days in a row. There was a woman on the food staff, Marlene, whom he suspected knew he was local, but she never said anything. She had somehow gotten the impression that he worked for some secret branch of law enforcement, which Tuper encouraged without actually saying so.

He came in the side door that entered directly into the dining area. The room held about eight dining tables and a long counter-height table that seated about twenty guests. Just to the right was another room where the food was set up as a buffet line. He strolled in there, dished up a plate of food, and sat down. Marlene was gathering up dirty dishes from the table next to him.

"Good mornin', darlin'," Tuper said, gently touching her arm as she passed.

"Nice to see you," she said, blushing from his touch. "Are you working on some big case?"

He leaned closer to her and lowered his voice to almost a whisper. "A missing boy."

Her face lit up. "Is that the boy who went missing from school a few days ago?"

"Shh," he said. "I can't really discuss it."

She clasped her index finger and thumb together and made a zipper motion across her mouth.

They made small talk for a few minutes, and then she went back to work. Tuper finished his meal and left the same way he came in.

~~~

Clarice answered her door in her work uniform. "Good morning, Tuper. Come on in. I'm about to leave, but there's some scrambled eggs on the stove and hot tea water. Lana is in the bathroom, but she's been up for hours searching for information for you."

Clarice entered the kitchen and poured him a mug of tea.

Shortly after, Lana came into the room and sat down at the table in front of her laptop. "Hello," she said to Tuper.

"Mornin'."

Clarice set his teacup on the table. "I'm in a bit of a hurry, but you can get yourself some breakfast if you want."

"Thanks, but I already ate," Tuper said.

"Residence Inn?" Clarice asked.

He nodded.

"You stayed at the hotel last night?" Lana asked.

"Nope."

Lana looked at him, shrugged, and went back to work.

"Have you found anything more about Nichole?"

"I found out she has lousy taste in men."

"That's easy to do."

"She's dated some real losers. Three of her breakups have been because the men went to prison. The first one was jailed; the guy after him was sent to prison. When the first guy was released from jail, she hooked up with him again until his crimes escalated and he was imprisoned again. That ended that one. She's always madly in love and talks about it constantly on Facebook."

"What did they serve time for?"

"The first guy was in for grand theft auto. He was out in a year, but less than four years later he was back in for armed robbery. The guy in between had served time before he met her for domestic violence. There's no record of violence with her— of course that doesn't mean there wasn't any—but he went to prison for manslaughter. Killed his own mother."

"What about Nichole? She got any kind of record?"

"Nothing. No convictions, not even any arrests—at least not in Montana—and the best I can tell, she has only lived here. I couldn't find any indication of drug use. Maybe she should."

"Should use drugs?"

"I'm thinking a little mind-altering drug might

improve her taste in men."

Clarice came through the living room wearing her coat. She grabbed her keys off the bar and picked up her purse. "I'm out of here. See you both later."

When the door closed behind her, Tuper said, "What about the new boyfriend?"

"His name is Alan Bowman. He's a little better than the rest. He has a misdemeanor for shoplifting ten years ago, and two years ago he lost his job for stealing supplies from the warehouse where he was working. They didn't press charges though."

"So he's a crook?"

"Right. Also, he had a drunk driving charge less than a year ago and hasn't completed his probation yet. His driving is restricted and he has no car registered to him. I'm guessing Nichole does the driving. She has a red 2012 Nissan. Oh, and he was arrested for peeing in public."

"That's illegal?"

"Not really, but indecent exposure is. They tried to pin it on him, but apparently they couldn't find any intent. He was drunk and had to relieve himself so he went on the sidewalk. They finally dismissed it."

"Can you tell if either one of them is connected to Randy Jenkins?"

"I couldn't find any connection on social media. Nichole was on the computer late last night at her mom's and I got into her email. I found nothing unusual. It could be she uses another email address that I haven't found yet, or that she erased anything that might be connected to Randy, but so far there hasn't been anything suspicious."

"And Alan?"

"I haven't been in his email yet, but I did find something interesting about Randy Jenkins."

"What?"

"He has no social media accounts."

"Neither do I. That don't make him odd."

"Yeah, it kind of does. I can only trace him back five years. Then he's not anywhere."

"What do you mean?"

"I can't find any information on him. You need to find out more about him from Denise, and then maybe I can do better. And you know how I said there was no divorce for them?"

"Yeah?"

"Find out when they got married because I'm not finding that either, at least not in Montana or any bordering states. And I tried Nevada, but there isn't anything there either."

CHAPTER FOURTEEN

Tuper found Squirrely at Humpty's bar. His buddy had been playing in the poker game the night before and spent the night.

"Squirrely, what you got for me?" Tuper asked.

"Not a whole lot. Everyone is aware of the missing kid, but the kidnapper doesn't appear to be any of the usual suspects. There's no local pedophile ring. I've got feelers out about the parents, and I also have people looking for that RAV4, but that hasn't shown up either."

"I have a hunch the car is in Great Falls," Tuper said. "I'm going there now to see what I can find out."

"Mind if I ride along? I'd like to check on my mother."

"Let's go."

Squirrely grabbed his jacket and a shopping bag with his clothes, and they left.

"How's your mother doing?" Tuper asked.

"She took a tumble the other day in the store, but she didn't break anything. I'm concerned because we're supposed to have a bad winter this year. She's not that stable, and if she falls and breaks a bone, she isn't going to be able to take care of herself. But she's too stubborn to listen."

"She's a tough old goat."

When they arrived at the car, Tuper chased Ringo into the back seat and Squirrely stepped into the front.

"Have you checked out the father?" Squirrely asked.

"Yeah, I've been watchin' him, but so far nothin'."

"The cops think it was him."

"His wife's pointing the finger at him too. I've been to his house and I've followed him a few times, but I haven't found any evidence of the kid. He has no toys, no photos, nothing belongin' to the kid, almost as if he's trying too hard to cover something up."

"Or maybe he doesn't have him."

~~~

When they reached Great Falls, Tuper dropped Squirrely at his mother's house. She was eighty-one years old and insisted on living in Great Falls where she had friends. She and her husband had lived in Nevada for a while with their daughter until her husband died. After that she'd become determined to return home.

After dropping his buddy, Tuper went to the address Lana had found for Nichole Walker and Alan Bowman. Although it was only a few miles from the nice neighborhood where Nichole's mother lived, the area was pretty run down.

He found the apartment with little trouble. A red Ford Focus was parked in the designated parking spot. Tuper drove around the area several times looking for the dark blue RAV4 but found nothing. He was hoping the car was there so he would know for sure that it was either Nichole or Alan who had it. Since Lana hadn't figured out who paid the ticket, Tuper couldn't confront Alan without the car.

Tuper waited and watched for another hour and a half and then drove to pick Squirrely up.

"Did you find the car?" Squirrely asked.

"Nope, but I thought we'd drop by again before we leave town. First, I need to stop and see a guy. He's meeting me at McDonald's."

Tuper pulled into the furthest parking spot in the

McDonald's lot. He took out his wallet and retrieved a ten-dollar bill and handed it to Squirrely.

"Get us each two of those little hamburgers. Make that five hamburgers. If you don't get an extra one, I'll have to share mine with Ringo."

Squirrely got out and went into the restaurant. Tuper walked to a car parked in a space two over from him.

"Thanks for comin', Glen," he said to the man in the car. "Any chance you could keep an eye on a house and watch for a car for me?"

"That depends. You know I work for the city, right?" Glen said with a smile. "I'm not your own personal detective."

"I know, but if this hunch pans out, you'll get another feather in your cap."

"Is it someone wanted by the law?"

"Not yet, but I'll let you know if it comes to that. So far, it's a guess. I'm trying to find a missing five-year-old."

"Mason Jenkins?"

"That's the one."

"Okay."

Tuper gave him Alan's and Nichole's names, their address, the make and model of the car, and the license plate number. They shook hands and the cop drove away.

When Squirrely returned with the hamburgers, Tuper took the meat off of two of them and gave the patties to Ringo. Then he ate the other hamburger and the two buns without the meat.

They drove back to Nichole's apartment, only to discover that the red Ford Focus was gone and no RAV4 was in sight.

~~~

Tuper dropped Squirrely off at Humpty's, and then called Denise and set up a meeting. She again chose the Mini Basket to meet, but this time she came by herself in a green Chevy Aveo. She parked next to Tuper's car and motioned for Tuper to come to her.

When he got in the car, she said, "It's warmer in here and we don't need to disturb Ringo."

"Okay."

"Do you know where my son is?"

"No, but maybe you can help."

"How?"

"I'm checking out a few leads, but I'm hitting dead ends. Do the police have any leads yet?"

"Not that they've told me. They're still looking for him, but I know they think it's too late. But it can't be, I'm sure he's alive." She choked back the tears. "You must help me."

"I'm trying. Tell me, does Randy spend much time on the computer?"

She frowned at Tuper. "No. Why?"

"Does he have any social media accounts?"

"No, he doesn't even own a computer. I have one, but I don't use it much."

"When were you two married?"

"Seven years ago."

"Where?"

Denise hesitated. "Why is that important?"

"Just humor me."

"Mexico."

"Mexico?"

"Yes, and unfortunately it's legal. I checked into it, hoping it wasn't because then I wouldn't need a divorce."

"Why Mexico?"

"Randy and I took a trip to San Diego to go to the zoo, Sea World, and the beach. Randy had a friend in the Navy stationed there who invited us. While we were there, we went to Tijuana just to see what it was like and we decided to get married."

"And when did you file for divorce?"

This time there was a long pause. "About that...." she said. "The papers were never actually filed."

"But you said the court gave you full custody and that made Randy angry."

"I just told him that. I told him I filed the papers and got a temporary order."

"And he took your word for it?"

She shrugged. "Yes. He's not too bright. I let him have visitation and that satisfied him for a while. But he threatened to get a lawyer. I knew he wouldn't do that though, so I wasn't concerned until Mason disappeared."

"Do you know a man named Alan Bowman?"

A slight change of expression crossed her face before she said, "No."

Tuper was pretty certain she was lying, but she was better than most at it.

"Do you think this Alan guy has something to do with the kidnapping?"

"Not sure yet."

CHAPTER FIFTEEN

Tuper and Lana sat in Tuper's car outside the house where Denise was staying. "Thanks again for letting me go with you on the stakeout," Lana said.

"You didn't really give me a choice if I wanted to find out what you learned today," Tuper said. "I'm surprised you wanted to go since you were so bored last night."

"It was kind of fun, except for the scene in the window."

"You're not doing that tonight. You're staying in the car."

"Okay," Lana said. "Why are you watching your client again? It seems you should be watching her ex."

"Because she's not telling me everything." Tuper shared with Lana the conversation he had with Denise earlier that day. He figured Lana needed to know if she was going to keep researching for him.

"Mexico, huh? That would explain why I couldn't find anything. Do you believe her?"

"About Mexico? Why not?" Tuper said.

"I guess it doesn't really matter where they were married or *if* they were married. And it doesn't matter if there was or wasn't a divorce. The thing is that she lied to you originally, and you think she's still holding something back, don't you?"

"Lying comes too easy for her. This isn't her first rodeo."

"That's kind of what I found out today. Her history online only goes back about five years, just like Randy's. They lived together in three different places. I have those addresses if you need them. But prior to that I can't find where they lived. I think there's way more to this than she's telling you."

"I think you're right."

"I guess we witnessed that last night. Don't you find it odd that this woman blames her ex for kidnapping her son and then goes to his house and sleeps with him?"

"I do, but the kid is still missing and she seems genuinely concerned about that. So maybe she doesn't really think it was him."

"Why would she try to steer you in his direction then?"

"Don't know."

Lana's eyes widened. "Maybe she was using sex to get information from him. Maybe she thought she could get him to give Mason up."

"That didn't work, or she wouldn't have had any reason to meet with me today."

Tuper started the car. "She's leaving." Just then another car came up behind them and passed before they could pull out. Lana glanced at the car and then leaned down as if she were putting her computer on the floor. Tuper thought she stayed there a little longer than she should have.

They followed Denise on the same route she had taken last night to Randy's mobile home. She seemed to be traveling even faster tonight, so they were again left in the dust.

As they drove into the double lane leading into the park, which had a line of trees down the middle, a black car sped out and onto Herrin. It was going too fast and was blocked by the trees, so they couldn't see it well.

"Sure some crazy drivers out here tonight," Lana said.

Once at Randy's, Tuper parked the car in the same spot he had the night before. Denise's car was parked next to the Dodge Daytona. Lights were on in the home. Tuper and Lana sat there for less than a minute before the door flew open and Denise rushed out. She jumped in her car and sped away. They tried to follow her but she was moving too fast. She seemed to be headed back home.

"What do you suppose happened?" Lana asked. Before Tuper could answer, she said, "She couldn't have been there long enough for them to have a fight. Maybe he had another girl in there. That would make her leave in a hurry—especially if they were doing the nasty. I bet that's what happened. Men, you're all pigs."

"Never denied it."

By the time Tuper and Lana arrived at Denise's house, the car was parked in the driveway and Denise was already inside.

"I think we should go back to Randy's and see what's going on."

Tuper didn't want to tell her that he was thinking the same thing.

"Why?" he asked as he drove back toward Leisure Village Mobile Park.

"Maybe Denise has a boyfriend."

His head turned quickly toward her. "What?"

"Maybe she caught her boyfriend with another woman." Her voice escalated. "Or with another man. What if she caught her boyfriend with Randy?"

"You're not makin' any sense, little lady."

"When I saw her going at it the other night, it might not have been Randy she was with. I couldn't see his face, just his bare butt. Maybe it was someone else."

"You're gettin' a little carried away. Why would she go to her ex-husband's house to have sex with her boyfriend?"

"I don't understand why she would go to a man's house that kidnapped her kid to have sex with him. This makes just as much sense to me."

"You may have a point, but I doubt if it's that far-fetched. Sometimes a campfire is just a campfire."

Lana lowered her head slightly. "And sometimes it's arson," she said softly.

"Are we still talkin' about this case?"

Lana didn't answer.

Tuper drove into the park and around the back way, watching for any sign of activity near Randy's home. His car was still parked to the side of the home, and the lights were still on inside. Tuper stopped the car and told Lana to stay put as he slipped on a pair of thin leather gloves.

"What are you going to do?"

"I'm going to knock on the door and have a chat with Randy. Think it's 'bout time." He looked directly at Lana. "Stay here."

Tuper walked to the front door and knocked. No one answered. While he stood there waiting, Lana left the car and dashed around to the back of the home.

When no one answered the front door, Tuper pulled out his Colt 45, slowly opened the door, and called out, "Anyone here?"

No answer.

He stepped inside the living room and quickly glanced around but saw no one. The curtain over the kitchen sink was open and Tuper saw movement out back. He ducked down and peeked out but saw nothing but a shadow. He waited for a few seconds before he proceeded toward the hallway. From his last visit there, he was aware there were only two more rooms, a bathroom and a bedroom. He moved as softly as his boots would allow. The floor creaked. He stopped. Still no one appeared. He pushed open the bathroom door. It was empty.

He crept along the wall for three or four feet to the open bedroom door. Just as he did, he heard a muffled sound. He dashed inside, gun drawn. Through the window he saw Lana in the oak tree with her hand over her mouth, about to fall out of the tree. Hanging off the edge of the bed was Randy in a huge red stain of blood.

Tuper leaned down and checked his pulse. There was none.

CHAPTER SIXTEEN

When Tuper returned to the car, Lana was already inside. She was shaking. He wondered how much was from the cold and how much was from what she had seen.

"Is he dead?" Lana asked.

"He's dead," Tuper said.

"What are we going to do?"

"Did you leave your mittens on when you were out there?"

"Yes."

"Did you have them on last night?"

"Yes, it was cold, remember?"

"Are you okay?"

"I think so."

"Okay, then," Tuper said, as he started the car. He drove out of the park and turned right.

"We can't just leave him, right?" Lana asked. "Do you think Denise killed him? I guess we should've gone in right away when we saw her run out; maybe he'd still be alive. Why would she kill him? And if he has her kid, how is she going to find him now? So much for the affair idea. Maybe not. Maybe she caught him in the act, killed him, and then left. His paramour could've left while we were gone."

"Paramour?" Tuper said.

"You know, lover."

"I know what the word means. It just seems like an odd word to use right now."

Tuper pulled into the small parking lot in front of a convenience store about a mile from the mobile park. Lana was still rambling. He pointed toward the glove compartment. "There's a burner phone in there. Hand it to me."

Lana glanced at the glove compartment, then at Tuper, and back to the compartment again.

"Today," Tuper said.

She opened the glove compartment, took out the phone, and handed it to Tuper. Normally he would've called his police friend, Pat Cox, and let him get some credit for finding out about the body, but since Pat was in the hospital he had to call someone else. He didn't want to call 9-1-1 because that would mean he'd have to explain too much. Besides, it might be detrimental to his client. He handed the phone back to Lana.

"Aren't you going to report the murder?" Lana asked.

"Do you want to call 9-1-1 and get involved?"

"No," she said a little too quickly.

"Didn't think so," he said. "Someone will find him."

"But that could take days."

"He ain't gonna get any deader."

Tuper pulled out of the parking lot and turned left back towards the mobile home park.

"You're not going back there, are you?" Lana asked.

Tuper shook his head.

"Where are we going then?"

"Takin' you home."

The sound of sirens blared. Just as Tuper and Lana passed the park they could see emergency lights flashing ahead of them. Tuper pulled over as he always did when emergency vehicles approached him. The vehicle in front of him had already pulled over and one coming from behind did the same. A pickup and an SUV passed from behind without stopping.

"Jackasses," Tuper muttered. "Don't they know they're supposed to stop?"

Two police cars approached, followed by a fire truck and an ambulance. Lana turned around so she could see where they were going.

"The cops pulled into the mobile park," Lana said.

"Guess we're done here."

~~~

It was nearly seven o'clock in the morning. Lana sat at the dining room table in Clarice's house pounding on her keyboard. She hadn't found anything yet about Randy Jenkins' death. She started wondering if those emergency vehicles were for someone else.

Clarice entered the dining area in her pajamas, robe, and slippers. "It's cold in here." She checked the thermostat and moved it up a couple of notches.

"Yeah, it got pretty cold last night," Lana said, as she continued to type on her laptop.

"You should've turned the heat up. You know, we could light the fireplace."

"I was fine once I got bundled up in bed. I heated that corn bag you gave me the other night. That was awesome. I've never seen one of those before. You called it a corn bag, so I'm guessing it has corn in it. Why doesn't it pop when you heat it?"

"It's different than the corn they use for popcorn. It's feed corn, the kind they use for feed."

"Whatever, it kept me warm," Lana said. "There's hot tea water on." The truth was that Lana didn't want to use the furnace and raise Clarice's utility bills. She was happy to have a place to stay and she didn't want to give her new friend a reason to ask her to leave.

Clarice joined Lana at the table with her cup of hot tea. "You're up early."

"I was looking for something on the Internet."

"Did you find it?"

"No." She looked up. "Is Tuper coming by this morning?"

"He should be here any time now. He just called and woke me up. He has no concept of time. He gets up in the middle of the night, stays up a few hours, and he thinks it's noon and everyone else is awake."

"He doesn't sleep much, does he?"

"Speak of the devil," Clarice said. She went to the door, unlocked it, and let in Tuper. "Now if you'll excuse me, I'm going to get dressed. I don't have to be at work until two this afternoon, but I have some errands to run before this snow storm hits."

Before Tuper could sit down, Lana said, "I couldn't find anything on the Internet about Randy Jenkins' death. Do you think they haven't found him yet?"

"They found him."

"How do you know that?"

"My buddy Glen called me from Great Falls."

"How would he know?"

"He's a cop there. We don't get too many murders in these parts so when there is one, the word spreads quickly, especially among law enforcement."

"Why did he call you?"

"Because he knows I'm trying to find Mason."

"Do the cops know where Mason is?"

"Nope."

"Did he tell you Randy's time of death?"

"They don't have an exact time for when he died yet, but it wasn't long before we saw him, but then we already knew that because he was still very warm when I checked his pulse."

"I'll bet Denise did it while we were outside his house."

"Maybe."

"What do we do now?"

"*We* aren't doing nothin'. You've seen way too much."

"Aw, Pops, you're concerned about me."

"I ain't your pops. If I was, you'd be hidin' from me for that stunt you pulled last night."

Lana looked at him and her lips turned up ever so slightly on each side in a sheepish smile. "You're not very scary, you know. Besides, you need my help." She turned back to her laptop. "I found something interesting about your client."

"What's that?" Tuper asked.

"So, *now* you want my help?"

"Just tell me already."

"Look at this," Lana said, turning her laptop so Tuper could see it. "Denise is on Facebook, but she hasn't said anything about her missing child."

Tuper looked at the screen. "Maybe the cops told her not to."

"No, look." She scrolled forward. "She has never said anything about Mason. Most people post photos of every little thing their kid does, but Denise hasn't. Nothing."

"Maybe she doesn't want to share her kid with the world. There's lots of perverts out there who like photos of little children."

"I thought about that, but I still think there's more to it."

"Maybe."

"I also found out that Alan Bowman is out of town."

"What do you mean?"

"I hacked into Nichole's emails and I found an email to a friend that said Alan was 'out of town' and that he left yesterday. She didn't know when he would be back."

Tuper didn't respond. He was wondering if Alan might have had something to do with Randy's death.

"Maybe Alan killed him. He's 'out of town,'" Lana said, making air quotes. "He left yesterday, so maybe he came here, killed Randy, and went somewhere to hide out."

"You have quite a vivid imagination, Agony." It bothered him a little that she was thinking the same thing he was. He hoped she couldn't read his mind the way she read the inside of that computer.

CHAPTER SEVENTEEN

Tuper pulled off to the side of the road to answer his phone. He didn't stop because he was concerned about driving while talking, but because his fading eyesight made it difficult to use technology.

"Yeah?" he said before he knew who it was.

"I need your help," the female voice said.

"Who is this?"

"It's Denise."

"Where are you?"

"I'm at the bus station."

"Don't leave. I'll be right there."

Five minutes later Tuper entered the bus station and spotted Denise sitting alone on a bench near the door.

"Where you goin'?" Tuper asked.

"I haven't decided. I thought about California. Randy and I had such a good time when we went there. But I don't want to go anywhere without my son."

Tuper didn't respond.

"Randy's dead," Denise blurted. Then a tear rolled down her cheek.

"I heard."

She went on as if she hadn't heard Tuper speak. "Someone murdered him last night. The cops came by this morning and questioned me."

"What did you tell them?"

"I didn't know anything to tell them. They think it's related to the kidnapping. They wanted to know if anyone had approached me for ransom. I told them I hadn't heard anything from the kidnapper. Up until last night, I still thought Randy had taken him."

"And now?"

She started to sob. "If he did take him, he stashed him somewhere and I may never find him."

Tuper didn't know whether to try and console her or not. He hated when women cried. It made him feel awful, and he never knew what to do to help them feel better.

"Why did you go to Randy's?"

She looked at him with a puzzled look. Then she said, "To convince him to tell me where Mason was."

"Two nights in a row?"

She sniffled, holding back the tears. "How do you know that?"

"I was there."

"What were you doing at Randy's?"

"My job."

Her eyes widened and she spoke sharply. "Did you kill him?"

"No. Did you?"

"Of course not." She began to cry again. "I loved him."

"I thought you hated him."

"I do. I did. But I still love him."

Tuper thought he'd never understand the way a woman's mind worked. He had given up trying a long time ago.

"Did you tell the police?" Denise asked.

"Tell them what?"

"That you saw me at Randy's last night?"

"No. Did you tell them you were there?"

"No," she snapped. "They always come after the spouse first. If they knew I was there, they'd try to pin it on me."

"You ran out in a hurry," Tuper said. "What happened?"

"I went inside expecting to talk to him."

"Like you did the night before?"

"Yes."

"Did you learn anything about Mason the night before?"

"No. He kept denying that he had taken him."

"And last night?"

"I knocked and he didn't answer. I tried the door and it was unlocked, so I went in and called to him. Still nothing. I thought maybe he was in the shower or had fallen asleep, so I went to the back of the house." She stopped talking and started to cry again. After a few moments, she contained herself and spoke. "He was hanging off the side of the bed and there was blood all around his head."

"Did you check to see if he was alive?"

"I checked his neck and his wrist. I couldn't feel a pulse. I took a mirror out of my purse and put it in front of his mouth, but he wasn't breathing."

Tuper must have frowned because Denise said, "I saw it on a TV show once. It made sense."

"Then what did you do?"

"I ran out and went home."

"You didn't call the police or an ambulance?"

"What was the point? He was already dead."

Tuper wondered if she was telling the truth about not calling the police, although he couldn't think of any reason she would have to lie about that. But then he was pretty sure she lied about other things he didn't understand either.

"Are you still going away?"

"Not without Mason," she said softly.

"Need a ride somewhere?"

"Could you take me to the Mini Basket? My friend will pick me up there."

"Sure."

Once inside Tuper's car, Denise asked, "Can I trust you?"

"I haven't done you wrong yet, have I?"

"That's true. You could've called the cops on me last night and you didn't." She reached inside her purse and pulled out an envelope. "If I give you this, will you promise not to open it unless something happens to me?"

"Somethin' gonna happen to you?"

"Probably. Someone already killed Randy. They could kill me too."

"Are you sure you don't know who killed him?"

"No, I don't know, but if someone kills me, I want you to open this, understand?"

He stared at her for a few seconds. "Okay."

"If I'm gone and you haven't found Mason yet, this might help you."

"Then wouldn't it be better if I knew now?"

"No. It won't help you now. Only if I'm gone. And if you do find Mason, please make sure he ends up with family."

"You're family?"

"You'll understand when you open this."

"You sure that's the way you want to play this?"

"I'm sure."

She handed him the envelope.

CHAPTER EIGHTEEN

"I need your help," Tuper muttered.

"What did you say?" Lana asked.

"I need your help."

"I know; I heard you the first time. I just wanted to hear you say it again."

He shook his head. "Why do I bother?"

"Because you need my help." She smiled. "What can I do for you? I'm guessing it's something on the web because I'm thinking you aren't ready for me to go undercover for you just yet. So, what is it?"

"If you'll stop talkin', I'll tell you."

Lana pretended to zip her lips.

"His name is Gordon Price," Tuper said.

"Who is?"

"Randy Jenkins. His real name is Gordon Price. He's also had a couple of aliases: Randy Price, Gordon Randall, and probably others. Can you search for him?"

Before Tuper finished listing his aliases, Lana had her fingers on her keyboard. "That explains why his online profile only goes back a few years. Do you know his birthday?"

"July 3, 1981." Tuper watched as her fingers flew across the keyboard. "How long will it take you?"

"Depends on what you want." She kept working as she spoke. "I can get you some basic information within minutes."

For the next few minutes, the only sound in the room was the clicking of computer keys.

"Gordon Price was born in Banning, California, in San Gorgonio Memorial Hospital to Stephen and Mary

Price. His father was a high school teacher. At some point, they must've moved to San Jacinto because he graduated in 1999 from San Jacinto High School."

"That's amazing."

"That he graduated?" Lana asked.

"No, what you can do with that machine." He paused and stared at her.

"What?"

"You know how you got into Nichole's mom's computer and fixed it so you could see when she's on there?"

"Yes?"

He hesitated. "Can you actually see her?"

Lana chuckled. "You have no idea how this works, do you?"

"Not a clue."

"No, I can't see her." She went back to work. "I can get a lot more information, but it'll be better if you tell me what you want so I can concentrate my efforts."

"Like what kind of stuff?"

"Like other schools he may have attended, criminal record, housing, who he has slept with…."

His head snapped up in surprise. "You can tell me who he has slept with?"

"No, I was kidding about that. Well, sort of. Sometimes they leave a tangible trail behind, like babies and stuff, but no, I can't see who they are sleeping with. So, what do you want to know?"

"All of it, but start with a criminal record and where he's been, especially around the time when he hooked up with Denise."

Lana smiled when he said "hooked up." Tuper saw the smile, but ignored it.

Tuper decided not to tell Lana about the envelope from Denise. He was pretty sure she'd want to open it and since he wanted to open it too, he was afraid she wouldn't stop buggin' him until he did. But he did tell her about Denise having him drop her off at the Mini Basket. Even though Agony could be annoying, she had a good mind and had already helped him figure out a few things. He wasn't about to tell her that she had impressed him, though. That would go right to her head.

"It sounds like Denise doesn't want me to know where she lives," Tuper said.

"It could be she has something to hide."

"But we've been there. Did you see anything unusual?"

"No, but whatever she's hiding might be inside."

"But she could easily control that by not inviting me inside."

"Maybe it's who she's living with. Do you know who that is?"

"No, she never said. It was a woman who brought her to the Mini Basket. That's all I know about her."

"We know the make and model of the car. If I had the plate number, I could check to see who owns the car."

Tuper spouted a numeric sequence starting with five. "It's registered in Helena."

"How do you know that?"

"Because I know five is the number for Helena plates."

"No, I mean the plate number itself."

"Saw it the other night."

"Were you already planning on looking that up?"

"Not necessarily. I just remember numbers."

"I'll look it up. The owner of the car might be the reason she doesn't want you there. Maybe she's someone important, like a senator or something. Or maybe she's her lover. Or she could have a meth lab in her house, or Denise could have Mason, or...." Lana rambled on. "Or it could be just that you're a man, an old man, but still a man, and she doesn't want you around." She gave Tuper a fake smile. "I'm guessing she doesn't trust men much right now."

Tuper thought about responding to the suggestions she made. Most of them were nonsensical. Although he did wonder about the possibility of Mason being there, he couldn't think of any reason why Denise would have him looking for her son if she had him. Besides, that was the one area where he was convinced of her sincerity. She seemed the most genuine when she spoke of Mason being missing. So, instead he murmured, "I'm not that old."

Tuper's phone rang. He looked at the number and, recognizing it, said, "Hey, Squirrely." He listened. "I'm going there right now. Thanks." He hung up.

"What's up?" Lana asked.

"The RAV4 was spotted at the Motherlode bar."

"I want to go with you."

"No, this could get messy. Besides, I need you here to find out about Jenkins or Price or whatever his name is. We need to find Mason."

Tuper walked out, not giving her time to gather her things and tag along.

CHAPTER NINETEEN

Lana did the dishes, cleaned up the kitchen, and put her bedding away in the living room. Then she sat down at the dining room table with her laptop. She was disappointed, but Tuper was right. Her time was better spent on the computer than tagging along with him. This was going to take a while. Besides, she didn't really want to be out in broad daylight.

Before she started her search, she checked one of her email accounts. She had about ten, and she was careful to never connect one to another. She used them for different purposes and people. One was for her hacker name Cricket. Only a few people had that one and she only received a few messages on it, although she checked it regularly. Nothing today.

She checked her Hotmail email address, one she'd had for years and her old friends used. She didn't communicate on it much anymore, and she wasn't really sure why she kept it except that it felt like home. She didn't have a real home now. She lived in cyberspace. Her old email account was as close as she got to home, and occasionally she heard from a friend in her old life.

She rifled through the junk mail, discarding as she went, and then she saw it. The email simply read, *I'll find you. I'm getting closer.* Her heart skipped a beat as she clicked out of it. She told herself the email didn't mean anything. If the threat had been sent to a newer email address, maybe, but this was just a bullying tactic.

She quickly checked the other email accounts and found nothing. She took a deep breath. "All is good," she said out loud, and then glanced around as if someone might hear her. Then she remembered she was alone in the house. Clarice and her sister Mary Ann were both at work. She wondered how long they would let her stay there. She had no money to pay them. As much as she hated housework, she had been cleaning up every day, hoping that might help. Every day she cleaned the kitchen, straightened up the living room, and made the girls' beds. In addition, she would do at least one other thing, like vacuum or clean the bathroom. She hadn't decided what she was going to do today, but right now she had work to do.

Lana ran the license plate number Tuper had given her for the car Denise was driving and came up with the name Jan Murray. The woman was a nurse at St. Peter's Hospital. She was renting the house where Denise was now staying. Her address prior to that was also familiar to Lana. It was on Lonesome Loop, the same area where Denise and Randy had lived five years ago. Lana looked at a Google map and saw that the backyards on their properties connected. Further investigation showed Jan was in nursing school at the time.

Everything she found seemed innocuous, but she would tell Tuper. Perhaps he would see more in it.

Lana had been sitting too long without a break. She hadn't slept well the night before and she was starting to feel it. She stood up, stretched, and decided to take a shower to revive herself.

When she finished, she scrubbed the tub and shower. She felt good that she had her cleaning done for the day. Wearing her bra and panties, she started to step out of the bathroom when she heard the front door open. She dashed back in, slipped on the pajamas Clarice had loaned her, and exited the bathroom.

"Hi, Lana," Mary Ann said when she came into the kitchen.

"Hi. I didn't know you were coming home."

"I decided to come home for lunch. I didn't have time to make it this morning. Want to join me? I'm having a ham sandwich."

"Sure, but I can make my own." Lana made a ham and cheese sandwich, without the ham.

They sat down to eat.

"Thank you, Mary Ann, for letting me stay here. You both have been so kind to me."

Mary Ann reached over and touched Lana on the hand. "Sweetie, I don't know exactly what your situation is, but I know you're a good person. To tell you the truth, Clarice is more trusting than I am, but she also reads people pretty well. I may not have been as generous at first, but now that we know you better, I'm good with it too. Clarice and I have both been in tight spots before and someone always helped us out. I'm glad we can do the same for you."

Lana wasn't sure she would be very generous either if someone were to come to her in need, but she was awfully glad Clarice had been. Without her friend's help, Lana wasn't sure where she would have gone.

"Well, thank you."

"Besides, this house looks better than it ever has. You've more than earned your keep."

Lana finished her sandwich and picked up the plates. Mary Ann started to help her, but Lana insisted she let her do it. "I'll clean up. You get back to work, or relax if you have some time."

"I do need to get going." She slipped on her coat. "You don't get out much, do you?"

"I don't really have any place to go."

"Maybe the three of us can go out sometime."

"Sure," Lana said and watched her leave. *Maybe someday.*

Lana got dressed and sat back down to her task at hand —finding more about Gordon Price.

CHAPTER TWENTY

Tuper found the RAV4 in the Motherlode parking lot. He glanced inside but all he saw was a coffee mug in the holder, an old pair of tennis shoes, and an open, empty shoebox in the back seat. The inside of the car appeared to have been recently cleaned, or Alan Bowman was a neat freak.

Tuper entered the Motherlode, stopped a second for his eyes to adjust to the lighting, and then looked around. It was Sunday around lunchtime so it wasn't very crowded. There couldn't have been more than fifteen people sitting around, including the ones at the slot machines. At the bar, there were two customers. An attractive woman in her mid-forties was sitting on a barstool at the middle of the bar, and a man was sitting at the far end. It was the same man who came to see Randy at the Motherlode, the man he called Dusty.

Tuper was glad Dusty had come to this bar because Tuper knew the owner, but then, he knew the owners of most of the bars. This one he happened to know better than most.

Tuper strolled up to the opposite end of the bar from where Alan was sitting. "Hi, Gene," he said to the bartender.

"Hey, Tuper, haven't seen you in a while."

"Sorry 'bout that. I've been tied up. I need a favor."

"Of course."

"There's a guy at the other end of your bar who may have some information about a missing kid. Do you mind if I use your back room to question him a bit?"

"A missing kid?"

"Yes, sir."

"Okay," Gene said. "Just don't break anything."

"I'll do my best."

Tuper sauntered down to the other end of the bar. When he passed the woman, she smiled at him. He wanted to stop and say hello and maybe buy her a drink, but now was not the time. He approached Alan, who was holding what looked like a glass of whiskey, and said, "Son, I need to ask you a few questions. Do you mind stepping into the office back there?"

"Who are you?" he said loudly.

"I don't think you want to do this in public, Alan. Or should I call you Dusty? I know you're driving that RAV4 that isn't registered to Alan Bowman. And I know about Randy Jenkins."

He looked scared, but he downed his drink and stood up. He glanced toward the exit.

"Don't even think about it," Tuper said.

Alan hesitated and then walked with Tuper to the back room. Stacks of boxes full of bottles filled with alcohol lined one side of the room. Two shelves above the alcohol held paper towels, napkins, and toilet paper. Other boxes were spread throughout the room, along with cleaning supplies, a mop and bucket, and a small step stool next to two folding chairs. There was ample empty space for the two men to have their "talk."

Tuper closed the door behind them. Alan must have mustered up a little courage because he said, "I don't have to talk to you. Are you a cop?"

"No," Tuper said softly. "All I want to know is where the kid is."

"I don't know what you're talking about."

"You picked up Mason Jenkins at school last Monday and no one has seen him since."

"No, I didn't."

"Yeah, you did."

"You're just fishing. I don't know why you think it was me."

"Because your car was used to pick him up."

"It wasn't my car. I don't even live in this town."

"Do you know Randy Jenkins?"

"No."

"Yet you met with him a few days after the kidnapping right here at the Motherlode."

"That wasn't me," he responded, almost sounding cocky now.

Tuper wondered if the liquid courage from the bar was taking hold.

"Jenkins put new tires on your vehicle a few weeks ago —a vehicle that is registered to Dustin Walker, your girlfriend's dead father."

"I don't know what you're talking about, old man. I'm leaving."

Alan took a step toward the door. Tuper grabbed his arm and twisted it behind him, brought his knee up into his back, and slammed him against the wall. "I don't like to be called 'old man.' Now, you want to tell me where the kid is?"

"I want my lawyer."

"You're not listening, kid. I ain't no cop. I don't care about your rights. I only care about finding the kid."

"I don't know anything."

Tuper pulled him slightly forward and slammed him into the wall again. Then he twisted his arm a little harder and jammed his knee into his kidneys.

Alan yelped. "Okay, I'll tell you what I know."

Tuper loosened up on his grip and slid him off the wall, turning him around so he was facing him. Still holding onto his arm, Tuper grabbed one of the folding chairs and opened it.

"Sit," he said, pushing him into the chair.

"Look," Alan said, "I don't know where the kid is."

"That's not a very good start."

"I really don't."

"But you do know Randy?"

"We've been friends for a few years. He asked me to pick the kid up from school because it was his day to have him and he wouldn't be able to leave work early. He and Denise were going through a divorce, and he was afraid he would lose his visitation if he didn't show up."

"When did he ask you to do it?"

"About a week before. That's when he put the tires on my car. I needed them, and I didn't think there was anything wrong with picking up his kid —except that he told me not to get too close to the teacher."

"Didn't you find that strange?"

"No, because he said the teacher had to think it was him because of Denise. And we look enough alike from a distance so no one would notice. So I waved to Mason, and he came running. It all worked out just as he said it would."

"Except it didn't."

Alan clasped his hands in front of him, twisting them back and forth in a nervous motion. "No, it didn't. I left school with Mason and drove to Randy's house, but when I got there, someone hit me over the head and when I woke up, the kid was gone."

"But you didn't tell the police that you were involved?"

"No, because Randy said it was to protect me. If we told them, I might go to jail. Since the car wasn't registered in my name and I didn't really think anyone could trace me, I went along with it."

"Did you see who hit you at Randy's?"

"No. I never saw it coming. We walked up to the door, Mason pulled it open, and Whack! I was clobbered over the head."

"Could it have been Randy?"

"I suppose, but why would he do that?"

"I don't know. You tell me."

"He had no reason to. It doesn't make sense."

"Did you kill Randy?"

"No," he said loudly. "He was my friend. Why would I kill him?"

Tuper remained standing and looked down on Alan. "Do you know Denise?"

"Yeah, she's pretty decent. At least she was up until this separation. I hadn't been around them much the past few months so I was surprised to hear they were splitting up. They always seemed to get along so well."

"Do you think she would go so far as to steal the kid from his father?"

"They lived for that kid, both of them, but I think Denise would do just about anything to keep her baby." Alan tried to stand, but Tuper pushed on his shoulder and he sat back down. "Can I go now? I've told you everything I know."

"What size shoe do you wear?"

"What?"

"What size shoe?"

Alan wrinkled his brow and said questioningly, "Ten and a half."

"Good. Can I have them, please?"

"You want my shoes?"

Tuper leaned down and looked him straight in the eyes. "I *said* please."

Alan removed his new tennis shoes, all the while watching Tuper as if he didn't know what he might do next.

"Socks too," Tuper said.

Alan shook his head, but he removed the socks, dropped them on the shoes, and stood up.

"You can go."

Alan stepped toward the door but before he could open it, Tuper said, "Take care of the registration on that car. If anything bad comes to that nice Mrs. Sally Walker, I'll find you."

Alan paused before he left. "Who are you?"

"Someone you don't want to mess with."

CHAPTER TWENTY-ONE

Tuper dropped the tennis shoes and socks off with Squirrely.

"Them's brand new," Squirrely said, admiring his new shoes.

"Just about," Tuper said. "Just saying thanks for letting me know where the RAV4 was."

"Did you find the kid?"

"Nope, but I got a lot of questions answered."

"How long has he been missing now?"

"It'll be a week tomorrow."

Squirrely didn't say anything. Tuper knew Squirrely was thinking the same thing he was; he hoped he wasn't looking for a murdered child.

Tuper said goodbye and drove to Clarice's. He was anxious to see what Lana had discovered. He parked in front of the house and got out. Snow was falling lightly on him and there was a thin layer of white on the ground.

Tuper came in and sat across from Lana at the table. She was so focused on what she was doing that when Tuper said, "Hello, Agony," all he got was a grunt. He waited because he preferred "quiet, focused Lana" and he knew the chatter would start soon enough.

After a few minutes, Tuper said, "Got anything interesting?"

She held her palm up to him for a second and then returned it to the keyboard. "One sec."

Tuper went into the kitchen and opened the refrigerator. "Want a sandwich?"

"Naw."

He took out the ham, mustard, and mayonnaise, and made himself a sandwich. He carried it to the table and sat down.

Lana looked up. "I don't think Randy, I mean Gordon, is Mason's father."

"Why?" Tuper asked.

"Because Mason was born three months after Gordon was released from jail and he served a year. So, unless they give conjugal visits in county jail, or he was a sperm donor, he can't be the father."

"Where was he in jail?"

"In Riverside, California. It's in Southern California about an hour from L.A. I know the area."

"What was he in for?"

"He scammed some woman out of $50,000. He took a plea deal to keep from going to prison. They gave him a year in county, which he served, and restitution, which he never paid."

"When did he meet up with Denise?"

"I haven't figured that out yet, but I can tell you that after high school he went to Mt. San Jacinto Community College. It's a local college in the same town where he went to high school. He was there for two years and got an associate's degree in criminal justice."

"And then he became a crook?"

"Pretty much. He got a job with security at Riverside Community College. The head of security knew Stephen Price, Gordon's father. I expect that helped him get the job. Gordon only lasted about a year and then got fired for what they called 'fraternizing with the students,' which didn't make any sense. What really happened was that he was selling the answer keys from the professors' computers to the students. I'm not sure why there was a 'cover-up,' but it was most likely for Gordon's father's benefit. At least that's all I can come up with."

"So he lies, steals, and cheats women. Nice guy."

"He worked in Shell gas stations for five or six years. It looks like he was a fill-in for a while at various stations and was then hired permanently. Eventually he became night manager of his own station, which didn't earn him much more than minimum wage. That's when he ventured out and scammed that woman out of her money."

"After he got out of jail," Lana continued, "he moved back home with his parents and somehow got a job at a facility called The Rosewood Home. I'm guessing his parents probably helped him with that as well."

"What is The Rosewood Home?"

"It's a home for people with mental health issues. I'll do more research on that later if you want. Gordon only worked there for two months. One day he left and never returned. That must have been when he became Randy Jenkins because there isn't any trace left of Gordon online except for a few posts on his Facebook page, but then he stopped posting there too."

"Was Gordon ever married?" Tuper wondered if Denise had married Randy or Gordon.

"I half-expected to find a marriage certificate for Gordon and Denise, but I couldn't find *any* marriage for Gordon. That doesn't mean there isn't one. I've checked all the states between California and Montana including Nevada, which would be the most likely, but it could be elsewhere, maybe even Mexico."

"Anything else?"

"I found out who owns the house that Randy was living in. His name is John Gavin. I couldn't find any other connection to Denise or Randy, other than that Randy was renting it, or to Alan or anyone else related to this case."

"Probably ain't any."

"I know there's a lot more I can find on Gordon Price. I haven't even begun to search for emails, study social media sites, or follow up on his friends."

"You do that. I'm going to see Denise."

CHAPTER TWENTY-TWO

"It's time to stop jacking me around," Tuper said to Denise. She had agreed to meet him at Nickels, and Clarice let him use the office so they had some privacy.

"What are you talking about?"

"Do you want me to find your son?"

"Of course." Tears rolled down her cheeks. "I'm going crazy without him, not knowing where he is or what's happened to him."

"Then you need to be truthful with me, woman. You got me chasin' my tail."

She sniffled back the tears and took a deep breath. "What do you want to know?"

"You told me you don't know Alan Bowman, but he seems to know you quite well. He was the man who picked Mason up from school."

"You mean Dusty."

"Yes."

She looked away for a second. "Sorry, I forgot his name was really Alan."

"How well did you know him?"

"Not that well. I saw him a few times. He was a pretty good friend of Randy's, but he didn't come to the house much or anything. He moved to Great Falls about a year ago."

"You're not surprised that he was the one in the RAV4?"

"No. Randy told me the other day."

"Did you know that when Alan picked Mason up from school, he took him to your husband's house?"

"Not until a couple of days ago. Randy told me the

night before he died. He confessed that he had set up the kidnapping in order to get Mason away from me. But then someone knocked Alan out and ran away with Mason. At least, that's what Randy told me."

"Did you believe him?"

"I'm not sure. At first, I didn't believe him, but now that he's dead, it makes more sense."

"I still don't see why the kidnapper would kill Randy."

"Unless he found out where Mason was. Or maybe Alan killed him so he wouldn't get implicated in the kidnapping. Or maybe Alan lied about getting hit, still has Mason, and he tried to get Randy to pay to get him back, and when he wouldn't, he killed him."

Denise had too many answers as if she was trying to lead Tuper away from her. It made him uncomfortable, but he was still convinced that her child was missing. She always got very emotional when she spoke of Mason or the kidnapping. Also, he couldn't come up with any plausible reason why she would've hired him if she had the kid. If anything, with parents like these, Mason needed him more than ever.

"What is your husband's real name?"

Denise moved a few strands of hair behind her ear. "Randolph Jenkins. Why?"

Unless they were pathological liars, most people had some telltale sign when they lied. Tuper thought Denise was lying partly because of the hair gesture, but it was possible she never knew his real name. He may have conned her too, so he let that go for now.

"Still no demands from a kidnapper?" Tuper asked.

"No one has called me, or tried to contact me in any fashion."

"You'd let me know, right?"

"Of course. I just want you to find my son."

"Are you still staying with friends?"

"Yes, I feel safer that way, but my friend drove to Grass Range to see her mother so I told her I'd house-sit and watch the dog until she got back."

"Do you feel safe there by yourself?"

"I'm good."

Tuper walked Denise outside and saw her get into a green Chevy Aveo, which was the same car she'd driven last time he saw her; the same one that he had seen earlier in front of her friend's house. Then he remembered the day he met Denise, when she had told him that's what she owned. He saw the license plate as she pulled away from Nickels and committed it to memory.

~~~

The important thing right now was to find Mason but Tuper was running out of leads. The best thing he had was Randy Jenkins aka Gordon Price. He was a criminal and had participated in at least the first part of the kidnapping, maybe the second part as well, if that's how it even went down. He needed to know more about Gordon before and after he became Randy. If he did take Mason, he was likely with someone he knew, and more likely that it wasn't anyone Denise knew. So someone from Gordon's past was most likely.

Tuper called Lana and gave her the license number from Denise's car. "Keep digging into Gordon's life," Tuper said. "See who he was close to. See if you can find anyone that he kept in touch with. I'm going to follow up on The Rosewood Home."

Lana's voice rose. "Are you going to California?"

"No, I know a guy. He owes me one."

Tuper left, got in his car, and started it up to get it warm. Then he made a phone call to California.

"Hello, JP. It's Tuper."

"Well, butter my butt and call me a biscuit. You're the last person I expected to hear from today. How's life in Montana?"

"Cold."

"That's a shame. It's 76 degrees here."

"Yeah, hot with a chance of traffic. You can have the city."

JP laughed.

"How are Sabre and Ron?" Tuper asked.

"Both doing great. They'll be excited to know I heard from you."

"It ain't really a social call. I could use your help with something," Tuper said, "if you're not too busy."

"You name it."

"How close are you to a town called San Jacinto?"

"About an hour and a half."

Tuper chuckled. "Why is it you Californians always give distance in time, instead of in miles?"

"I suppose it's because of the traffic and the stoplights. Miles don't really matter here. It can be two miles away, but if you have fifteen stoplights in between, you aren't getting there in two minutes."

"Another reason not to live there," Tuper said.

"So, what can I do for you?"

"I'm looking for a missing five-year-old boy."

"And you think he's there?"

"It's possible, but even if he's not, a man who's involved is from there."

"Let me get my notebook," JP said. "Okay, shoot."

Tuper gave him a brief description of what was going on and told him everything he knew about Gordon Price. "The last place he worked was The Rosewood Home. He was only there a few months, then left abruptly. Maybe you can find out why."

"I'll get right on it," JP said. "I know you're not much with technology, but is there any way you can get me photos of Gordon, Denise, and the boy?"

"Not me, but I know someone who can," Tuper said. "I know you're a busy man, JP, so I really appreciate this."

"You caught me at a good time. I'm between cases right now."

"Oh, and my client doesn't have any money."

"I wouldn't expect any. I owe you big time, Tuper. I could never repay you for what you did for us. Besides, you had me at 'missing five-year-old.'"

CHAPTER TWENTY-THREE

JP was a private detective. He worked for an attorney who represented abused children in juvenile court. This kind of case was right up his alley.

He and Sabre had met Tuper when a case took them to Montana. Tuper never spoke much about himself so JP never even knew what he did for a living, or if he had any family. He did learn that the man had more connections than a chain-link fence, and he seemed to know just about everybody in the state of Montana. He learned that Tuper liked guns, gambling, and women, and that's about where it ended. Tuper had helped him through some rough times on that trip. He had saved their lives on more than one occasion, so JP owed him big time.

JP related well to Tuper because JP was born and partially raised in Texas and was a cowboy at heart. As his girlfriend, Sabre, would say, "You and Tuper wear the same uniform—a western hat, jeans, and boots." Except Tuper had had the same hat for over twenty years, and his boots were pretty worn as well. JP, on the other hand, wore a clean, black Stetson and the best boots he could buy. Tuper called him a citified cowboy. JP and Tuper were close in height, but JP was some twenty-plus years younger than Tuper.

JP drove to the address he had for Stephen Price, Gordon's father. Who would be better to keep his child than his grandparents? JP rang the doorbell, but no one answered. He waited a few minutes and tried again. Still nothing. He was about to leave when a thirty-something woman in a black BMW pulled into the driveway.

"May I help you?" she asked as she stepped out. JP noticed she wasn't carrying a purse.

"I'm looking for Stephen Price."

"That's my father." She swallowed. "He passed away two weeks ago."

"I'm so sorry, ma'am. I didn't know. Did Gordon make it home for the services?"

"Gordon? No. He's been missing for years. What do you know about him?"

"Not a whole lot, ma'am. I know he was living in Montana for a while."

"Was? Is he somewhere else now?"

JP hated to be the one to tell Gordon's sister that her brother was dead, but he didn't want to lie to her either. "I'm afraid he recently passed."

She closed her eyes for a few seconds as she reached her hand up to her forehead and rubbed it as if to make pain go away.

"That would explain the calls on Dad's voice mail. I just listened to them this morning. He had several calls from the police department in Helena, Montana." She shook her head. "I'm glad Dad didn't know; at least he still held hope that he would see him again."

"I'm sorry to bring you such bad news."

"Is that why you're here? Are you a cop?"

"No, ma'am. My name is JP Torn. I'm a private detective." He reached his hand out to shake.

She reciprocated. "Lenore Webster."

"I'm here because I'm looking for a missing child."

"And my brother had something to do with that?"

"I'm afraid so. Did Gordon ever tell you he had a son?"

"No. Is it his son who is missing?"

"Actually, it's more complicated than that. His wife or girlfriend, we're not sure which, had a son who may or may not have been his, but he raised him as his own. They weren't getting along and he took the boy. Now that he's dead, we don't know where the child is. We were hoping he was here." JP didn't think it would do any good to explain any more so he left it at that.

"I didn't have any idea. He hasn't been in contact for about five years. As an adult, he was always closer to Mom than he was to Dad or to me. We were real tight as kids, but our lives changed as we got older. It was only a few months after Mom died that he left. He came by and gave me a little gift."

"What kind of gift?"

"Just something to remember him by. He told us he had to get away and he was starting a new life. We never heard from him again. After a while, we didn't know if he was dead or alive. I think Dad blamed himself for not having a good relationship with his son. He spent quite a bit of time and money trying to find him, and he never gave up hope. But Gordon was on probation when he left, and they issued an arrest warrant for him for a probation violation, so I'm sure he didn't want to be found."

"He was using a different name," JP said. "Did Gordon have a girlfriend the last time you saw him?"

"He was seeing someone, but I don't remember her name. He seemed pretty crazy about her, but with him, we never knew for sure."

"Do you happen to know if she was pregnant?"

Her face seemed to lose color for a second. "I wouldn't know. Gordon never said anything about that, and I never saw her. He wanted to bring her for Christmas and Dad asked him not to."

"Why's that?"

"Because it was the first Christmas without Mom and he thought we should spend it alone—just the family."

"Could the girlfriend's name have been Denise?"

"I don't think that was it, but maybe." She shook her head. "No, I'm sure that wasn't it."

"Do you know any friends who he had when he was living here in town last?"

"He spent a lot of time with Sonny Lynch. He owns Chippies. It's a bar on San Jacinto Avenue, not far from here. Gordon was also friends with Bob Blake. They were real close in high school, but I think Bob outgrew him. The more he got in trouble, the more Bob pulled away." She gave him a couple of other names, but she didn't think they would be much help.

JP thanked her for her time, got directions to The Rosewood Home, and turned to go to his car.

"How did he die?"

JP's stomach tightened up. He had been hoping she wouldn't ask that.

He turned around. "I'm sorry, Lenore, but it appears he was murdered."

She clasped her hand over her mouth and muttered, "Oh, no. Oh, my." She shook her head. "He just couldn't stay out of trouble."

JP hung back and waited, hoping Lenore would leave so he could follow her. He didn't expect Lenore to stay long in her father's house since she hadn't brought her purse in with her. It was his experience that many things could be deduced from what women did with their purses. He knew that wasn't an absolute, especially since he met his girlfriend, Sabre, who never carried a purse, but this time it panned out. Lenore was in the house for less than a half hour. JP didn't know if the information she had given him was truthful or not, but he wanted to make sure she didn't have Mason. She appeared nervous but that could have all been from the news he had just dropped on her.

He followed her onto South Victoria Avenue where she parked in front of St. Hyacinth's Elementary

School. He waited as she went inside. Approximately five minutes later, she walked out with a young boy about five or six years old. They got in the car and drove away.

CHAPTER TWENTY-FOUR

On his way to The Rosewood Home, JP called Tuper to report what he had seen.

"The kid was about the same age as Mason, but I'm sure it wasn't him," JP said. "He had the same blue eyes, but he has dark hair and is taller and thinner than Mason. I can send you the photos that I took of the boy if you'd like."

"That'd be good," Tuper said.

"Have someone text me the number where you want them sent and I'll get them to you the next time I stop."

~~~

JP turned right onto San Jacinto Avenue and noticed an old neon sign with a chipmunk protruding from a very old building. The sign read *Chippies*. He veered to the right, parked in front of the bar, and went inside.

The inside of the bar matched the name and the sign, a stereotypical dive bar from its schizophrenic wall décor down to the beat-up red Naugahyde booths. It was dark and smelled of cheap booze. It had a long bar about ten feet from the front door. Behind it was a large room with pool tables, some chairs, and blacked-out windows. A few more tables and chairs were scattered throughout the bar.

Even though it wasn't noon yet, six people had found their way to the bar and were drinking. JP didn't judge. Whatever their reasons, he was just glad he didn't have them. Behind the bar was a tall, blond man with tight, wavy hair cut close to his scalp. He served a drink, took the money and put it in the cash register, and then picked up his own drink and took a sip.

JP walked up to the bartender. "I'm looking for Sonny Lynch."

"You found him."

JP sat down.

"Can I get you a drink?" Sonny asked.

"Coffee, if you have it," JP said. "Black."

"Just made a fresh pot."

Sonny brought him a large coffee mug. JP must have looked at it a little too long because Sonny said, "When they need coffee here, they really need it. It saves me from making too many trips."

"I thought you were serving all of Texas."

Sonny chuckled. "Now, what can I do for you?"

"I understand you're a friend of Gordon Price."

"I am, but I haven't seen him in a long time. Are you a cop?"

"No, I'm a private investigator. Gordon has been murdered and I'm looking for his missing son." JP found that if he was going to lie to get information, it was always better to stick as close as he could to the truth. That way, it was easier to remember. He also used the story he thought worked best for his audience.

"That's not good," Sonny said.

"You don't seem that surprised."

"Not that he got murdered. I always thought he would get shot by some jealous husband or jilted woman. I'm more surprised to hear he had a son. Sorry to hear he's missing. How long has he been gone?"

"About a week."

"How old is the boy?"

"Five."

He shook his head. "Poor kid. What can I do to help?"

JP took out his phone and showed Sonny a photo of Mason. "Have you seen this kid around town with anyone?"

"You think he's here in San Jacinto?"

"We hope so. If he is, he's probably safe."

"So you think someone Gordon knows has him?"

"Maybe."

"Which means Gordon had something to do with the kid's disappearance."

"We think that's possible, which doesn't really matter to him at this point since he's dead. We just need to find the boy."

"Wait a minute," Sonny said, taking a step back. "You don't think I have him, do you?"

"Do you?"

"No."

"I stopped here because Gordon's sister told me you and Gordon had been friends for a long time. I was hoping you might know something about those last few months that he lived here."

"Like what?"

"I understand he had a girlfriend. Did you know her?"

"No, I never met her, but she had quite a hold on him."

"How do you mean?"

"Gordon was always calling the shots with women. He never really fell for any of them, which seemed to make them want him more. But it was different with this one. He was hooked right from the start. Before her, he would come into the bar almost every night, often with a different woman on his arm. But after they met, he totally stopped. The last couple of months before he left, he came in here, maybe three times. I told him to bring her in so I could meet her but he never did. The last time he came in, it was to tell me he was leaving."

"Do you know if he was leaving with the girlfriend?"

"He didn't say. He was very serious at first and he told me he was starting over. At first, I thought she had dumped him and he didn't want to be around where he might see her, but actually he was in very good spirits. He was laughing and joking. So I figured they were starting over together."

"Did he say where he was going?"

"No. I was pretty busy so I didn't get to talk to him very long."

"Do you know his girlfriend's name?"

"Since you asked about her, I've been racking my brain trying to think of it, but I'm sorry, I have nothing. He talked about her all the time—the few times that I saw him. You'd think I'd remember, but I don't." He picked up his drink and held it up. "Probably too much of this stuff burning up the brain cells." He took a drink before he sat it back down.

"Did you ever see or hear from him after that?"

"No, not a word. I'd ask his father now and again when I would see him around, but he never heard from him either."

"And Lenore? Ever see her?"

"No, she moved out of town. I know she'd come home once in a while to see her father but I never saw her."

JP took out a business card and handed it to Sonny. "If you think of anything, especially the girlfriend's name, please call me."

"I will."

JP paid for his coffee and stood up.

"How well do you know Lenore?"

"I've known her most of my life, but unlike her brother she was pretty straight. I can't imagine she'd steal a kid, or help Gordon, for that matter, but Lenore always wanted kids. She never had any of her own as far as I know. I heard she adopted a baby a while back."

JP drove to The Rosewood Home on San Jacinto Avenue, about a mile from Chippies. His first encounter at the desk was with a woman with gray hair and a pained look on her face who was writing notes on some documents as she stood at the counter.

"Who you here to see?" she growled without looking up.

"I'm looking for a missing child." JP decided to lead with that since most people were empathetic to children.

"We don't have any children here, just adults."

"His father worked here about five years ago. I was hoping to get some information."

She stopped for a second and looked at him. "Are you a cop?"

"No, ma'am. I'm a private investigator. My name is JP Torn."

"Sorry, JP Torn," she said with the same angry tone, "but we have privacy laws. I can't tell you anything without a warrant. Now if you'll excuse me, I have work to do."

The woman picked up her papers, turned to another woman, much younger than herself, sitting at a small desk a few feet from her. "Anna, make sure this gets entered in the computer. I'm going to lunch."

As soon as she left, Anna approached JP, the papers still in her hand. "Don't pay any attention to her," Anna said. "She's not a happy person. Maybe I can help. What do you need?"

"Thank you," JP said. "A five-year-old boy has been missing for about a week. His father was recently murdered and we think there's a connection. The father worked here about five years ago for a very short time."

"I've been here for almost six years so I may

remember him. I knew most of the staff, unless they worked the graveyard shift. I work eight to five, and the night shift comes on at eleven and is gone by the time I get here. What's his name?"

"Gordon Price. I have a photo of—"

"No need." She smiled. "I know Gordy." Suddenly her face became solemn. "Gordy's dead?"

"I'm afraid so."

She shuddered. "That's awful. His father just died too. Did he know about Gordon?"

"No, Gordon died after him."

"Well, that's good. Mr. Price didn't need that. He was such a good man and a good teacher." She took a deep breath. "Sorry, it just kind of hit me."

"I understand."

"I went to high school with Gordy. He was a senior when I was a sophomore. I had a mad crush on him."

"Did you date him?"

"Only in my mind. I would daydream about our dates, what he would say to me, where we would go. I even had him walk me down the aisle, had three children, two girls and a boy, and a new Honda in the driveway of our two thousand-square-foot house with a lake view." She laughed at her own joke. "No, Gordon was way too popular for me. I wasn't one of the 'cool kids.' He was always nice to me, though, and would say 'hi' and smile at me, but that was about as close as we got. When he came to work here, he didn't even remember me from high school."

"Were you still interested in him when he came back here?"

"Came back here? Actually, Gordy never really left San Jacinto, until this last time about five years ago. I mean he did for a year or two at a time, but even then, he was here a lot, and he always ended up back at his parents' house. He couldn't seem to get his life together. He was even in jail for a while."

"You knew about that?"

"It's a small town."

"Did you *ever* date him? The last time he was here, I mean?" JP asked.

"No. I dodged the bullet on that one. He flirted with me at first. I was flattered by it for about two seconds, the *Mighty Gordon Price* flirting with me, but I realized I wasn't interested. It wasn't that he had changed; it was because he hadn't. He never grew up. I did."

"Gordon was seeing someone while he worked here. Do you know who it was?"

"Someone here at Rosewood?"

"I don't know. Possibly."

"I don't remember him dating anyone here. He flirted with everybody and most of the women liked him. He was a very charming guy. But to tell you the truth, I started dating my husband around that time, and that's where all my focus went."

JP opened his phone and brought up a photo of Denise that Tuper had someone send him. He showed it to Anna. "Do you know this woman?"

Anna studied the photo. "I don't think so. She may look a little familiar, but I couldn't tell you for sure."

"That's okay," JP said. "One more thing. Was any of the staff pregnant when Gordon was working here?"

"Not that I would know. What I mean is, since I've been here there was never anyone here who was visibly pregnant."

JP thanked her and left. He found Bob Blake, the other friend Gordon's sister had suggested, at his work. He wasn't able to provide any more information than JP already had. So he called Tuper and reported what he had learned.

CHAPTER TWENTY-FIVE

Clarice, Tuper, and Lana sat around Clarice's dining room table. Tuper was stumped and he thought more brains might help bring this little boy home, so he brought Clarice and Lana up to speed on everything he knew, except he didn't tell them about the envelope. He knew Lana would want to open it, but he had given his word.

"By the way, Tuper, the green Chevy that Denise was driving is registered to her," Lana said.

"Thought so."

"What are you working on?" Clarice asked Lana who was parked behind her laptop.

"I've been researching The Rosewood Home. It took some work but I finally got into their employment records. They have a decent firewall there, but once you're inside, it's a piece of cake. They have their entire employment file online; every document is scanned and placed in their file. I was able to find that Gordon worked there from December 1st through January 28th, so I've been concentrating on those dates. Let's assume for a minute that the woman he was in love with was Denise. If he met her while he was working there, they could have left together and started a new life, and she could have changed her name just like he did."

"But why would they just leave?" Clarice asked. "People don't just get up one day and decide to leave everything behind —their friends, their family —and go off on an adventure. Except maybe in the movies."

"Things aren't always what they seem," Lana said. She looked over and saw Tuper studying her face. "But you're right, the reason they left might be important."

"Still, there is Mason," Clarice said. "Where did he come in? He was born on Valentine's Day; his mother would've had to be showing in January, yet no one remembers a pregnant employee. She must not be from there. I think it's more likely that he left, met Denise, and she was already pregnant."

"Does he really strike you as a man who would hook up with a pregnant woman?" Lana said. "By all accounts, this guy was the ultimate ladies' man. Besides, his friend Sonny said Gordon was crazy about this woman, more so than any other one. This was different."

"That's true," Clarice said. She walked over behind Lana. "Do you have a photo of Denise? I'd like to see what she looks like."

"Sure," Lana said as she opened up an image from her Facebook page.

"She's pretty, and she has beautiful hair," Clarice said.

"From a bottle," Tuper said.

Lana and Clarice both looked up from the computer. Clarice said, "What?"

"The hair. It ain't natural."

Clarice smiled. "Most of us aren't."

Lana went back to her task at hand. "So, I have a list of all eighteen of the employees during that time frame. That includes the kitchen staff, nursing staff, everything."

Tuper spoke up before she could say anything else. "Don't suppose any of them are named Denise."

"No. That would be too easy. Seven of the employees are men, so we have eleven women. For now, I've eliminated the three women who were fifty or over. So I have eight women aged nineteen to forty-three. Several of them are married, but I left them in the group because I don't think that would matter to Mr. Casanova. Besides, that might explain why they left. They could've been running from an angry spouse or something."

Tuper let them chatter on. As usual, he waited until he had something worth saying, but this was taking too long. "Agony," Tuper said, "your point?"

She stopped talking for a few seconds and then started again. "Okay, so we have eight. Anna and two others still work there, so we're down to five. Out of those five, one terminated her employment two weeks before Gordon."

"So that must be her," Clarice said. "What's her name?"

"Jessica, but it's *not* her," Lana said. "I was able to track Jessica to another facility in Northern California near Sacramento. She left because she had MS. She's a patient, not an employee."

Tuper twisted his mustache. "So, you got nothin'?"

"Pretty much," Lana said. "But I'm not done."

Tuper's phone rang. He answered it and said, "Yeah?" He listened for a few moments, said, "Thanks, JP," and then hung up.

Both girls looked at him waiting to hear what he had just learned.

"Name is Jessica," Tuper said.

"Gordon's girlfriend's name was Jessica?" Lana asked.

"Yeah. Sonny remembered her name and called JP."

"That's the woman's name with MS?" Clarice said. "That can't be. Right, Lana?"

Lana was refocused on her research. "Huh?" she said.

"Is it the MS woman?" Clarice asked.

"I don't know how it can be, but I'm looking again."

"If she wasn't an employee of Rosewood, where else do you have to look?" Clarice asked.

"Not sure yet," Lana said, then turned to Tuper, "but I think it's time you have a heart-to-heart with Denise."

"Probably," Tuper said, and stood up. That's as close as he could get to acknowledging Lana was correct.

~~~

Lana was glad to have peace and quiet so she could concentrate. Tuper had left to try to find Denise, and Clarice had gone to work. Lana spent the next few hours re-tracking Rosewood's employee, Jessica. Everything was in order. The employment records showed the last two evaluations had indications of her illness. The reason she gave for quitting was that she had been diagnosed with multiple sclerosis and could no longer do her job. There was no indication that she might be pregnant and no birth by her. Her address for the next three years was that of her parents. When the illness progressed, she moved to the facility in Sacramento.

It had to be a different Jessica. Lana had only ever met two girls named Jessica, but when she looked up most common names for the time period, Jessica was on the top ten for most of the 1980s and the 1990s. Gordon could have met her anywhere. San Jacinto was too big a town to just start looking for a "Jessica, without a surname." That could take her years. And she may not even have been living there. She could've been commuting from a nearby community. Lana was frustrated. She was good at what she did, but if Jessica wasn't from Rosewood, Lana had nowhere to start.

She decided to do a more in-depth look into

Gordon Price, in an attempt to find any Jessica in his life, working for the moment under the assumption that Denise and Jessica were the same person. She found a few Jessicas, mostly in high school, but only one fit the height requirement and she was African-American.

She needed more information if she was going to find her. Hopefully, Tuper would get Denise to 'fess up. Meanwhile, she went back to the Rosewood records; maybe she had missed something. She started with the original list of employees, subtracted all the men and women who were still working there, leaving her with eight. This time she left the women over fifty in her list.

One by one, she checked their employment records looking for anything that might be a clue. Stella, the oldest woman, had recently retired. When Lana extended her search on Stella she found she had two daughters but neither was named Jessica.

The next employee was April. She left about a year after Gordon was there and went back to college to get her degree in business. She was now working in Worker's Comp for the state, married a year ago, no children.

Ashley was next. She left fourteen months after Gordon did. No reason given for her departure, which seemed strange. The records showed she walked out one day and never returned. Lana couldn't turn up any evidence of a childbirth, but even with that and the late unemployment, this was the most promising so far. It's possible she joined him in Montana later. Then there was her physical appearance. Lana found a couple of photos of Ashley. They weren't recent and they didn't look like Denise. They were about the same height and both blonde, although according to Tuper, Denise wasn't a natural blonde. But their noses were very different and their lips. So unless Jessica underwent some intensive plastic surgery, she and Ashley were not the same person.

The search continued with one rejection after another until she came upon a woman named Trinidad Andrade. Her employment terminated closer to Gordon's than anyone else's. She quit the company six weeks after Gordon. Lana started through each page in her employment file. She had worked there for seven years and had only missed two days, once for a funeral and another time when she got food poisoning from a local restaurant. She had worked her way up from emptying bedpans to nurse's assistant. She had taken a number of nursing classes and was just short of getting her degree as a Licensed Practical Nurse.

Lana was more intrigued. Why would she leave when she was so close to getting her degree? She hoped it wasn't for a man. She got frustrated with women who didn't live their own lives, giving up theirs for what their husbands or boyfriends wanted. Compromise was one thing, but she had known women who stopped living their own lives when they fell in love. If she was pregnant, perhaps she needed bed-rest or something. However, a thorough search of the employment records showed no indication of a pregnancy. And she certainly was diligent about not missing work.

Lana was becoming convinced that Trinidad, Jessica, and Denise were the same person. Or at the very least, Trinidad was Jessica. She continued to read every piece of information in the employment record until she found a hand-written note by a supervisor in the margin of an evaluation report. It said, "Jessica is a true self-starter. Consider promotion."

From there, Lana did a DMV search for Trinidad and discovered her middle name was Jessica. She downloaded a photo of her and brought it up on her computer next to a photo of Denise. Then she picked up her phone and called Tuper.

"I found her. Denise's real name is Trinidad Jessica Andrade."

CHAPTER TWENTY-SIX

"I'm going to start searching for information on Jessica Andrade," Lana said to Tuper on the phone.

"You're sure they're the same person?" Tuper asked.

"I'm sure. I put dark hair on Denise's photo, compared them side-by-side, and there's no mistaking it; Denise and Jessica are the same person. Besides that, Jessica actually left just a few days before Gordon. She had some vacation time and some comp time on the books so she didn't technically terminate until five weeks later. At first, it looked like she was still working there, but she wasn't. So, why do you suppose Jessica changed her name when they left?" Before Tuper could say anything, she answered the question herself. "I'm thinking it was to protect Gordon, because if anyone knew they were together, he'd be too easy to track. I hate when women do that. He was probably just using her anyway. I know he claimed he loved her, but..."

"Lana," Tuper tried to interrupt her.

"Look what he did," she said. "He set up a kidnapping to steal her child away from her. It wasn't even his kid. That's not love."

"Lana," Tuper said a little louder. He couldn't help but wonder what man had done her wrong.

"She should've known better," Lana continued ranting. "She must have known he had been in jail and that he scammed that other woman out of $50,000. Otherwise, why would they change their names? Why would he treat her any better than he did other women? Gordon was a pig."

"Agony," Tuper said in a loud voice. "We're all pigs. What's your point?"

There was silence for a few seconds, and then Lana said, "I don't understand sometimes why people do things that are so destructive to themselves."

"A conversation for another time."

"Right. What did you learn from Denise?"

"Nothing, yet. I've left her three messages. She's not answering her phone."

"What are you going to do?"

"Gonna keep tryin'," Tuper said.

He hung up the phone and tried calling Denise again. It went to voice mail. This time Tuper didn't leave a message. Instead, he drove to Denise's house. It looked quiet. Only the green Chevy Aveo was in the driveway. He figured she was probably home alone, since her roommate was going on a road trip. He exited the car, walked up to the house, and rang the bell. No one came to the door, but he heard a dog bark. He waited about thirty seconds and rang again. Still nothing except the dog. This time he tried knocking even though he could hear the bell when it rang. Still no Denise. He decided to wait in his car and see if he could see any activity coming from the house.

An hour later, Tuper hadn't seen anyone come or go from the house. The curtains were all closed so he couldn't see inside, but at one point he thought he saw the curtain pulled back as if someone was peeking out. A few minutes later, Denise came outside carrying a suitcase. She opened her trunk, flung the suitcase inside, and drove away.

Tuper followed her onto Canyon Ferry Road, but she was already putting distance between them. His old car was not made for a chase. He could still see her when they passed Wylie Drive, until a car pulled out in front of him and blocked his view. He had to wait for two cars to pass before he could go around it. By then, he couldn't tell if she was in front of him or had turned. She was headed in the direction of the airport and since she had a suitcase with her, he figured that was a likely scenario, but he also knew it was probably a waste of time to try to find her at the airport.

He passed Canyon Ferry Mini Basket, glancing to see if she may have stopped for gas, but her car was not there. He continued toward the airport and decided to make a quick drive through the parking lot.

He considered other possibilities. One was that she was leaving town in her car, in which case he had no idea what direction she went. She could be on Interstate 15 by now and he had no way of knowing if she went north or south. She could be going to stay with another friend, or she could be going to a hotel. Since she didn't have her son with her, he figured she probably wasn't leaving Helena, unless she'd gotten word that he was somewhere else.

Tuper tried calling her again, but it went to voice mail. He didn't leave a message. He thought about going back to her house, breaking in, and looking around to see if he could find a clue as to where Mason might be. His concern was that the roommate might come home—and then there was the dog. Instead, he drove to Clarice's house to regroup, hoping Lana had some new information that would help him.

CHAPTER TWENTY-SEVEN

After several hours of flying around cyberspace, Lana checked her own Hotmail email account with trepidation for what she might find, but she had to know. He had already sent one email; he could send another. *What if he does know where I am?* She realized it was better if she knew what he knew. The fifth email from the top of her list had come in about two hours earlier.

It read: *I'm not bluffing. I'll be there soon. Get ready.*

She wanted to tell him to go to hell, but she refused to engage him. That would please him and that was the last thing she wanted to do. Besides, if he really knew where she was, he would just show up. Or would he? He loved the cat-and-mouse game. She closed the email account with her shaking hand. She hated the effect he had on her. She told herself to breathe. She took three deep breaths, blowing each out slowly, dismissed the thought of her old life, and resumed her research just as someone knocked on the door. She jumped. The knock had startled her, but then she heard Tuper say it was him. She unlocked the door and let him in.

Tuper looked at her and immediately noticed something was wrong.

"You okay?" he asked.

She waved her hand in a dismissive gesture. "I'm fine. Did you talk to Denise?"

"Afraid not. She won't answer her phone, and now she may have left town."

"How do you know that?"

"I saw her leave her house with her suitcase and head toward the airport."

"Without Mason?"

"I don't think she would leave without Mason, but I don't know where she is either." Tuper watched Lana's demeanor. He knew something was wrong, but she apparently didn't want to tell him so he didn't ask again. "Did you find anything that will help us?"

"I think it'll help. My search for Trinidad Jessica Andrade provided only two social media accounts, Facebook and Twitter. She had eighty-two friends on Facebook and twenty-four on Twitter. She was listed as Jessica Andrade on both." She glanced up and saw the blank look on Tuper's face. She made another dismissive gesture with her hand. "That doesn't really matter. Anyway, she didn't have any relatives listed. Of course, that doesn't mean she doesn't have any. But she had two friends on Facebook who called her Trini; everyone else referred to her as Jessica. There were a few posts she made before she left the account that indicated big changes were coming."

Lana read the Facebook posts.

--I'm finally going to get what I've wanted all my life.

--I've been blessed. God is good.

"That was her last entry," Lana said. "She never closed the account, but there are no more posts. She may or may not lurk around reading what others are posting."

Lana started clicking her keyboard as if she was looking for something. Then she said, "I found an old

Yahoo account belonging to Gordon Price that dated back to before he was incarcerated. It was silent for the year he was in jail, but became active again while he worked at Rosewood. He used the email account sporadically throughout the last five years, but nothing seemed relevant. There was never any mention of Mason in any of the emails. The account included a couple of emails to and from Jessica just before they left Rosewood."

She looked at the screen. The first one was from Gordon.

It read: *I can't wait to be together full time. Goodnight my sweet.*

Jessica responded with: *It won't be long now. Everything is in place. The rest is up to nature. See you tomorrow. Love you. Goodnight.*

Then Gordon said: *I love you too.*

"That was it for any correspondence between them, unless they used other email accounts, which I'm still looking for." She paused. "Oh, and I scrolled through Jessica's emails. There were tons. I couldn't read them all. It was filled with junk mail too. Other than the few emails with Gordon, she had the most exchanges with two other people before she left, a girl named Judi who sounds like a BFF, and someone named Mel, not sure if that's a man or woman. The emails were all very innocuous. One to Mel sounded like they were meeting for lunch or dinner. That's about as exciting as they got."

Before Tuper could say anything, Lana spoke again. "In the email when Jessica emailed Gordon and said '*The rest is up to nature*' she was probably talking about the birth of the baby. So, was Jessica pregnant, and about to give birth when she left Rosewood?"

Tuper started to say something, but Lana continued, "There's nothing in her employee records that indicates that she was pregnant, and you'd think if she was pregnant she would've stated pregnancy as her reason for leaving her job, but that's not the reason she gave. She said she left for other employment. So, was she pregnant or not?"

"If you'll stop talking for a minute, I'll tell you," Tuper said. "JP called Anna at Rosewood. She said she didn't know Jessica because she was on a different shift, but she asked around and people who worked with her said she was not visibly pregnant."

"If she wasn't far enough along to have a baby two weeks later, maybe Mason is younger than she says. Maybe he wasn't born on Valentine's Day. But why would she lie about his birthdate?" Another rhetorical question because she answered it herself. "To keep him from his real father, I bet. But that can't be right because then she would say he was born later instead of earlier than he was. But we know that's not true, because she wasn't pregnant two weeks before the baby was born."

"Do you always have these conversations with yourself?"

"I always try to talk to the smartest person in the room."

Tuper chuckled. He believed she really meant that.

"But what if Jessica had a jealous boyfriend and she got pregnant by Gordon? They may have picked up and left as soon as she found out she was pregnant. If her jealous boyfriend had any inkling that she was pregnant, and traced the birth certificate somehow, she may have said he was born earlier to throw him off." Her eyes widened as they did when she seemed to think she was on to something. "He must be a cop. I'll check to see if I can find out if she was seeing anyone."

"You have quite the imagination."

"When I'm trying to gather information, I try to imagine every scenario, that way I won't miss anything."

"Even the absurd?"

"Sometimes things seem absurd at first, until they're not."

Lana started to rattle on about other even more far-fetched possibilities. Tuper just listened. When she finally took a breath, he said, "Or maybe it wasn't *her* baby."

"So where did Mason come from?" Lana asked. Then her eyes widened again as if she was having an "ah ha" moment.

Tuper wrinkled his brow. "What?"

"I can't find a marriage for Randy and Denise. I know Denise said they were married in Mexico, but *she lies*, so we don't really know. I can't find a marriage certificate for Jessica and Gordon. The divorce papers you saw were for someone else, but changed to make it look like they were for Randy and Denise, which also means *she lied*. What else is she lying about? I'm thinking maybe she didn't have a baby. She has no photos of him on Facebook, nor does she ever mention him on social media."

"What are you saying?"

"I'm saying, maybe Mason doesn't exist."

"Then why would she have me look for him?" Tuper asked, thinking this was as far-fetched as anything she had come up with yet. She didn't answer his question, apparently refocused on her computer search. "Besides, Randy's death is real. Someone murdered him."

"And as far as we know, it might have been Jessica. We saw her at his house. And if it wasn't her that killed him, it must have something to do with what she wants from you. It's too coincidental."

Tuper hated to admit that she might be on to something. The more he thought about it though, the more she made sense. "Unless..."

"Unless she wants you to find something or someone else."

"The first thing we need to do is find out if Mason is real. Can you get me the addresses for every place where Jessica and Gordon lived?"

"Already on it."

CHAPTER TWENTY-EIGHT

Tuper thought about what Lana had said about Mason. It was possible that Mason didn't exist, but Tuper wasn't totally convinced. He saw the look of despair in Denise's eyes when she spoke about him. And he remembered that his friend Jerome at Johnson Tire had seen Randy with a child a couple of times. It's possible he wasn't Mason, but more than likely he was. Nevertheless, he decided to investigate further. If there was no Mason belonging to Denise/Jessica, he was done with her.

He could go see Jerome and show him the photos to see if that was the child he had met, but that wouldn't really tell him anything. All he would know was that it was the same child as the photo, not whether or not it was Denise and Randy's child. He had to talk to neighbors at their previous residences.

Lana had found the addresses where Denise and Randy had lived since they came to Montana. She told Tuper what they were, and he recognized both neighborhoods. Then she wrote both of them down for him in large print. Perhaps she thought he couldn't see.

Tuper drove to the most recent address, which was a mobile home in a small park on Valley Dr. He knew the neighborhood well because he had a woman friend, Louise, who had lived there for years. It was a casual relationship, but she always welcomed him into her home and gave him breakfast before he left. She drank a little too much for his taste. It wasn't that he cared that she drank. It was just that she would get ornery when she had too much, and had even hit him a few times with her shoe or whatever she happened to have handy.

The park was a huge step down from the home Denise and Randy lived in on Lonesome Loop when they first came to Helena a little over four years ago. They had lived in the mobile park for less than a year before they split. From what Lana could gather, they left that home less than a month before Mason disappeared. New tenants already occupied the mobile home.

As Tuper drove, he wondered how Lana could get so much information from that machine. It frightened him a little. He had heard about identity theft and all that goes with it. It was no wonder, when all your information was out there for people to steal. He yearned for the "good old days" when everything was paid with cash, and no one knew what actually went on behind your closed door. Now, it was as if someone was watching you all the time.

He pulled into the park and drove to the space number Lana had given him. It was only two doors down from his friend Louise. He debated whether he should stop and see her. He didn't need to get involved with another woman. He already had trouble juggling what he had. When he was younger it was much easier, but the older he got, the more conventional he became with his relationships. Besides, he didn't even know if she still lived there. On the other hand, she may have information about Denise and Randy and he was sure she'd be truthful with him. There hadn't been much of that in this case so far.

He drove forward, stepped out of his car, and told Ringo to stay. He almost changed his mind by the time he got to the door. He tried to remember just how it had ended with her. When he did, he realized she might not be too happy to see him. Before he could ring the doorbell, the door opened.

Louise stood there for a second with her mouth agape. Then she smiled. "Well, if it isn't the wayfaring stranger knocking at my door."

"Hello, Louise."

She opened the door further for him to enter. "Come on in, Tuper. How the heck have you been?"

"Good, and you?"

"Same ol', same ol', just a little older and probably not any wiser."

"Well, you're still as beautiful as ever."

Her face turned pink, clashing with her red, poufy hair.

"You're always a charmer, Tuper."

He did know how to charm the ladies, but he meant this compliment. That wasn't always the case, but he always thought it never hurt to make a woman feel good, so he often did it even when he didn't mean it. But Louise did look beautiful; he had forgotten what a looker she was.

Louise broke his train of thought when she said, "What brings you here? I'm guessing it's not to see me, but I'm glad you're here just the same. Can I get you something to drink?"

"No, I don't have much time. I'm looking for a lost child."

"And you think I can help?"

"Did you know your neighbors in #18? Denise and Randy Jenkins?"

"Yes, they were lovely people. I got to know them quite well, especially Denise. She didn't have any family here and often came to me for advice."

"What kind of advice?"

"Mostly cooking stuff, or how to get stains out, that sort of thing."

"Did you know their son?"

"Of course. His name is Mason. He's a sweet,

adorable little boy. A little skittish sometimes, but I think that was his parents' fault. They doted on him, particularly Denise. She never wanted him out of her sight. I think I was the only one she ever left him with." Suddenly her face grew solemn. "Don't tell me it's Mason you're looking for?"

"Afraid so." He retrieved the photo from his pocket and showed it to Louise. "Is this him?"

She put her hand over her mouth for a second. "That's him. What happened?"

"He was snatched from school his first day back at kindergarten after the holidays."

"That poor little boy." She shook her head. "How are Denise and Randy holding up? They must be going crazy with Mason missing."

Tuper took a deep breath. "It's hard for Denise. Randy was murdered a few days ago."

"Oh no! That's just awful." She sighed. "How can I help?"

"Just answer a few more questions."

"Of course."

"When did Denise and Randy move?"

"About three or four weeks ago."

"Did you ever see them fighting? Or did Denise ever complain about him?"

"No, in fact, they seemed like the perfect couple. They were always so kind to each other and appeared to be so much in love. I admired their relationship and often wished I had one like it myself. Denise never said anything bad about him—quite the contrary. She always sang his praises. She was concerned that he had trouble finding good work but she never blamed him for it."

"Do you remember what kind of cars they drove?" Tuper asked.

"Randy drove an old, cream-color Dodge Daytona.

I don't know the year."

Tuper remembered it to be tan, but that was close enough.

"And Denise had a green Chevy. I'm not sure what model."

"Did you ever see either of them drive a dark blue RAV4?"

"No, but I saw one at their house a lot, especially the last few months. I even met the guy who drove it. His name was Alan something."

"How did you happen to meet him?"

"I went to see Denise to give her a zucchini bread that I had just baked and some cookies for Mason. Alan was there and Denise introduced him to me. At first, I thought it was Randy. They looked a lot alike, similar hair, build, and height, but when he turned around, their faces were very different."

"And she called him Alan?"

"That's right."

"Did she ever call him anything else? Like Dusty, maybe?"

"No, just Alan. I saw him once after that. Denise was at my house and he came looking for her."

"For *her*? Not Randy?"

"No, not Randy. He asked for Denise."

"How often would you say he was at their house the last month?"

"It seems like almost every day. At least four or five times a week."

"Thanks, Louise." Tuper said. "You don't happen to have anything that belonged to Mason, do you?"

"As a matter of fact, I do. I have an old hairbrush. He kept it here because he liked me to brush his hair. He didn't like it combed. Let me get it." Louise left and returned within a few minutes and handed him the brush. "Here, I hope it helps you find Mason."

"Me too," Tuper said as he opened the door to leave.

He took a step away from the mobile home when Louise said, "Hey, Toop, don't be a stranger. I've missed our evening meals and our breakfasts."

He turned and winked at her. "You'll be hearing from me, darlin'. But first I need to find Mason."

CHAPTER TWENTY-NINE

Although Tuper was satisfied Mason was real, he drove to the house on Lonesome Loop. According to Lana, they had rented this house on March first. If someone remembered her when they first moved in, he could find out if she was pregnant. Lana had theorized that Mason wasn't born on Valentine's Day but rather later, which seemed far-fetched to him, but it also supported his theory that Mason was not Jessica's baby.

Lonesome Loop was in a relatively new housing development. Each home sat on two acres of land, which meant the houses were not close to one another. Some of them still didn't have lawns or fences, and all but one was occupied. He knew it would be more difficult to get information since the neighbors weren't that close. Besides, he didn't know anyone who lived on this street. He did have a couple of friends on Kaitlyn Loop very near here, but they were too far away to see what might have gone down on this street.

Lana had told him that she had researched the homes to see who was near the Jenkins. She already knew that Denise's friend Jan Murray was living in the house on the street behind them when Denise and Randy moved in. Jan was only there for a month but, apparently, she and Denise had hit it off. Their rear fences abutted. Jan and Denise probably met in their backyards over the fence. Perhaps she did the same with the people who moved in there when Jan left. At least it was a place to start.

He passed the house where Denise had lived, drove around the loop to the other side and parked in front. He knocked on the door and a man in his forties answered.

"Can I help you?" he asked.

"I hope so," Tuper said. "I'm looking for a missing five-year-old boy."

"Was he lost in this neighborhood?"

"No, but until last year he lived behind you. You may have known his parents, Denise and Randy Jenkins."

"Yes, I met them a few times, but we have acres between us. It's not like we were next door. My wife knew them better than I did. Our gardens are against the back fence and they both liked gardening so they talked some."

"Who is it, honey?" a woman called from another room.

"It's someone looking for the little boy who used to live behind us. He's missing."

The woman dashed to the door, wiping her hands on a towel. "Oh no! Not Mason!"

"I'm afraid so."

"What happened?"

"He was abducted from school," Tuper said. "When did you last see Mason?"

"Last year, before they moved. We haven't kept in touch."

"How well did you know Denise?"

"We met when we first moved in here."

"When was that?"

"It'll be five years in April. April first," the man said.

"That's right. It was spring and we were just starting our gardens. We had a mild winter and were able to get the gardens planted fairly early."

"Is that how you met? At your garden?"

"Yes, we were both in our backyards and excited about getting started. She had just moved in as well, about a month before us, I think. We started talking and she invited me to coffee. She was new to this area so she didn't have many friends."

Tuper twisted his mustache. "Was she pregnant at the time?"

"No, Mason was already born. He was about two months old at the time, a cute healthy little baby. I was envious of Denise's shape. She sprung back so fast. You couldn't even tell she had had a baby. I still haven't got my shape back, and my daughter is twelve." She chuckled and then became somber again. "I watched Mason grow throughout the years. Such a sweet little boy."

"How is any of this going to help you find him now?" the man asked.

"The truth is we're grasping at straws trying to find anyone who may have some information," Tuper said. "Did you know any of her friends?"

"No. Denise was real nice but we didn't socialize beyond the occasional neighborly coffee. That only happened a couple of times. Mostly we had backyard meetings in our gardens whenever we both happened to be there. Mason always helped her or played near her when she was there. Denise was very protective of him. I can't imagine what she's going through."

Tuper thanked them for their help and left. Then he drove to the home of a friend who owned a DNA lab, which was on the other end of town.

It was getting late and he probably should have called first but he didn't much like talking on the phone. Besides, he wasn't sure he could find his friend's number on his phone.

The light was on in the living room when Tuper drove up in front of Brad Bergstad's house. The curtain was partway open and he could see the television was on. He knocked.

Brad came to the door in his sweats. "What the heck brings you here this late?" he said jokingly, then quickly added, "Everything okay?"

"It's all good. I didn't expect you'd be in bed for another hour or two."

"You're right. Come on in."

Tuper stepped inside, holding two plastic bags in one hand. The bags contained Mason's hairbrush and the toothbrush Tuper had taken from Randy's mobile home the night he broke into it.

"I need a favor," Tuper said.

Tuper and Brad's father had been good friends for many years. Tuper had taken them both in and given them a home for a month or so when Brad's father and mother split up. Brad was a teenager then and had some trouble adjusting without his mother. Tuper managed to keep Brad out of trouble on more than one occasion. He grew up to be quite successful.

"Sure, shoot."

"You still own that DNA lab, right?"

"Yes."

Tuper handed the bags to Brad. "I have a hairbrush from a missing five-year-old boy and a toothbrush from the man who claimed to be his father. Can you run a paternity test for me?"

"What happened to the kid?"

"He was abducted from school. We don't know where he is now."

"You know you won't be able to use this in court?"

"Don't plan to go to court. Just need to know if he's the father or not. I don't expect he is. Just need to know for sure."

"I'll put a rush on it, and I'll let you know as soon as I have the results."

CHAPTER THIRTY

Tuper drove through Clancy and headed for his cabin in the Elkhorn Mountains. He needed to go home to check on the place and pick up a chainsaw he had borrowed from a friend who needed it back. A storm was going to hit pretty hard within the next few days and once it did, Tuper wouldn't be able to get to the cabin for a while.

He passed a clearing and then some trees and turned left in front of Elkhorn Health and Rehabilitation. After he followed the pavement for about five miles, the road turned to gravel. It was always difficult getting from the road to the cabin, and it would be impossible when the snow hit.

He was tired, but the bumpy, curvy road kept him awake as he bounced along, climbing the mountain through the mass of fir trees. When he had driven about four miles, he slowed down and watched for his turnoff, as it was difficult to see at night. He turned and drove about sixty feet through the filled ruts up to the cabin, his headlights illuminating the tools, car parts, and other junk surrounding the small, dilapidated home. *I really need to get that junk cleaned up*, he thought.

Tuper stepped out of the car, letting Ringo out as he did. Ringo darted across the yard and around the corner toward the old outhouse with the crescent moon window that sat about ten yards behind the cabin.

Tuper breathed in the cold, mountain air as he approached the door with his gun in one hand and a flashlight in the other. He reached down and turned the handle. The unlocked door squeaked when he pushed it open. Shining the light quickly around the twelve-by-sixteen-foot room soon told him it was empty. On more than one occasion Tuper had returned home to find someone or something in his cabin. Once it was a bear. That time, he backed away slowly, leaving the door open, and waited in his car with his shotgun pointed at the door until the bear decided to leave.

The cabin was cold and dreary but it was home. Tuper liked it here. He was most at home when he was among wildlife and nature.

It had been over a week since Tuper had been here but nothing looked disturbed. The one-room cabin had a small wooden table with two chairs and a big armchair in front of a large cookstove flanked by two completely full woodboxes. Tuper had filled them before he left. There was a sink with a water pump, a chest of drawers, and a twin bed against the wall. There was one window above the table but it was usually too dirty to see out of. An ax stood in the corner behind one of the full woodboxes. On top of the dresser there was a bag of unshelled peanuts, two empty shell boxes, and a deck of cards.

When Tuper removed his jacket, he saw the envelope Denise had given him. He laid it on the table. He could have looked at it but he had given his word that he wouldn't, and looking wouldn't have made any difference anyway.

He lit the propane lamp that sat on the table, put some wood in the cookstove, and started the fire. Then, using the water from the pump over the sink, he filled the old, blue-and-white speckled teakettle and placed it onto the stove. Then he paused for a few moments while he held his hands over the hot stove, rubbing them together to warm them up.

When the teakettle began to boil, he made himself

a cup of hot tea and sat down in the chair in front of the fire. Before long, he dozed off. He started when the door creaked. He turned toward the door with his gun drawn. The door creaked again and Tuper felt the breeze from outside as Ringo pushed his way inside. Tuper rose, walked to the door, stuck his head out, and glanced around. He put the wooden latch he had recently built across the door. He never locked it unless he was home, and then only at night. He had nothing in the cabin worth stealing, and if someone needed a place to sleep when he wasn't there, he was fine with that.

It was late, and Tuper was tired. He pulled his boots off, left his clothes on, stirred the fire, and lay down on his bed bundled up in his blankets. He was asleep within minutes.

It was still dark outside when Tuper woke up. He turned his flashlight on inside the cabin, let Ringo outside to run, and then made himself some tea. Ringo returned just as the sun began to rise. Tuper changed his shirt and put on his boots. He went outside to use the outhouse. Then he went to the shed and picked up the chainsaw and put it in the car. A light snow had fallen through the night. Scatterings of green and brown peeked through the white blanket of snow.

The snow had let up but the sky was still dark with clouds, and Tuper wanted to get down the mountain before the worst of the storm came in.

"Ringo, let's go," he called. Ringo ran up to him, jumped in the car, and they started down the mountain. As usual, he admired the view he had from his cabin. He could see for miles most days, but today he couldn't see much for the snow that was falling and the cloud cover.

The snow was falling hard by the time Tuper was halfway down the mountain, making it difficult to see the road. He kept moving forward, hoping he wouldn't get stuck before he hit the highway. He shivered as the wind whistled through his window that wouldn't close tight.

He was glad when he reached Clancy. The roads were already being plowed and he could pass through with ease. He reached in his shirt pocket for his phone and he realized he had left the envelope on the table that he had received from Denise. The snow was falling too hard to go back now. He only hoped he wouldn't need the envelope before he got a chance to go back.

CHAPTER THIRTY-ONE

This missing kid thing was eating at him. It was taking too long. He knew the likelihood of finding Mason alive was slim, but as long as there was a chance, he'd keep looking. He was running out of leads and was upset at himself for losing Denise yesterday. He decided to go back to the airport to see if her car was parked in the lot, just in case he had missed it before.

When Tuper couldn't find Denise's car at the airport, he drove to Clarice's. Her kitchen and dining room lights were on, which meant she had the early shift this morning and would be good for a hot cup of tea.

Clarice answered the door and let him in. Lana was still lying on the sofa. Tuper wondered if he woke her when he knocked on the door.

"Good morning," Clarice said. "Tea water is on. Help yourself. I need to get ready for work."

As Tuper walked toward the kitchen he heard a voice from the sofa.

"It's the middle of the night."

"To me, the day is half over. All in how you look at it, I guess."

Lana rolled off the sofa, grabbed her bag, and headed toward the bathroom. Tuper went into the kitchen, made himself a cup of tea, and sat down at the table. He was sitting there contemplating his next move when Lana returned. She had changed from her pajamas to jeans, a sweatshirt, and her boots. She sat down in front of her laptop and started it up.

"Jessica was not pregnant when she moved into

the house on Lonesome Loop," Tuper said. "And she lied about how well she knew Alan Bowman."

"How did you find that out?" Lana asked.

"I know someone who lived near her when she was in the mobile park."

"Of course you do." She rolled her eyes. "Do you know everyone in town?"

"Don't know that pretty little filly who was drinking at the Motherlode when I paid Alan a visit. But I'd like to."

Lana shook her head. She didn't know Tuper well enough to know when he was joking, or if he ever joked. "What's her game?" she asked.

"The woman at the bar?"

"No, Jessica aka Denise. You'd think if she came to you for help, she'd tell you the truth."

"Just 'cuz she needs help don't mean she doesn't have something to hide." His look lingered on Lana a little longer than usual.

Lana's eyes turned toward her computer. "True," she said, and then started tapping on her keys like she was looking for something. "Tell me what else you learned."

"That was about it," Tuper said.

"Tell me everything that was said. It might help me when I'm looking for information."

Tuper gave her as detailed an account as he could, leaving out the part about Louise asking him to breakfast.

Before long, Lana started chattering in a soft voice, without looking up. "So, where do we go from here? We know that Jessica did not give birth to Mason. She wasn't pregnant when she left Rosewood and Mason was born around mid-February. He was about two months old when the neighbors moved into the house on Lonesome Loop and he was a healthy-looking baby, so the birthdate we have is probably pretty close. We know that Gordon Price is not the father since he was in jail when Mason was conceived. So where did they get Mason? We need to find out where he came from."

"Are you talking to me?" Tuper said. He thought she was since he was the only other person in the room, but she never looked away from her laptop and she was muttering.

"No," she said, looking at Tuper. "I was talking to myself, but you can listen if you want. Being a cyber engineer is a lonely business. I've learned to talk to myself. Sometimes, when I say things in my head, they sound plausible, but when I say them out loud, they sound foolish. It steers me in the right direction."

"Most of what you say sounds foolish to me, but that may be because you're from a different planet."

"You know I've been a big help to you in the search for Mason."

"Ain't found him yet."

"We will. And you have to admit I've given you some pretty good information."

He stroked his mustache. "Don't have to admit nothin'." But he knew he wouldn't know nearly as much without her chopping or hacking or whatever it was called. Suddenly, Tuper felt a cramp in his leg and stretched it out under the table to break it. He didn't want Lana to see. Maybe he *was* getting too old for this. Maybe it was time for the young'uns to take over. But he wasn't about to tell her.

"You're a strange little thing, aren't you?" Tuper said.

"So I've been told."

"As far as Randy/Gordon being Mason's father, we don't know that for sure."

"But Gordon was in jail when the baby was conceived, so he couldn't be the father."

"Just the same, since we don't know for sure when that baby was born, I'm getting a DNA test done."

"How are you doing that?"

"I know a guy."

"Of course you do."

Tuper's phone rang and when he answered it, he heard a panicky voice on the other end. She was so loud that Lana could hear her as well.

"Do you have it?" she yelled.

"Denise?" Tuper asked.

"Yes. I want the envelope back. Have you opened it?"

"I told you I wouldn't."

"I need it."

"Are you okay?" Tuper asked.

"I just need the envelope."

"Where are you?" Tuper asked. "I'll bring it to you."

"I gotta go." She hung up.

Tuper sighed as he closed his flip-phone and put it back in his shirt pocket.

"What envelope?" Lana asked.

"It's not important."

"It's important to Denise. It sounds like she gave it to you and told you not to open it, right?"

"It's on a need-to-know basis. You don't need to know. Besides, I don't have it."

"You told her you would bring it to her."

"Whatever it takes to get her to meet me, at this point. She doesn't know I don't have it."

"What did you do with it?"

"It's in my cabin near Clancy."

Just then Clarice entered. "I'm leaving for work. Mary Ann's still asleep so please try to keep the noise down."

Tuper stood up and retrieved his jacket from the back of his chair. "I was just leaving too."

155

"Where you going?" Clarice asked.

"To get some breakfast."

"At the Residence Inn?" Clarice asked.

Lana got her coat and pulled her beanie over her head, covering her ears.

"What do you think you're doing?" Tuper asked.

"I'm going along."

"No, you're not."

Lana unplugged her laptop, stuffed it in its case, and tucked it under her arm as she walked out the door to a blanket of white. She shivered when she stepped into the cold, damp air but she kept moving toward Tuper's car which was already topped with snow. He and Clarice were close behind her. Clarice's car was right in front of her house so she was in her car first.

"Agony," Tuper called, but Lana kept walking.

Tuper zipped up his leather jacket and got in his car. Ringo ran around, took care of his business, and then dashed up to the car. Tuper reached across and opened the passenger door, calling Ringo at the same time, to avoid his snowy, wet paws bouncing across him. Ringo jumped in and Tuper pulled the door closed behind him. Ringo spun around trying to get comfortable and then shook. The loose snow flew everywhere before he settled into the seat.

"Move over, Ringo," Lana said as she opened the passenger door and got in.

Tuper just frowned at her without saying anything.

"I'm bored," Lana said, "I need the fresh air, and I'm hungry."

CHAPTER THIRTY-TWO

"Brr, it's cold out there," Lana said as they entered the Residence Inn. They came through the side door into the dining area. A lone man sat at a table in the corner watching the news and drinking a cup of coffee.

"There's hot drinks over there," Tuper said, pointing across the small room. "And a fireplace if you need to warm up." He nodded his head to the left.

"Hot chocolate sounds good," Lana said.

"Get me some too, will you?"

Lana frowned at him. "I'm not your lackey."

"Then sit down and I'll get the hot chocolate."

"No, you sit, old man. I'll get it."

Tuper stopped arguing with her, but he wondered why he had let her come along. He sat down at the table closest to the hot beverage counter. Lana went straight to the counter and made them each a cup of hot chocolate.

Marlene must have spotted Tuper as soon as he came in. She came directly over to his table.

"Good morning, Tuper. Back at work I see."

"Yeah." Just then Lana returned with the drinks and set them on the table. Marlene had a funny look on her face when she saw Lana, so Tuper said, "This is —"

"His assistant," Lana said. "We're working on a very important case. What did you say your name was?"

"Marlene," she said. "What are you working on?"

"I'm afraid we can't talk about that, but it's so nice to meet you, Marlene." Lana started to reach her hand out, but Marlene was holding a large box of honey packets.

Marlene lowered her voice. "I understand. Hush, hush, huh? I promise I won't tell anybody."

Lana struggled to find something to compliment Marlene about. She had found that if you can get the conversation back on the person, it took it off yourself. Marlene was wearing a boring tan uniform, so she couldn't say much about her clothes. Her hair was pulled back in an awkward little ponytail, and her teeth were sparse. "Are you the only one working here this morning?" Lana glanced around the small room. "Oh, there's another employee, but you seem to be doing all the work. I see you buzzing all over the place, picking up dishes, offering coffee."

Marlene grinned. "Thank you for noticing. Sometimes I feel like I'm the only one working."

Tuper reached out and touched Marlene's arm. "You always take good care of me."

Marlene blushed. "I'd better get back to work."

"That was smooth," Tuper said. "How did you know what to say to her?"

"That was easy. People always think they do more work than their fellow workers."

"My assistant?" Tuper grumbled. "An assistant would bring hot chocolate without complainin' about it."

"Would you rather I had said 'daughter' or 'granddaughter,' Pops?"

"I'd rather you didn't talk at all."

Tuper got up and went to the buffet table. He loaded a plate, taking two extra sausage patties for Ringo. Lana followed suit. To Tuper's delight, they ate in silence. He was just about done when his phone rang and Denise's photo appeared on his screen.

"Where are you?" Tuper said when he answered.

"Near the air—"

Suddenly he heard a loud smash and breaking glass on the phone. Denise screamed.

Tuper jumped up and ran out the door. Lana grabbed Ringo's sausages and followed him.

"Denise, where are you?" Tuper yelled into the phone.

"You," she yelled. He heard a loud clunk, as if she had hit something with her phone, and then another scream. Then he heard what sounded like a struggle, a thud, and another scream, but this one was further from the phone. All of a sudden it was quiet.

Tuper and Lana were about to get in the car when a gold Honda Accord sped through the parking lot from behind the Inn. It was going so fast it almost didn't make the turn at the end of the lot. Whoever was driving didn't stop at the corner that put them onto Custer Ave. A car coming from the left slammed on his brakes, spun around on the icy road, and slid onto the shoulder facing the opposite direction. The gold Honda turned to the right and headed toward the highway.

Tuper dashed around to the back of the Inn with Lana close behind him.

"Go back to the car," Tuper yelled, but Lana kept coming.

Just as he rounded the corner, he spotted Denise's car across the parking lot. He ran toward it and saw the smashed window and Denise's bloody head hanging out the window.

CHAPTER THIRTY-THREE

A man was standing in front of Denise's car with his cell phone to his ear. Tuper could hear he was calling 9-1-1.

Tuper stepped closer to Denise and Lana followed. Lana took one look at the bloody mess and turned her head away. Tuper reached around to the back of Denise's head and plucked a few hairs out. Then he took a couple of steps toward the man on the phone and waited for him to finish his call.

"Did you see what happened?" Tuper asked.

"No, I heard some commotion from my room." He pointed to the room by the door. "I was just getting ready to leave for the airport, but I thought I heard screams so I came outside. It was too dark to see much and I didn't know exactly where the noise came from because it had all stopped. Then I saw a car come from over there." He pointed to the left, further behind the Inn. "He almost hit me as he sped past."

"He? It was a man driving?"

"I don't know. It was pretty dark, but he or she came pretty close to me. Now that you ask, he or she was wearing a beanie, but I didn't see a face. I guess I just assumed it was a man. It's harder to imagine a woman doing something like this." He paused and looked at Tuper. "Are you a cop?"

"No. Just happened to be leaving the hotel when I heard all the commotion."

The sun was creeping onto the horizon providing more light. A couple pulling suitcases came out of the Inn and walked across the parking lot toward them. The man asked, "What was all that hullabaloo a while ago?"

The man with the cell phone pointed toward Denise. The man with the suitcase wrapped his arm around the woman he was with and led her in a different direction. Sirens could be heard in the distance, and more people started to gather.

Tuper turned to Lana. "It's cold out here. Let's go."

As they went back to the car, Tuper said, "Let's get some more hot chocolate."

Lana looked at Tuper, tipping her head. "Really? That made you thirsty?"

"I have my reasons."

Lana shivered and said, "Good idea, but I think I'll have tea. And then let's go before this place is swarming with cops."

Tuper was impressed that Lana hadn't fainted or screamed. It had obviously upset her but she was a tough kid.

"Can you show me the photo of Denise on my phone?" Tuper asked just before they reached the side door.

"Sure." Lana looked at him curiously but took the phone, opened it, and brought up the photo. "Here you go," she said as she handed it back.

They got inside just as a police car sped through the parking lot. Lana went to get the tea, and Tuper stopped Marlene and took her off to the side. She was visibly shaken. He could tell by the buzz in the room and the curious looks on the faces of the people around that word had already gotten inside. A man in a suit came from the office behind the front desk and hurried past them and out the door.

"Marlene, do you know what's going on outside?" Tuper said softly.

"I heard some woman was killed."

"I need you to look at this photo and see if you

recognize this woman." He held up the phone for her to see.

"It's not a very good photo, but that looks like the woman who came in here this morning. Is that the woman that got killed?"

Tuper didn't answer her. Another siren blared. Tuper glanced out the large plate glass window at the end of the lobby and saw a firetruck pass. "Did you talk to her?"

"I did. The coffee wasn't out yet and she asked when it was coming. She was the only one in the room at the time. It wasn't long before you got here. I went and got the coffee pot and set it up. She went to get her coffee and I went around the corner toward the storage room to get some honey packets because we were all out. She passed me up and headed down the hallway. She seemed to be in a big hurry."

"Did she go to a room?"

"No, she went out the door."

"Did you see anyone else?"

"No, nobody. Wait, yeah, I saw some woman go out right before her, but nobody after her. Then I reached the storage room and went inside. After that, I came back and saw you."

"Can you describe the woman you saw go out before her?"

"Not really. I just barely saw her. She was medium height, medium weight. She was wearing a furry, white coat and a beanie. I think her hair was lighter. Not sure."

Lana came up to Tuper carrying two cups of hot tea.

Tuper touched Marlene on the shoulder. "It's very important that you keep this little talk to yourself. Can you do that?"

"Of course."

Tuper was pretty sure she wouldn't keep quiet, but it didn't matter that much.

"One more thing. Do you have a plastic baggie?"

Marlene left and returned right away with a baggie and handed it to Tuper.

"Thanks," he said.

More sirens and more emergency response vehicles were filling the lot as they walked out to the car. Lana handed him one of the teacups. Tuper shoved the baggie in his pocket and took the tea.

"You didn't have to get my tea. You're not my *lackey*, you know."

"I know, but you looked cold," Lana said.

Before getting in the car, Tuper handed the baggie to Lana. "Open this, please," he said.

When she opened the baggie, Tuper dropped in the four or five strands of hair he had taken from Denise's head that he still held in his clenched fingers.

"Where did you get these?"

"From Denise's head."

"You took hair from a dead woman's head?"

"It's not like she felt it."

Lana grabbed her stomach and shook her head. "We better get out of here. I really don't want to be questioned by the cops."

Tuper looked at her and wondered what it was she was hiding.

CHAPTER THIRTY-FOUR

Tuper drove a couple of blocks and then pulled into a gas station, but he didn't go to the pumps. Instead, he parked, leaving the car running, and took out his phone.

"What are you doing?" Lana asked.

"I'm calling someone," Tuper said.

"And you had to stop to do that?"

Tuper tapped the number into the phone and waited for it to ring.

"Hello, Denis," Tuper said. He paused. "Can you meet me at McDonald's on North Montana? I have some information about the murder at the Residence Inn this morning." Tuper hung up.

"Was that the cops?" Lana asked.

"A friend."

"A cop friend?" She sounded skeptical.

"I have those." Tuper started the car and drove west on Custer Ave.

"Why are you calling the cops?"

"Because they will soon know I was there and I don't want them to think I'm hiding something."

"Are you?"

"I won't tell them everything, but if they can find Denise's killer, they might find Mason, and that's what we want, right?"

"Right." Lana got quiet.

Tuper turned left onto North Montana and made an immediate right into the parking lot near McDonald's. He didn't want to break the silence because it was so peaceful with "quiet Agony."

"Stay here. I'm doing this alone."

"Okay," Lana said.

Tuper got out of the car and then stuck his head back in. "Agony, there's no need for me to tell him about you."

She sighed. "Thanks."

Tuper sat down at a table toward the back and waited until Denis Castro showed up. Less than five minutes elapsed before a man about five-foot-eleven with dark, curly hair and a mustache came in. He glanced around the room and then walked toward Tuper.

"It's been a while, Toop," Denis said.

"Sure has."

"You're not in trouble, are you?"

"No. I've been helping someone look for that missing five-year-old, Mason Jenkins. I'm sure you know that was his mother who was killed this morning."

"I do. And his father last week." He eyed Tuper. "What do you know that I don't?"

"I don't want to get caught up in the middle of this."

"You won't if I can help it. What have you got?"

"I was talking to her when she got killed."

"You were with her?"

"No, on the phone."

"What did she say?"

"Mostly, she just screamed. Once she said, 'You.'"

"You what?"

"No, it was more like an accusation in her tone. Like *it's you*. She didn't actually say *it's*, but from the inflection, I think she knew the killer."

"They usually do," Denis said. "What else?"

"I'm sure you'll discover it soon enough, but I think her real name is Trinidad Jessica Andrade and she's from Southern California, your old stomping grounds. And her husband, Randy Jenkins, is really a guy named Gordon Price, which I'm sure you already know.

They both came here from San Jacinto, California."

"You're just a wealth of information. I don't suppose you want to tell me how you know all this?"

"Nope."

"Do you know who the killer is?"

"If I knew that I woulda led with it."

"I suppose so." Denis chuckled. "You're still the same ornery old goat, aren't you?"

"Humph."

"You got anything else?"

"Yeah. I don't think either of these people are Mason's real parents."

When Denis left, Tuper went back to the car and found Lana working on her laptop.

"Anything interesting?" he asked.

"Denise's murder is all over Facebook. They don't get a lot of excitement in this town, do they?"

"Not many murders, if that's what you mean."

Tuper started the car but before he could move his phone rang. The photo of Denise that Lana had put in popped up. Lana's mouth dropped open.

"Someone is calling you from Denise's phone," Lana said.

Tuper started to pick it up but Lana hit the speaker button. "I want to hear."

"Hello," Tuper said. There was no response. Again Tuper said, "Hello."

"You'll never find him," a woman said.

"Who?" Tuper asked. He could hear road noise so he knew she was driving.

"My baby boy. You call him Mason, but that's not his name anymore. It's a good strong name, but it's not his. My sweet boy will have a new name." She sounded eerie. "I have him now. He's safe. He'll never feel pain again, so stop looking for him."

"I'm afraid I can't do that. Tell me where you are

and I'll help you."

"I don't need your help," she said calmly. Then in a loud voice, she said, "Just stop looking!"

Suddenly he heard a lot of static on the phone, possibly created by wind in the background, a swishing sound, and a clunk.

"Are you there?" Tuper asked, but the line went dead.

"What happened?" Lana asked.

"I think she threw the phone out the window."

Lana shook her head. "That was creepy." Tuper didn't respond. "What do you think she meant when she said, 'He'll never feel pain again'? Do you think she killed Mason?"

"I don't know, but I'm not stopping until I find out."

CHAPTER THIRTY-FIVE

Lana sat at the table in front of her laptop with a soft, fuzzy throw blanket wrapped around her legs. She had warmed her hands and her body in front of the fireplace, but she couldn't quite shake the chill she had gotten outside. She continued to wrap her hands around her hot teacup between typing bouts. Her body longed for Southern California, as did her mind from time to time.

Lana started digging back further in Jessica's life, hoping to find Mason's mother. She read through her entire Facebook page, from the time she joined to date, which she found totally boring and a little gloomy. A thread of significance throughout was her interest in someday becoming a mother, but it was innocuous. She didn't appear to be obsessed with it, and posts about it stopped about a year and a half before she met Gordon at Rosewood. She seemed to replace them with happy, flowering images and quotes, like she had found something wonderful in her life. None of the posts revealed what it might be.

Lana checked her list of friends to see if that would lead her anywhere. It wasn't a long list, but it became way too time-consuming for the return she was gaining, so she went on to Jessica's other interests. She found she belonged to a group page called "A Mother's Love." She had joined the group about six months before her change of heart on Facebook, so that wasn't likely her reason for the turnaround. Lana clicked on the group and looked at its members. There were only eight, and the group page stopped a few months later.

It wasn't much, but Lana thought it might be a

connection to Mason, so she pursued it. She discovered that "A Mother's Love" was a local non-profit organization that no longer existed. It had only lasted a year and then stopped, apparently because of a lack of funding. She knew much of the financial information of non-profit organizations was available for public viewing but she didn't want to take the time to file a Form 990 with the IRS. So she took a shortcut. Hacking most public records was a lot easier than those of the private institutions. Some sites just took longer.

A Mother's Love was initially funded by one donor, a woman named Susan Adams. That name seemed familiar to Lana, but she couldn't recall where from. It was a common name so maybe it was nothing. She kept digging, but the name was nagging at her. She decided to Google it and see what she got. With the name, Susan Adams, she found a Senior Editor at Forbes, a professor at UC Davis, a property manager in San Diego, a former beauty queen, and several obituaries. She narrowed the search to Riverside County, California, and it turned up an artist, a lawyer, and Bingo! There it was.

"Wait until Tuper hears this," Lana said aloud.

~~~

Tuper entered Definitive DNA, the lab owned by his friend Brad Bergstad.

"May I help you?" the receptionist asked.

Tuper smiled at her, always happy to see a pretty face. "Is Brad in?"

"May I tell him who is asking?"

"Tuper. The name's Tuper."

"Okay, Mr. Tuper, please have a seat. I'll check to see if he's available."

She left the room and returned shortly. "He'll be right with you."

Brad stepped into the doorway. "Come on back, Toop."

Tuper followed him.

"I don't have the results yet."

"I brought you another one." Tuper handed Brad the baggie. "It's hair from the mother. I want it tested against the little boy."

"You're questioning maternity? That's unusual. Most of the time, people know who gave birth to the baby."

"It's a strange case."

"I take it you still haven't found the boy?"

"No, and every day it gets harder."

"I'll get right on this. I should have the other one back for you by tomorrow. I put a rush on it. I'll do the same with this one."

"Thanks, Brad."

Tuper left the building and just before he reached his car, his phone rang. Lana's photo popped up on the screen.

Tuper wondered when she had put that on there. It annoyed him at first, but actually it was pretty handy seeing who was calling. He couldn't always tell who it was, otherwise. *Maybe I'll have her do that with my other contacts,* he thought. *But that would mean asking her for a favor.*

"Hello, Agony."

"Don't call me that."

"You got some information for me?"

"I do. Several things, actually."

"I'm only about ten minutes away."

Lana got up and stretched, used the bathroom, and got herself a glass of water before she went back to work. She had a hunch that involved the Riverside

County jail system. She had hacked other jails before. Most of them weren't nearly as well protected as they should be, but even so, she couldn't get the information she needed.

"Fudge!" she said, just as Tuper came in.

"Not much of a welcome," Tuper said.

"Not you. The Riverside County Jail. I'm trying to get into it."

"Go there and commit a crime. They'll let you in." He sat down.

"Very funny."

"What do you have that is so interesting?"

"I've spent a lot of time on Jessica's social media accounts. Both on Facebook and on Twitter, but mostly Facebook because she didn't do that much on Twitter. Both of them showed the same thing, so I think it means something. And so did Pinterest, but that one is really kind of empty. It only has a few posts, but all the same kind."

"Agony, speak English."

"On Jessica's social media accounts she was kind of gloomy, or at least neutral, but then all of a sudden, well over a year before she met Gordon, she started posting all these cheerful things. It was all kind of ach..." She stuck her finger up to her mouth in a vomiting gesture. "But I think it means she suddenly had a change of heart about life because that's what people do."

"Like what?" Tuper hoped he wouldn't be sorry he asked.

"I figured she had found religion, fallen in love, or maybe just got laid." She glanced at the laptop. "But since there was not a bunch of religious quotes, except for the occasional 'I've been blessed,' I ruled out religion. So, that left falling in love or getting laid, or both."

"So?"

"So, she either met someone she was crazy about or she found a way to get a baby. People get all giddy when they fall in love. And yes, I said people, not just women. Men do it too. They may not exhibit it in the same ways, but they do. Anyway, it appears she was crazy about Gordon when she met him, so either she does that with every guy she meets or—"

Tuper interrupted, "Or she met Gordon before he went to jail."

"Or she found a way to get a baby."

"Or both," Tuper added.

"That's why I was trying to get into the jail system to see if Jessica ever visited Gordon when he was there."

"But you couldn't get in?"

She frowned at him. "Oh yeah, I got in. It's just that they weren't logging their visitors in the computer back then. And I can't see a log-in sheet. We'd have to go there for that."

"Okay," Tuper said.

"You're going there?" Before he could answer, she added, "Let me guess, you know a guy?"

"I know a guy who knows a guy."

Lana gave him an "of course you do" smile. "And that's not all. Jessica belonged to a group on Facebook called 'A Mother's Love.' It's a non-profit organization that was in existence for only a year or less. And get this, it was funded by a woman named Susan Adams."

"That supposed to mean something to me?"

"It's the same Susan Adams who was bilked out of $50,000 by Gordon Price."

CHAPTER THIRTY-SIX

Tuper called JP and asked him if he could check the visitor log for Gordon Price while he was serving his time, which JP was glad to do. He also gave him a quick synopsis of what they knew so far.

"Our main goal is to find Mason's parents," Tuper said, "with the hope it will lead us to Mason. Or if they're not involved, then I expect they're still looking for their little boy and would want to know."

"What else can I do?"

"We think we have a current address on Gordon's fraud victim, Susan Adams. I was hoping you could talk to her as well."

"Where is she?"

"Palm Springs. Is that asking too much?"

"Not at all. I'll go to Riverside, then Palm Springs, and back home. It's a big circle and I can do it in one day. San Jacinto is along the trail as well if you need me to stop there."

"I know someone who is real good on the computer and she's looking for the whereabouts of Jessica's best friend. If she finds it, I'll let you know. She may be worth talkin' to."

~~~

JP sat down with the log for the dates that Gordon Price was in jail. It was only five years ago but the system seemed archaic. Now, every visitor is listed in the computer and all you have to do is bring up the prisoner's name and see who visited him. The plan, according to the clerk, had been to get all the old information put in the computer as well, but lack of funding put a quick damper on that.

It took JP longer than he had planned but he found what he was looking for. He got in his car and started his drive to Palm Springs to see Susan Adams. Once on the road, he called Tuper.

"I checked the entire record for Gordon. During his year there, he had only two visits from his father, one from his sister, and his mother came once a month like clockwork, always on the first Saturday of the month. He had no visits from Jessica or Trinidad Andrade."

"None?" Tuper said.

"But he did have visits every Saturday, except the weeks when his mother came, from Denise Jenkins."

"Well, I'll be," Tuper said. "They go back before his jail time, and she was using the same name. That puts an interesting twist on it all."

"I'm on my way to Palm Springs to see Susan. I'll keep you posted," JP said. "Hey, I heard on the news that you're having some pretty cold weather there."

"It was three degrees below this morning."

"Dang, it's supposed to be in the nineties today in Palm Springs. That's a difference of nearly a hundred degrees. How do you stand that cold?"

"Better'n the heat."

~~~

The sun continued to shine as JP drove along I-10. He watched the temperature rise on his dashboard thermometer and was thankful he was a southern boy. He had spent some time in Montana in the winter a short time back and he had no desire to return there this time of year.

He turned onto California State Route 111 and followed his GPS to Susan's home. He had spoken to her earlier and she had agreed to meet with him.

He walked up to the stucco house with the red tile roof, past the garage and a row of hedge and some succulents until he reached the front door. Two glass and metal tables with chairs, a chaise lounge, and a small barbeque sat out front on the large slab.

Susan answered the door and stepped out, pulling the door closed behind her. She had beautiful blue eyes, mousy blonde hair, very dark eyebrows, and perfectly formed lips. She also had a rather large nose. JP gave her credit for not spending her money on plastic surgery.

Susan said, "We can sit out here. It's a lovely day."

JP didn't blame her for not inviting him inside. He was always surprised when strangers brought him into their homes with all the crazies out there. He wondered if she had become more cautious after her experience with Gordon.

JP took a seat and she sat across from him. "Thank you for seeing me today. I wouldn't have bothered you if it wasn't for the missing child."

"I just don't know how I can be of help."

"I understand that about six or seven years ago you funded a non-profit organization called 'A Mother's Love.'"

"That's right."

"How did you happen to get involved with it?"

"A friend of mine told me that a friend of hers was associated with this group of women who were trying to form a support group for women who couldn't have any children of their own. My accountant had suggested that I give some money to charity, so I accepted a proposal from them. I was moved by the concept because I understood what these women were going through. I guess I felt kind of guilty because I could give birth but chose not to. I loved the idea of helping these women reach their dreams or deal with their losses. They had some great ideas, and so I had my lawyer set it all up. It was all legit."

"Did you ever meet the two women who wrote the proposal?"

"Yes, I met with them several times beforehand as well as after. Very nice ladies."

"Do you remember their names?"

"Yvonne Burkhardt was the main one. We've remained friends even though I didn't continue with the organization."

"Why did you stop?"

"I was a wreck after the incident with Gordon. I went into a deep depression, almost became an agoraphobic, but I had support from a few good friends who helped me out of it. Yvonne was one of them."

"Who was the other woman who proposed the idea to you?"

She sighed. "I can't remember her name."

"Could it have been Denise or Jessica?"

"No, I don't think so. I think it started with an N."

"Do you remember what she looked like?"

"She was a very attractive woman, dark hair, and quite tall."

"She was tall?" JP asked, a little surprised.

"Yes, she must have been near six-foot."

JP took out his phone and showed her a picture of 'Denise.' "Do you recognize this woman?"

"She looks familiar, but I'm not sure."

Then he remembered Tuper had sent a photo of 'Denise' when she was Jessica, a younger version with dark hair. He showed the photo to Susan.

"How about this woman?"

She looked up quickly with wide eyes. "That's the same woman as the other photo, isn't it?"

"Yes. Do you know her?"

"That's Gordon's sister. She's the one who introduced us. What does she have to do with this?"

JP didn't respond right away.

Susan's face turned pale. "She's not his sister, is she?"

"No, I'm afraid not."

She shook her head from side to side. "I should've known. I was such a fool. I was skeptical when we were introduced because he seemed to be giving her some interesting glances. But then he was so flirtatious with me and I'm afraid I sucked it up. I saw them together once after that and when I look back, I realize they didn't act like siblings, but I guess I was too much in love to notice back then."

"And her identity never came up with the court case?"

"It was never an issue. It might have been if we had gone to trial, but he took a plea. Was *she* part of the scam?"

"She may have been. We expect so, but we're not sure," JP said.

CHAPTER THIRTY-SEVEN

JP drove to see Judi Snider, Jessica's best friend in San Jacinto. She met JP at a coffee shop called The Hot Spot at Farmer's Corner Shopping Center on South San Jacinto Ave. When he walked in, she was sitting at a table, wearing a red ribbon in her hair as she said she would be. Her natural beauty struck JP. It was easy to see why she was crowned Miss San Jacinto some fifteen years ago.

"Hi, I'm JP. Thanks for seeing me."

"You said you had some information about Jessica."

"I do." He sat down at the table.

"Is she okay?"

"I'm afraid not."

"Is...is she dead?"

JP nodded.

Tears began to roll down Judi's cheeks. "I knew she couldn't be alive after all this time. She would've called me if she could."

"Have you had any contact with her since she left here five years ago?"

"No. Nothing."

"Did you know she was leaving?"

She hesitated before she spoke. "I promised her I wouldn't tell, but I guess that doesn't matter now." She swallowed. "She told me she was going away but she didn't say where to. She said if anyone came looking for her, she didn't want me to have to hide it. I begged her to tell me, but she said what I didn't know, I didn't have to lie about."

"Did she say *why* she was leaving?"

"Not everything, but I know it had something to do with Gordon Price."

"Did you know him?"

"Everyone knew Gordon. We were just freshmen when he was a senior, so I'm sure he didn't have any idea who we were. He was the hottest thing in high school, football quarterback, baseball pitcher, and very good-looking. Jessica had a big crush on him back then, but so did all the other girls. He was very charming and flirtatious, made a good impression when he was around parents, but never took any girl seriously. Even when he dumped them, he did it in such a way that they kept coming back."

The waitress came to the table and gave them menus.

"Just coffee for me," JP said. "Black, please."

"I'll have a skinny latte, please," Judi said.

"Did *you* have a crush on him?" JP asked when the waitress left. He wanted to make sure there was no animosity about Jessica being with him.

"I suppose I did in high school, but that faded pretty quickly, and my lack of interest was reinforced after high school. He couldn't live on his glory days anymore and his charms didn't work on me."

"But they did on Jessica?"

"Yes, she started seeing him a couple of years before she left."

"A couple of years, not months?"

"Years, but it was a big secret. She told me, but I think I was the only one who knew it. She fell hard for him. She had only been seeing him a few months when she told me they were going to get married and have a baby. She wanted a baby more than anything, even more than having Gordon. When I reminded her that she couldn't have children, she said Gordon would make it happen, and they would have their 'love child.'"

"Did you know what she meant by that?"

Judi didn't respond right away because the waitress was there with their coffee. She set the cups down and placed the bill on the table.

Judi took a sip of her latte and then said, "No, I didn't know what she meant by that, and the more I pushed, the more she withdrew until eventually she stopped talking about it. She wouldn't talk about him at all after that, and she started spending less time with me. Then he got arrested for conning some woman out of her money and he went to jail. I saw her a little more often while he was in custody, but our relationship was never the same."

"Did you know she was visiting him in jail?"

"I suspected as much, but she always denied it. Although she said she was through with him, I never believed it."

"And then they got back together when he was released from custody?"

"I suspected that as well, but she said no. When she came to me and told me she was leaving, she asked me to not worry about her. She would be fine, and she wanted me to just be happy for her because she was finally getting everything she ever wanted."

"Did she say anything about Gordon?"

"I asked her right out if she was leaving with Gordon, and she said no. Then she said she was leaving for something 'more precious.' I remember those were the exact words she used. It struck me as odd, so I asked her if she was pregnant. She just laughed and said, 'You know I can't have a baby.' Then she hugged me and left. I never saw or heard from her again."

JP brought up a photo of Mason on his phone. "Any chance you've seen this little boy in the last two weeks?"

She looked closely at the photo. "He's adorable. Is he Gordon's son?"

"Why do you ask that?"

"Because he looks like him, especially the eyes."

"We don't know for sure, but Jessica and Gordon were raising him."

Her eyes opened wide. "Is he Jessica's?"

"We don't think so, but do you know anyone who Jessica would trust enough to leave a child with?"

Judi looked down at the table. "Only me. I would be her most likely choice. At least, five years ago I would've been. Although she obviously didn't trust me enough to let me in on her secret." She looked up at JP. "I'm sorry, I'm rambling. I was her closest friend, as I told you, but I never heard from her after she left here."

"Does Jessica have any family she would maybe leave him with?" he asked.

"No." Judi sighed. "Jessica had no family left. She had a rough life. She was only five when her mother divorced her father and left them. I think she was better off because her dad really loved her. A few years later, he married a woman with a daughter three months older than Jessica. I don't think it was too bad at first, but then her father was killed in a car accident less than a year after they were married. He was on his way to pick Jessica up from a birthday party that her stepsister wasn't invited to. I guess her stepmother didn't want Jessica to go, and she and her husband had a fight about it before he left. Jessica never forgave herself for her father's death, and I don't think her stepmother forgave Jessica either."

"Did she get along with her stepsister?"

"No, not at all. They fought all the time. After Jessica left home, she and her stepsister completely cut ties."

JP picked up the bill.

"You said Jessica and Gordon were raising the boy?"

"Yes."

"When did she die?"

"Just a few days ago."

Judi's eyes filled with tears. "And Gordon doesn't have the boy now?"

"I'm afraid he's gone too."

"How did they die?"

JP wished she hadn't asked. He hated to tell people their loved ones were dead, but it was always worse when it happened like this.

"I'm sorry to say this; they were both murdered."

Judi started to cry again. She choked back the tears and said, "At least she had her child for a while. That's what she always wanted."

CHAPTER THIRTY-EIGHT

Tuper hung up the phone after his conversation with JP. He related everything he had learned to Lana and Clarice.

"JP was sure Judi didn't have the boy?" Clarice asked.

"As best he could be. Judi seemed pretty surprised by the whole thing. He said he was going to trail her some to see if he could find any Mason sightings."

"So it sounds like Jessica and Gordon were plotting to abscond with a kid somehow, but we don't know who the kid is or how they did it. And even if we did, how is any of this going to help us find Mason?"

"Don't know, but it's all we got," Tuper said.

"If they were planning this whole thing before Gordon went to jail, they must have had new IDs made," Clarice said. "They probably didn't do that themselves. Is there any way to find out who did that for them?"

Lana perked up. "That's it."

"You know how to find out who made their new IDs?" Clarice asked.

"No, but we need to follow the money. Everything they did would have cost them money. I need to dig into their financials. Maybe they bought the baby on the black market. We might even uncover a whole baby-selling thing going on." Her voice gained excitement as she spoke. "Who knows? Maybe that 'A Mother's Love' group is just a cover for a bunch of baby thieves?"

Tuper rolled his eyes. "Who knows?"

Clarice looked at Lana. "No one could ever accuse

you of not thinking outside the box."

"She don't even know there is a box," Tuper muttered.

"That's what I'm going to do—find out where the money went, starting with that $50,000 that Gordon got from Susan Adams. We know from the court case that he cashed the check, but no one seems to know what he did with it after that."

"You would think the cops would've found it," Clarice said.

"The reports say that Gordon claims he gambled it away. Besides, they didn't have the information we have. I have a hunch." Lana buried herself in cyberspace.

Lana continued to search for financial information starting with Susan Adams. She had previously gone phishing for Susan's account information and had gathered enough to get into her bank account. She had set up malware on Susan's computer as well.

Once she got inside Susan's bank account, she was able to look at old statements until she found a check written to Gordon Price for $50,000. With a little more effort she was able to see that the check was cashed the same day it was written and deposited into another account, which Lana was able to trace to Gordon.

Gordon's account showed that all the money had been withdrawn seven days later, which corresponded with the time hold the bank put on the check. A few days later, Gordon's account was closed. With a little more work, she found Bank of America accounts for Randy Jenkins and Denise Jenkins, both opened at the end of January.

Lana was making progress, but it was taking longer than she had hoped. And she had to avoid Bank of America if she could. She sent an email from her

"Cricket" account to her friend, Ravic.

--R U busy? Could use your help.

It only took seconds for him to respond. She knew he received a signal when he got a post in his hacker account. She had her account set up the same way. Only a handful of people, all of whom were hackers, had that email address.

Ravic's response: *Always 4 U, Cricket. Talk to me.*
Lana opened a chat window. *I need to get into a bank account and I'm running out of time. It's not 4 me. Still trying to save the little boy.*
Ravic: *What bank?*
Lana: *B of A.*
Ravic: *Still a little gun shy?*
Lana: *4 sure. Can't afford to leave my digital footprints there.*
Ravic: *Of course. B glad 2. What do U need?*

Lana gave him the information she had and told him what she was looking for. She didn't like sneaking around Bank of America for fear someone might be watching her from inside. A while back she had created access while working with an insider from B of A and that could have come in handy now. If she could just have bopped in and out, she might have done it. But this search could take a while. She was thankful Ravic was there for her. It wasn't always like that. He had caught her in cyberspace when she was just a novice. He figured out pretty quickly that she wasn't a Black Hat. He helped her out of a few jams. She sometimes wondered what his life was like in the real world, where he lived, if he had a real job, but she never asked. None of them did; the less they knew about one another the better for all.

Trinidad Jessica Andrade had a closed account in a small, local bank. It was in existence for six years, but was closed a few weeks after she left San Jacinto. The smaller banks were usually easier to crack than the big conglomerates, but this one was proving difficult. Lana tried getting past the firewall using several different methods. She attempted to load malware in to exploit a back door but was unsuccessful. Had she known someone with an open account, she might have been able to upload a compromised file allowing her to execute script or code. In the past, she would have tried a brute force attack, but they weren't effective any more.

"That's it," she said aloud.

Clarice started. "What?"

Lana waved her hand in a dismissal. "Nothing. I think I know how to get in."

San Jacinto wasn't that large a town and a lot of people probably used the local bank. She started with the names of those involved somehow in Gordon's or Jessica's lives: Sonny Lynch, Bob Blake, Lenore Price, Judi Snider. None of them worked, so she moved to their families and friends on social media, eliminating those who weren't locals until she got a hit. Sonny's wife, Kelly, was on her computer. Lana zeroed in and got lucky. Spear phishing got her the information she needed. She was always amazed at how easy it was to get people to give personal or financial information when she sent bogus emails to them.

"I'm in!" she shouted.

No one said anything, but Tuper and Clarice watched in awe as Lana's fingers danced across her keyboard.

When Lana slowed down and finally looked up, Tuper said, "Whatcha got, Agony?"

"I found the money." She grinned like the Cheshire Cat.

Clarice set a bowl of salad on the table. The smells of garlic and marinara sauce filled the air.

"You made dinner while I was working?" Lana asked.

Clarice nodded.

"How long have I been at this?"

"Quite a while," Clarice said. She stepped into the kitchen and brought back bowls for the salad.

"Where's the money?" Tuper asked.

"There was a $50,000 deposit made into Jessica's account seven days after Gordon cashed the check from Susan."

"And no one knew to look there," Clarice said, "because no one knew about their relationship except Judi, who either didn't tell or wasn't asked."

"Too big a coincidence to be from anywhere else," Tuper added.

"I want to look through the statements from a few months before and up until the time when the account closed, but that's going to take some time. Maybe we'll see where the money was spent."

"You can dish up your own spaghetti," Clarice said. "I made both meat and meatless sauce."

Lana stood up and just as she was about to close the lid on her laptop, the sound of an ahooga horn came from it.

Tuper was already in the kitchen. He turned around. "What the heck was that?"

"It's an alert from one of my email accounts."

Lana checked her email. Ravic had emailed her saying he had info. She started a chat with him.

Lana: *What did you find?*
Ravic: *Found a joint account for Denise and Randy*

Jenkins. It was opened with $4,124.

Lana: *Any big purchases or withdrawals?*

Ravic: *No. It was all downhill after that. That's the most they ever had in the account.*

Lana: *Were there any individual accounts for either of them?*

Ravic: *No.*

Lana: *Thanks.*

Lana related the information to Clarice and Tuper and then said, "Let's eat. I'm starving."

Before they could begin their meal, Tuper's phone rang. He answered it, listened, and thanked the caller. He looked up with wrinkled brows.

"That's a surprise," Tuper said.

"What is it?" Lana asked.

"That was Brad at the DNA lab. Gordon Price was Mason's father."

CHAPTER THIRTY-NINE

"How could Gordon have been Mason's father?" Lana asked.

"Ever heard about the birds and the bees?" Tuper said.

"I'm talking about timing. If he was in jail when this child was conceived," she said, "unless he wasn't."

Tuper knew she would continue to explain her thoughts so he waited.

"We don't know for certain when Mason was born because we can't find a record of his birth. We know he couldn't have been born nine months after Gordon got out of jail because the neighbors on Lonesome Loop saw him when he was a baby and he wouldn't have been born yet. Unless," Lana put both hands out in front of her, palms up, "it's not the same baby. Maybe they lost that baby somehow and got another baby." She scrunched her mouth. "No, that's not very likely. But if Mason was a preemie, or just a small baby, he could've been conceived before Gordon went to jail, and he might be able to pass for the age they said he was when they moved to Lonesome Loop."

Tuper and Clarice looked at Lana without saying a word. She was on a roll. Sometimes when she did this, she actually came up with a good idea so they let her rant.

Her shoulder dropped and she continued. "But that doesn't make any sense either. Because why would they lie about his age? What difference did it make? No one knew them here." She perked up again. "Unless they did. Maybe someone here knew them. Nah. Are you sure they can't have conjugal visits in the Riverside jail?"

"I'm sure," Tuper said.

"Maybe the mother is a guard at the prison, or someone that works there that he had access to."

Tuper frowned.

"You're right," Lana said. "That's not very likely. But it's possible."

"Or maybe they used his sperm," Tuper muttered.

"There's that," Lana said.

"Is it possible Jessica got pregnant before Gordon went to jail?" Clarice asked.

Tuper shook his head, and Lana spoke. "No, JP's sources at Rosewood said she was never pregnant, at least not visibly, while she was working there. Her employment records show she never had any leave during that time. And besides, we know from several people that Jessica couldn't get pregnant." Lana waved her finger in the air. "But that's not a bad idea; I'll see what I can find in her medical records."

"So Gordon got someone else pregnant, one way or another. Then they stole the baby and took off," Clarice said.

"Which would explain why they had to change their identities and maybe pretend the child was born at a different time." Suddenly her voice rose. "That's it."

"What?" Clarice asked.

"I bet Mason's mother found him and stole him back. Remember Marlene said a woman in a beanie left the hotel ahead of Jessica. And that witness at Jessica's murder scene said the driver was wearing a beanie."

"Why wouldn't Mason's real mother go to the police?" Clarice asked.

"Maybe she did and they didn't believe her or something. She could have claimed dozens of other children before, and they just started ignoring her.

People go a little whacko when they lose their children. But maybe this time she was right, and she took it too far."

"You sure have an imagination," Tuper said. He didn't want to admit it, but she might be onto something. "Can you check for missing babies around the time Jessica and Gordon became Denise and Randy?"

"I'll get right on that."

"I wish I knew who killed Denise, I mean Jessica," Tuper said. "I feel like I should be out there, looking for Mason or for Jessica's killer."

"Where would you look?" Clarice said. "Besides, you wouldn't be able to see a thing out there right now with this storm."

Through the open blinds, they could see the snow pounding down. The wind had started to blow, making the snow fall at an angle.

"That storm's getting pretty bad," Clarice said.

Tuper put his jacket and hat on. "I best be going before it gets any worse."

"You're not going up the mountain, are you?" Clarice asked.

"Never make it."

Clarice walked over to the window. "It may be too late even for town. It's pretty nasty out there. You're welcome to stay here if you want. Lana can sleep in my bed. I'll sleep in Mary Ann's room, and you can have the sofa."

Tuper went to the door. "A little storm don't bother me. Let's go, Ringo." Ringo jumped up from the spot on the carpet in front of the fireplace where he had curled up earlier and ran to Tuper. "See you in the morning."

Clarice followed him to the door. The wind howled when the door opened. The cold sent a shiver down

Lana's back. She wrapped her arms across her chest and squeezed to help herself keep warm, never taking her eyes off her computer. She had so much to do.

"Sorry about that," Clarice said.

"It's okay." She had already started the search for missing babies who were now about Mason's age.

"I'm going to bed," Clarice said. "Stay up as long as you'd like. Oh, and there's extra blankets in the hall cupboard. You may need one tonight."

"Thanks," Lana said. "Is Mary Ann coming home tonight?"

"No. She called and said she was staying at her boyfriend's. She didn't want to drive in this weather."

As soon as Clarice left, Lana focused completely on her task. She started by Googling *missing children* and found websites for the National Center for Missing and Exploited Children, the Polly Klaas Foundation, the National Missing and Unidentified Persons System, and numerous other organizations dedicated to finding children. She was impressed that so much energy was spent on finding these kids, and totally bummed by the huge numbers of kids who were missing. Some of them were runaways, a lot were taken in family abductions, and others were taken by strangers. She was struck hard by a statistic on one of the sites stating that one out of six runaways was a victim of sex trafficking.

Mason was supposedly born on February 14. So Lana started to look for missing babies born around that date, a few months after, and for the entire previous year. That would certainly cover the time period, she thought.

Some of the sites had lists and search engines where anyone could check. She started with those first. It would be simpler if she didn't have to get inside. Most of the public registries were limited to a single state rather than a national search. She started with California. Some asked for the date or the child's name. So she decided to see if Mason had been listed in the most recent abductions. She couldn't find him on any list that was open to the public.

Most of the national sites she would have to hack. She could fill out forms and email them or make phone calls in the morning, but that would take too much explanation and time, so she continued with the California list.

She found a baby boy who was born in Riverside, California on December 23rd and disappeared on the 25th. Riverside was approximately thirty minutes from San Jacinto, so it was a likely possibility. The mother was also missing. Lana Googled their names and found that mother and baby were last seen leaving the hospital. Lana followed the story and found that the woman's abusive husband, the father of the child, was the main suspect. It took the police six months to charge him with kidnapping and murder. He ultimately confessed to the crimes and took a plea to avoid the death penalty, even though it had been over ten years since anyone was executed in California and there were over seven hundred inmates on death row.

Another little boy born on January 4 in Fontana at Kaiser Permanente disappeared a month later. Lana perked up at the possibility that he might be Mason. With further investigation, she discovered the baby was found three days later at the paternal grandmother's house, safe and sound. The grandmother didn't trust her daughter-in-law, and when her son was deployed, she freaked out and took the baby to protect him. Lana wanted to follow up and see what happened to the grandma, but this was already taking too much time.

Lana found several children missing from northern California, but none of them panned out. She was almost done with this site when she came across a baby boy who was born on March 1 in Victorville, California, which was only a little over an hour from Jessica's hometown. The mother came home from grocery shopping with her month-old son, Aiden. She was struck on the back of the head just as she stepped inside her house, and when she woke up, her baby was gone.

Lana dug through public records to find more information about Aiden, but nothing turned up. The mother had several active social media accounts prior to the abduction, but they all stopped when her son went missing. She appeared, at least, to have been a happily married woman—lots of photos of her with her husband on Facebook, and the last month with her child. This didn't quite fit with Gordon being the father, but everything else pointed to a good possibility that it was Mason. At least this was the most likely candidate they had so far.

CHAPTER FORTY

It was five-ten in the morning and Tuper had already been awake for almost an hour. He had come in late to Stacy's the night before and slept on the sofa. He had considered going to see Louise but decided to wait on that. He didn't need the distraction from finding Mason and besides, Stacy lived closer and had a carport.

Stacy was still asleep when he got up, so he didn't make tea for fear he might wake her. Instead he decided to go to Clarice's house, hoping Lana had made some progress.

When he left, it wasn't snowing very hard, but the wind was whipping, creating a flurry of white. It was blowing so hard that Tuper had trouble getting the front door closed and Ringo could barely move against the wind. Tuper picked him up and carried him to the car.

Tuper backed out onto York Road. A light blanket of snow covered the road even though it had been recently plowed. He suspected the snowplows had been out all night. Where he had to turn off York Road, the plows had run a lot less. He inched along the last mile until he reached Clarice's house, glad to see the lights were on.

"Get in here, before the door blows off," Clarice said as she answered the door in her work uniform.

Tuper stomped his feet to get the snow off his shoes. Then he stepped in and yanked the door closed behind him.

"I'm not sure you should be going out in this weather," Tuper said.

"I'm supposed to open this morning but the boss

called and said he would do it, and for me to call him in an hour to see if he needs me."

Lana was sleeping on the sofa.

"Oops," Tuper said, and then lowered his voice. "Guess I shouldn't be so loud."

Clarice spoke softly as well. "I think she was up pretty late last night."

"Three-fifteen," Lana said in a sleepy voice from the sofa. She rolled out of bed, picked up her bag, and walked down the hallway.

"Since I have time, I think I'll make some breakfast. You want some oatmeal?"

"You bet," Tuper said.

Tuper sat at the counter and visited with Clarice while she made breakfast.

"We haven't had a storm like this one in a long time," Clarice said.

"Worst I've seen for a decade or so."

"The power is out in most of the northeast according to the news this morning. They've already attributed two deaths to this storm."

Just then Lana returned.

"I thought you were gonna sleep all day," Tuper said.

"I bet I got more done today than you have."

"Probably so, but I made it out of bed. That's pretty good."

"I found a missing kid who might be Mason, but I haven't been able to get much information on him yet. His real name is Aiden Master. I tried for hours last night to crack the national registry for missing kids, but that thing is tighter than Fort Knox. I haven't given up, though. My eyes were starting to lose focus, and when I started nodding off, I decided it was time to call it quits."

Lana relayed the information she had found on

Aiden and added, "From what I can tell, he's still missing."

Lana went back to searching on her computer until the oatmeal was ready. Clarice brought two bowls of oatmeal to the table and then went back for hers.

"Dang," Lana said.

"Did you find something new?" Clarice asked.

"I don't think Aiden and Mason are the same kid." Her fingers flew across the keys. She stopped for a second and looked up, her sleepy eyes now wide open. "But I think I know where Aiden is."

"Where?" Clarice asked.

"I think he's on a small ranch in a place called Bonsall. It's a small town in Southern California, east of Oceanside and west of I-15."

Tuper looked up, but didn't say anything.

Clarice raised her eyebrows. "What makes you think he's there?"

"Because, among other things, several kids, including Aiden, keep leading me to suspected kidnappers Joe and Grace Waters. The cops can't find the Waters couple, but I'm pretty sure they're living on that ranch in Bonsall. They were living in Banning when they became suspects in several kidnapping cases. The authorities apparently couldn't get enough on them because there was never a trial. And then they took off. And now they're in Bonsall."

"Why haven't the cops picked them up?" Clarice asked.

"Because they don't know where they are."

"How do you know that?"

Lana lowered her head and rolled her eyes.

Clarice continued, "How can you find them if the cops can't?"

"Because they looked in the wrong place. I was tracking several different missing kids who seemed to lead in the same direction. Different agencies are trying to solve each of these cases, and even where there is some collaboration, they're still looking at them from different angles. And I got lucky. The cops do too sometimes. They're searching for one kid and find others with him or her, but most of the time, it's bodies they find."

"But you think these kids might be alive?"

She shrugged. "Maybe."

"Either way, you have to let someone know," Clarice said.

"And just how do I do that? If I report it, they're going to want to know how I know. I can't very well tell them I hacked into their server and read their files, but it was all very innocent because I was really looking into other businesses and the private lives of citizens." She waved her hand from side to side in a dismissive manner. "But it's all okay, because I'm trying to find a missing kid."

Clarice sighed. "I understand, but if there's any chance those boys might be alive, you have to report it."

Lana slammed her laptop closed and jumped up. "That's what I hate about this. I'm always finding something I don't really want to know." She paced a few steps back and forth without leaving the room. "Of course, I want to save those kids if I can, but I can't risk getting caught. And they may already be dead anyway."

Tuper finally broke his silence. "Maybe there's another way."

"What's that?" Lana asked, a little calmer.

"How about if I tell JP? He don't know nothing about you, and he don't need to. He can pass it on to his cop buddies or do his own investigation, but you'll be off the hook."

"Are you sure you can trust him?"

"No doubt in my mind."

"Let me think about it," Lana said.

"Don't take too long. You don't want a dead kid on your conscience."

CHAPTER FORTY-ONE

"You're right," Lana said to Tuper. "Call JP. We'll tell him what we know and he can do what he wants with it."

"Good."

"Do you want me to write out the information for you so you can tell him?"

"I can do it," Clarice quickly volunteered.

Tuper handed his phone to Lana. "Can you call and put him on speaker?"

"Sure," Lana said.

"I'll talk to him first and then you can give the information he needs." Tuper said. "He won't know who you are or anything else about you, but that way we'll make sure he gets it right. That okay with you?"

Lana looked in the contacts for JP, dialed the number, put it on speaker as it was ringing, and then laid the phone on the table between her and Tuper.

"Hey, Toop. If you're calling about Judi, Jessica's friend, I've been following her pretty much non-stop since we last talked."

"Get anything helpful?"

"Not really, except maybe to rule her out. I haven't seen any sign of Mason around."

"Thanks. That was a long shot anyway." Tuper paused. "I have something else for you. It doesn't have anything to do with Mason, just something we come across in our investigation that might save some other kids."

"You've piqued my curiosity. What is it?"

"You can do whatever you think best with the information I give you, but I need your word that you won't reveal where it came from."

"Of course. I ain't got no dog in your fight."

"I knew I could count on you. We think we found a couple who are wanted for stealing babies. They're living in Bonsall on a small farm. Do you know where Bonsall is?"

"You bet."

"I have you on speaker so my friend Agony can give you the information." Tuper winked at Lana when he called her Agony. She shook her head and gave him a half-smile.

Lana told JP the names of the people, the address of the home, and the names of the boys she believed to be there.

"That's some very specific information," JP said. "Can I ask why you think the children are there?"

"I know the adults are there," Lana said, "but I can't tell you how I know. I have reason to believe that all three of these boys, and maybe others, have at least passed through this home. I can't tell you whether or not they are still alive, although I think at least one of them is."

"And they were all babies when they were taken?"

"Correct. All three were abducted in Southern California as much as six or seven years ago. Two of them lived in Southern California, and one was there on vacation from Kansas."

"Thanks. I'll make good use of this information. I have a good friend who's a deputy sheriff in North County. I know he'll be glad to check it out for me. And as far as where it came from, you can be sure I'll be as quiet as a one-handed clap."

Tuper hung up but before he could get his cell phone back in his pocket, it rang. He answered it, listened, and said, "Thanks. I don't expect any surprises." Clarice and Lana both looked at him.

"It was Brad from the lab. He apologized for taking so long on Jessica's DNA test, but the weather has slowed everything down. He still hopes to have it to us today or tomorrow."

All of a sudden, Lana said, "Hey, old man, where's the envelope?"

"What envelope?" Clarice asked.

"The one Jessica gave him and made him promise not to open unless something happened to her." She looked directly at Tuper. "Well, something happened to her."

"It's in Clancy."

"Where's Clancy?" Lana asked.

"South of here, about ten miles or so."

"What's it doing there?"

"It's in my cabin in the mountains near there. I left it there before the storm. Can't go and get it now."

"Did you read what was inside the envelope?" Lana asked.

"Nope. Promised her I wouldn't."

"That's too bad. It might just have the information we need to find Mason or Jessica's killer."

"It might, but that storm is in charge right now. And it don't seem to care much about no envelope."

Tuper stood up and put his coat on.

"Where you going?" Lana asked.

"To get more firewood. It's gonna be a long, cold night."

CHAPTER FORTY-TWO

Lana walked to the window, pulled back the curtain, and looked out. All she could see was white. The deck was several feet deep in snowy mounds, and as far as she could see, everything was colorless: the cars, the ground, the trees, the trash cans, all were a heavenly white.

"I've never seen so much snow," Lana said. "When will it stop?"

"Not any time soon," Tuper said.

Clarice came into the living room and turned on the television to the local news. There were photos of cars, lined up on streets that had been blocked by accidents or fallen trees, and were covered with snow. Others were of drivers trying to make U-turns and going off the road, some overturned. The reporter said that every person with an available snowplow was asked to volunteer to help clear their own roads and driveways because the government plows would be too busy. The snow was falling so hard and so fast that the plows couldn't keep up. The cameras spanned a block in downtown Helena. Many offices and businesses were closed. The reporter said some were closed because employees couldn't get to work, and others because customers couldn't get to them.

Clarice turned the volume down but left the picture so they could get a glimpse of it if they chose.

Lana retrieved her laptop and sat in the living room on the sofa. She had two doors she was trying to break through that had proved challenging. One was the National Center for Missing and Exploited Children, the other was Jessica's bank account. She had worked a good part of the night on the missing children site so she set it aside and went back to checking the bank statements in Jessica's account, starting with the $50,000 deposit and working forward. Before the deposit, Jessica had sixteen grand in the account, so the new balance was $66,000.

Lana stopped her search for a second and reported her findings to Tuper and Clarice.

"It looks like the money remained in the account for only a few days before an initial withdrawal of $10,000." She clicked on her keyboard. "A month later, another ten grand was withdrawn."

Clarice grabbed a notebook off the counter and said, "Just a minute. Let me make a timeline."

Lana kept looking through the account.

"Okay," Clarice said. "I have that down."

"She spends some on rent, credit cards, and utilities. She also has her work check deposited into her account," Lana said. "Okay, here's another withdrawal for $20,000 in May."

"That would be while Gordon was incarcerated, right?"

"Right."

"There's a cash withdrawal in late November, the day after Gordon's release, for $1,000."

"Which could be Christmas money or it could be for Gordon."

"There's another $20,000 taken out in early February just before they disappeared."

"Nothing in between?"

"Just living expenses. A few days later, the account was closed with a withdrawal of just over $4,000, which is close to the deposit used to open the Denise and Randy Jenkins account."

"Any way to trace the cash?" Tuper asked, but he knew the answer.

"Not really," Lana said.

"Seems like the money was spent before they came to Montana."

"That's what I'm thinking. They didn't come here and buy a house or anything. No car, or any other big purchases," Lana said. "So I'm thinking they used it to buy the baby."

"But it was Gordon's baby. Why would they have to pay for it?" Clarice asked.

"Maybe he had to pay the mother off. Maybe it was easier than fighting for custody, which he probably would have lost. He just got out of jail, so unless the mother had worse problems than he had, he wouldn't have gotten custody." Lana was on another roll. "And if Jessica wanted it to be her baby, and not share it with anyone, they had to get the baby for themselves. But how did he get her pregnant?" She looked at Tuper. "I know you said they could have used his sperm, and that makes sense if you look at the cash withdrawals. They would have had to pay for that, but why the secrecy? And they would have had to use a doctor or a facility."

"Maybe they did," Clarice said.

"Naw, I still think we should check out the guard or employee situation at the jail. Lots of things go on in those jails that nobody talks about. And if someone did get pregnant there, they aren't going to claim Gordon as the father, and they may not want to keep the child."

"So how do we find out?"

"We could have JP see what he can find, but I think it's a waste of time," Tuper said.

Lana was already typing. "Or we could see if any employee took maternity leave around that time."

No noise came from the sofa for the next twenty minutes or so except the tapping of keys until Lana said, "Uh huh."

"What is it?" Clarice asked, as she walked over to Lana.

"Maria Gonzalez took maternity leave in December. According to her file, she needed to be on bedrest." Another five minutes passed before Lana spoke again. "Her baby was born on March 8, which works because we only know for sure that Jessica and Gordon had the baby by April 1, when the neighbors moved next door on Lonesome Loop."

"But the neighbor told us Mason was about two months old," Tuper said. "He must've been a pretty big baby when he was born if he was only three weeks old and passed for two months."

Lana continued typing. A few minutes later, she said, "Maria took two months of maternity leave and another three weeks of saved vacation or comp time before she returned to work." She shook her head.

Clarice leaned in so she could see the computer screen. "What is it?"

"If this is Mason, they went to a lot of effort to cover it up."

"How's that?" Clarice asked.

"All I'm looking at is her employment record from the county. I don't have medical records or anything like that. Maria took several days off work shortly after she returned from her leave. Then she takes off once a week for six weeks due to her child's illness. At first I couldn't tell what it was, but when he was about eighteen months old, there's a comment in Maria's record that her son was a diabetic."

"So it can't be Mason then, right?" Clarice asked.

"Unless it was a cover-up," Lana said. "But probably not, what would be the point? Unless she was so upset about losing her child that she kept taking time off. Besides, everyone knew she was pregnant. She would have had to explain if she suddenly didn't have her child. Unless this was her way of avoiding that."

Tuper shook his head. Even Clarice thought it was a little far-fetched.

"You're probably right," Lana said. "I'll keep looking. I think I'll go backwards in Jessica's account now and see what she was spending money on before she got the fifty grand. Maybe it'll tell us something."

Tuper answered his phone, had a brief conversation, and hung up. "That's a good idea, Agony, because I think you're barking up the wrong tree."

"It's possible," Lana said. "We can't really rule it out yet."

"Except that that was Brad on the phone with Jessica's DNA test results, and Jessica is Mason's biological mother."

CHAPTER FORTY-THREE

"That changes things a bit," Lana said. "So, if Jessica and Gordon are Mason's parents but Jessica couldn't get pregnant... or maybe she could." Lana paused. "But even if she could get pregnant, no one saw her pregnant so she still didn't carry that baby. Unless she didn't show until the very end and Mason was born a little later, maybe she was pregnant. But Mason couldn't have been born much later because he looked two months old on April 1." Lana stopped talking again for just a second and turned to Clarice.

"Is it possible to be pregnant and no one know it?"

"Highly unlikely," Clarice said. "I've heard of it happening, but the mother was always already overweight with a large stomach, didn't gain that much more with the pregnancy, and so it wasn't as noticeable. Never with a woman Jessica's size. The baby had to be somewhere, and on her skinny body, it would show for sure."

"Maybe the birds and the bees weren't involved for either one of them," Tuper mumbled.

"I thought about that," Lana said. "If they used a surrogate, they would need some medical professionals. I guess that's where I'll concentrate for a while."

Lana stood up and stretched. Clarice walked to the television and turned the sound up to check on the storm. More devastation filled the screen. Sections of the highway were displayed as clear for a short distance and then drifts of snow two or three feet high suddenly appeared, all difficult to see because of the whiteout.

The reporter announced that a weather advisory was in effect for the storm, and that schools were all closed until further notice. Just then a loud blare came out of the television and the screen read *Emergency Travel Only* in big red letters. Instructions filled the screen defining the alert:

--Refrain from all travel;
--Comply with emergency measures;
--Cooperate with law enforcement, public officials, and disaster services personnel enforcing emergency procedures and plans;
--Deviation from the plan may result in substantial fines.

A few seconds later, Clarice's and Lana's phones both beeped an alert as well through the Wireless Emergency Alert system. Tuper's didn't have that function.

The alert stopped and the television reporter commented on the "Emergency Plan," which basically amounted to "just stay home." Then he went on to show more destruction the storm had caused, including a semi and a small car that had crashed, causing themselves and two other vehicles to go off the road on Interstate 15. Only a few miles down the highway was another semi carrying crushed cars that had slid off the road and scattered the cars. The already crushed cars were strewn about the highway blocking any possible passage.

"I guess I'm not going to work today after all," Clarice said. "I better call Mary Ann and see how she's doing." She went back to her bedroom to make the call.

Lana unplugged her laptop and carried it back to the table. "I need to change positions for a while," she said to Tuper.

Tuper stood up, walked to the sofa, and lay down. He had dozed off a little earlier, and he wondered if Lana had seen him and that was why she gave up her seat. He didn't ask because he figured she'd never admit it if she had. That would be too much like an act of kindness toward him.

~~~

Lana's fingers flew across the keyboard with the same intensity as the storm that blew outside. She was zoned in and focused, unable to see much around her, just as the emergency workers were in the whiteout. She wanted as much information as she could gather before the storm let up. She knew as soon as it did, Tuper would be venturing out to see if he could find Mason and, hopefully, Jessica's killer. He was pretty convinced that if he found one, he'd find the other. All Lana could do was try to find the reason for the kidnapping, the murders, and whatever else went down, which she hoped would lead to Mason.

Who knows where that little boy is right now? He could be out there somewhere in that storm, if he was even still alive. She had a feeling that he was, just as she believed those boys in that home in Bonsall were alive. But her gut feelings weren't always right. Sometimes, they were just wishful thinking. She was quite certain she didn't possess any psychic powers, as she was wrong about this sort of thing more than she was right.

Lana brought up Jessica's bank statements, glanced through them, and then downloaded the statements for February, the month she left San Jacinto, and for January, the previous month. Then she left the bank program. The longer she stayed in there, the more she was at risk of being discovered.

The February statement was only a partial. Her rent was paid, and her utilities, and a credit card balance. She traced the card, only to discover it was closed immediately following the February payment. The card was mostly used for gas and groceries. A few items of baby clothing and some diapers were purchased at Target.

The January statement was very similar except for the baby items, covering rent, utilities, and a credit card payment, as were the months preceding, until Lana went back a year and five months. The July statement had a check written out to Healthy Babies for $2,000. Lana Googled *Healthy Babies* and discovered it was an in vitro clinic, owned and operated by Dr. Melinda Richards.

There were no other payments by check or by credit card to Dr. Richards, and no other checks of any kind that seemed of any interest or concern.

Lana started researching the clinic through a legitimate Internet search. She discovered that the clinic opened in June of 2011 and closed a few weeks after Jessica's $2,000 check was rendered. The clinic had eight lawsuits filed against it. Five were dismissed early on, two appeared to have been settled, and one withdrew the complaint after only a few weeks. The clinic's debts were such that it appeared the clinic had shut down for financial reasons, perhaps as a result of all the lawsuits.

Lana couldn't find any evidence of Dr. Richards still practicing, at least not in California. She looked the doctor up on breeze.ca.gov, a website that shows action taken against doctors. Her profile didn't show that any disciplinary action had been taken and her clinic was the last place listed for employment. Lana would have to go to the deep web once again.

CHAPTER FORTY-FOUR

Lana took a deep breath and then checked her own Hotmail account. Nothing new today. She breathed a sigh of relief. She thought about not ever checking because it upset her so much when she received an email from him, but it bothered her more not to know what he was up to. It was all about the game to him.

She spent the next couple of hours gathering information on Dr. Melinda Richards, and trying to gain access to the National Center for Exploited and Missing Children. She had tried everything from phishing to a brute force attack and nothing worked. Finally, a kluge put her in.

"I pwned it," Lana said aloud just as the front door opened and Tuper stepped in with Ringo, Caspar, and Izzy Bear. All three dogs shook vigorously and snow flew everywhere, hitting her in the face.

"Sorry," Tuper said. "They all had to go out."

Clarice grabbed a couple of towels from the hall closet. "No problem. Thanks for taking them out for me." She wiped the dogs off and then cleaned up the wet floor. "And thanks for getting the firewood in earlier."

"What did you pawn?" Tuper asked.

"Nothing. I didn't pawn anything. I pwned it...Sorry, it's just a term meaning I beat it. I pwned the system." Lana shivered from the cold air that came in through the open door. She retrieved a lap blanket from the sofa and wrapped it around her shoulders. Then she refocused, concentrating on the time period when Mason was born. She came across the same children

212

she had seen before on the public site, including Aiden. She was appalled at the thousands of missing children across the country. She decided to focus on California and nearby states; otherwise she would never get through.

Two other baby boys went missing within the parameters she had set, one month before and after Mason's alleged birthdate. Upon further investigation, she determined that one had been found a few days after he went missing, unharmed.

The second one caught Lana's attention because he was taken from Hemet Valley Hospital, the hospital that served San Jacinto. A mentally ill woman named Elizabeth Strong had stolen him, claiming the baby was hers.

"I think I might have something," Lana said.

Clarice came to the table. Tuper, who had been pacing, followed her.

"What is it?" Clarice asked.

"There was a baby stolen from the hospital in Hemet, which is right next to San Jacinto. It's the nearest hospital and it was on February 24."

"And they haven't found him yet?" Clarice asked.

"No, they found him two weeks later. The woman who took him, Elizabeth, was trying to care for him, but she wasn't really able to. He was emaciated when they found him and they nursed him back to health."

"So that wasn't Mason?"

"Right, but since Elizabeth claimed her child was missing and there was no listing in the national registry for her child, I started to dig further. Sometimes I go off on tangents that are interesting, but they don't take me anywhere. This one was different. I found Elizabeth's file in their program, but her child was never added to the missing children list because they didn't believe she actually had a child, nor did the police. Here, let me read what is in the file about why she was rejected for a place on the list."

Elizabeth had made several claims previously about her missing son or daughter; she wasn't exactly sure which sex it was, but she thought he was a boy. She claimed he was born on Valentine's Day, but not in a hospital. She didn't know where exactly he was born but she thought it was in someone's home.

She said she woke up one morning and she was pregnant, then these nice women helped her, a doctor and her nurse. They helped her have her baby, but then the baby disappeared.

Since he was born on Valentine's Day, Elizabeth named the baby Valentin, which she was told meant 'strong' in Spanish, so he only needed one name since his last name was Strong too. He could go through life like Cher or Madonna with only one name. Otherwise his name would be Strong Strong. That's the kind of bizarre thinking she had.

Elizabeth had previous mental illness history, and since there was no record of the birth of this child, he was rejected for placement on the "Missing Children List."

"So they didn't think Elizabeth ever had a baby?" Clarice asked.

"They thought she was delusional, but what if she wasn't? What if she had her baby boy and Jessica and Gordon took him?" Before anyone could answer, she said, "We know Jessica visited an in vitro clinic. We know Jessica and Gordon are the biological parents, yet they couldn't have created him the old-fashioned way. So, what if Jessica and Gordon fertilized the eggs and Elizabeth served as a gestational surrogate?"

"Suppose that's possible," Tuper said. "Except

there's no connection between Elizabeth and Jessica."

"If there is, I'm going to find it," Lana said.

CHAPTER FORTY-FIVE

Jerome had been driving the snowplow for twelve hours straight, fighting the worst storm he had ever seen. The wind howled and screeched as he edged his plow down the highway attempting to get a glimpse of the reflectors on the posts to guide him so he could stay on the road. The whiteout was so bad that he had to be within a few feet to even see the reflectors.

Jerome moved slowly, plowing the snow and dumping it to the side of the road, just trying to clear it off enough to allow emergency vehicles through. With the Emergency Travel Alert in effect, no one else should have been on the highway, but there were always the idiots who didn't think the rules applied to them. One of them was heading in his direction on the opposite side of the road in a Dodge RAM 2500. At least he was in a decent vehicle, not a VW bug or something.

The heat was turned down low in the cab of his snowplow. Too much warmth and Jerome was afraid he would fall asleep. It was chilly, but far warmer than it was outside. He shivered as he pulled off the highway onto an off-ramp, plowing as he descended. He was almost to the bottom when he saw a car parked on the side. The rear of the car was sticking up higher than the front. He pulled up as close as he could and shined a light into the vehicle. A woman sat in the driver's seat. He couldn't tell for certain if there was anyone else in the car.

This was the fourth stranded vehicle with passengers that he had to call in today. He got on the radio and called Dispatch in Butte, giving them the description of the car and location.

"It looks like a lone woman. I haven't spoken to her." Jerome moved up a little and shined his flashlight so he could see better. She turned toward him and he saw her face. She looked to be about thirty-five or forty.

"She's moving around inside, but that car isn't going anywhere. The snow is too deep."

"It's going to be a few hours. We're on an 'Immediate Priority' or 'Mass Casualty' response. There was a fatal crash on the highway a little north of you, a van full of teenagers and three other vehicles. There's another semi down with a gas spill. The emergency vehicles are all dispatched. I can put you on the list, but you'll be listed as a 'Significant Call' and it'll take a while to move up."

"I'll get out and talk to her and call you back."

Jerome pulled a beanie over his head and got out of his truck. His door flew open as he stepped down. It took all his strength to get it closed. The wind felt like cold needles on his face. He pushed against the wind as he plodded around his plow and to her car.

"Are you okay?" Jerome asked as he shined his flashlight into her car, avoiding her face so as not to blind her.

The woman cracked her window about two inches. "I'm stuck here. I'm not that far from where I'm staying. I'm just over there." She pointed off to her right. "My son is asleep in the back seat."

Jerome moved his light to the back and saw a bundle under the covers. His nose and his closed eyes were exposed along with a wisp of blond hair.

"If I was alone, I'd try to walk but I can't carry him all the way. And the snow is so deep in spots that I'm sure it would cover him. I tried myself, but I didn't even make it to the end of the off-ramp before I came back. It was so cold."

"How long have you been here?" Jerome asked.

"About an hour." She shivered. "I left the engine on and ran the heat for a while and then I turned it off. Every twenty minutes or so, I turn it back on to take the chill off, but I don't know how long I can do that because my gas is getting low."

"Have you called for help?"

"I tried to get a tow truck, but most of the ones I called I just got a voice mail message. The two I reached said it would be four or five hours, if they can even get to me at all. And my phone is almost dead. Can you help me?"

Jerome hesitated. It was against protocol to take anyone in his truck, but he couldn't leave them there to freeze. He wanted to ask her why she was out there in the first place, but what good would that do? She was there, she needed help, and he was all there was to help her.

"Please," she begged. "Just get me to my friend's house. It's not far."

He looked at the woman and then at the child. He could get in a lot of trouble, especially if anything went wrong. And it would take time away from plowing the highway so emergency vehicles could get through. It wasn't like him to break the rules.

"Please," she pleaded. "Don't let my little boy freeze to death."

"Okay," Jerome heard himself saying. He immediately chastised himself for his choice.

He opened the woman's car door and helped her out.

"Just a minute. I need my purse." She reached back in and grabbed her purse off the seat.

"I'll get your son," Jerome said.

"No," she barked. Then she lowered her voice. "He'll be afraid. He...he has some issues and he gets confused. I'll get him."

Jerome opened the door and held it for her, letting her reach inside to get the boy. She used a soft, tender voice as she woke him up--too soft for Jerome to hear the words.

The boy was still a little groggy when she got him out of the car, leaving the blanket wrapped around him to shield him from the cold. She continued to whisper in his ear as she carried him. He had perked up a little by the time she put him in the truck.

"You'll have to hold him since there's only one seat. As you can see, the console takes up a lot of room."

"We're just glad to be out of there."

Jerome helped the woman in, closed the door behind her, and trudged around to take his seat behind the wheel. The woman reached across the child to buckle the seatbelt just as Jerome got inside. He noticed a big red blotch on her white furry coat sleeve.

"Is that blood? Did you get hurt?"

She looked at the sleeve and then back at Jerome. "Oh, that. No, my son got a bloody nose and I guess I got it on me when I was trying to clean him up."

She finished buckling herself in and then wrapped her arms around the child and pulled his head into her bosom.

"Can you take me to my friend's house?" she asked. "It's really not too far off the highway."

"I'll try. Where exactly is it?"

She gave him the address.

"You're right," Jerome said, "that's pretty close."

The little boy sat in complete silence as Jerome inched his way down the off-ramp, dumping snow on the sideline.

"I'm Jerome, by the way. What's your name?"

"Liz."

"And what's your name, young man?"

Before the boy could answer, the woman said, "Valentin. His name is Valentin. It's a strong name. It means 'strong' or 'valiant.' He's a strong and valiant young man. He's been through a lot, but he's been very valiant." She wrapped her arms a little tighter.

Jerome found her comments very odd, but figured she was probably a little uncomfortable being in this storm with a stranger and her child.

He made a right at the bottom of the off-ramp and worked his way down the Frontage Road for three blocks before he turned left. The address they were looking for was the first of three houses on this street, all a few acres apart. This one sat another eighth of a mile from the street. The road was covered with several feet of snow; more had drifted in areas. He couldn't leave her here. He'd have to plow his way to the front door without reflectors or any knowledge of the road itself.

"Are there any obstacles along this road that I should be aware of?"

"I don't think so, and it's pretty straight. There's some trees on the left and a fence off to the right a bit, none of which I can see right now."

When they got closer, Jerome could see a light on inside and that helped steer him toward the house.

When he finally reached the front, Jerome offered to see her inside but she flatly refused. He walked around and held the door for her as she picked Valentin up and pulled him out. She wrapped the blanket around him covering his head, but he pushed his head up as she stepped away. He was a frightened little boy.

CHAPTER FORTY-SIX

Lana decided to follow Elizabeth Strong's history, to see who she was and if she truly was delusional. She wasn't on social media of any kind. Her birthdate and birthplace were listed in the notes she got from the National Center for Missing and Exploited Children so Lana started with that. Elizabeth and her younger sister were raised in Yucaipa, California, the daughters of a successful businessman and a chiropractor. She attended public school and graduated from Yucaipa High School at the age of nineteen.

"Are you okay, Toop?" Clarice asked.

Lana's concentration was broken. She looked up to see Tuper pacing the floor.

"I'm gettin' cabin fever."

"You can't go anywhere in this storm," Clarice said firmly.

"I'm thinking with this weather, Jessica's killer can't have gotten too far either. I should be out lookin' for her."

"And where would you look?" Clarice said. "You have no idea where to start."

"Humpff."

"Why don't you take another nap?" Lana said. "Let me concentrate on getting you some information so you can find Mason."

"It's hopeless," Tuper muttered.

"Probably, but I'm trying anyway. Look what I've found on Elizabeth Strong."

"What?" Tuper asked.

Lana told him what she knew so far about her childhood as she continued to follow her trail. "Now this is interesting." She paused for just a second. "She moved to San Jacinto shortly after she graduated from high school, to an address on... Well, I'll be."

"What?" Clarice asked.

Lana kept typing and flipping to other screens. "That's what I thought."

"What did you think?" Clarice was standing over her shoulder now trying to see.

"She was at a mental facility there."

Tuper stopped pacing around and came back to the table. "Was it Rosewood?"

"No, it was Brentworth, but it was in Hemet, which is right next to San Jacinto. She could've known Jessica. She was there for almost three years. She left the facility about eight months before Jessica left Rosewood. Which means she could have been pregnant with Mason." Lana kept tapping into different sites, looking for more information on Elizabeth.

"Do you know where she went from Brentworth?" Clarice asked.

"There's no forwarding address and she just kind of disappears. She didn't give a reason for leaving and no one checked her out. According to her file, she snuck away on her own. But what else are they going to put? If it appeared to be foul play, it would make Brentworth look bad."

Clarice and Tuper waited to see what else she would find.

"The next time I see evidence of Elizabeth is when she files a police report about her missing child. There are a number of similar reports filed with other police agencies in bordering towns as well as the notes in the National Center for Missing and Exploited Children. It appears no one took her seriously, probably because there was no record of a baby being born, and she was a 'runaway nut case from a mental health facility,' as one police report stated."

"Did they bring charges against her for stealing that baby?"

"Yes, I'm looking at that right now. Give me a sec."

About five minutes later, Lana said, "They locked her up in Patton State Hospital in San Bernardino, California."

"She still there?" Tuper asked.

"I don't know. That might take some work. Give me some quiet. I'll see if I can find out."

Tuper put his coat on and walked to the door. "Ringo, Caspar, Izzy Bear, let's go play in the snow." He opened the door and the dogs dashed out.

Lana tried everything she could to open a back door to Patton, but with no luck. She knew she could get in eventually, but it would take some time. Instead, she decided to find one of Elizabeth's family members on social media. People loved to share their dirty laundry on there. She continued her search for about fifteen minutes, oblivious to Tuper and the animals returning, until she got hit with a flurry of cold snowflakes. "Dang," she said, and then pulled her blanket tighter around her and continued. She was onto something.

"There it is," Lana exclaimed. "I found her sister on Facebook. On December 29, she posted: *I picked my sister up from the hospital today. It's so wonderful to have her back home.*"

"I see she doesn't mention what kind of hospital," Clarice said.

Lana read the post that followed.

January 1: I woke up this morning and my sister was gone. Please help me find her. She isn't well.

"Many of her friends shared the post and

commented about how badly they felt," Lana said as she scrolled through the pages of responses. "A post from yesterday indicates that she's still missing."

CHAPTER FORTY-SEVEN

"Hi, Toop," JP said when he answered his cell. "How are you holding up in that storm?"

"It ain't easy," Tuper said. "Worst part is I'm stuck inside."

"I heard it's cold as a banker's heart, and the wind's blowin' like perfume through a prom."

"That 'bout sums it up."

"I don't suppose you want to hear that it's 73 degrees and sunny here."

"No. I sure don't."

"Then I won't tell you. By the way, I'm in Bonsall at the address you gave me for the Waters' ranch trying to see if there are any children here."

"You in the house?"

"No, I'm outside on the street. The house sits back on the lot and there's a lot of eucalyptus trees, small sheds, and junk around so it's difficult to see. And it's all fenced in. I'd go up there and give some bogus reason for being here, but I don't want to spook them. All I need to do is get a glimpse of a kid or two and it'll be easier to get the cops out here."

"Thanks for followin' up. I need one more thing if you can."

"Sure. What is it?"

"See what you can find out about a Dr. Melinda Richards. It doesn't seem like she's practicing anymore. She kinda fell off the radar about five years ago." Tuper explained how she might be connected to Mason and Jessica.

"If I find her, do you want me to talk to her?"

"Maybe put a little pressure on her and see if we're

right about what went down."

"You bet."

JP drove up the street about an eighth of a mile and turned off the road. He parked his car and walked back through the trees carrying his binoculars. He reached the fence that surrounded the Waters' property and moved north alongside it. He had to be careful because there weren't enough trees to keep him completely hidden from view, especially if someone on the other side was using binoculars.

He found a spot behind a fallen tree and crouched down so he couldn't be seen. He smelled a slight odor of garbage and manure in the air, but he was uncertain where it came from. Through his field glasses he observed ten or fifteen chickens in the front yard; perhaps that was some of the smell. Toward the back of the house, he saw three goats, a billy and what appeared to be two females. The billy goat climbed up on a pile of junk about four or five feet high and parked himself on an old washing machine. JP moved his binoculars so he had a more expansive view. Mountains of junk filled the yard. A little off to the west there stood a pile of garbage.

He moved a little farther north, staying as close as he could to the fence line without being seen. The further he went north, the stronger the stench. It was definitely coming from the pile of garbage on the property.

He found some tree branches in a pile, making a good spot to stop. He hid behind them and peeked through the fence with his binoculars. The goat was still playing "king of the mountain."

The stillness was almost eerie as he crouched down in a comfortable position, trying to see through the branches. Suddenly he heard a twig crack. JP didn't move. Leaves rustled. With his hand on his shoulder holster, he slowly turned his head in the direction of the noise, making eye contact with a squirrel that very quickly scampered up a tree. JP took a deep breath and went back to his surveillance.

Three or four minutes later, a heavyset woman came around the side of the house carrying a large bucket. She went directly to the garbage pile, emptied the contents, and then disappeared behind the house. Although he couldn't see the door, JP assumed she had come out of the house and then gone back inside.

Shortly after that, two young boys around eight or ten dashed across the yard and climbed up with the billy goat. Two younger boys followed them up the pile. JP zoomed in on them. The children were dirty and their clothes raggedy. All of them were barefoot. He wondered how they climbed that trash pile without getting hurt.

JP removed his phone from his pocket, zoomed in his camera as close as he could, and took photos of the boys. He panned around and took more photos of the yard. Just as he started to put his phone away, another child came onto the scene. He was still a toddler, three at absolute best, but more likely two years of age. He snapped a few photos. The little boy was barefoot as well, and JP wanted to run and grab him when he headed for the junk pile. When he started to climb it, one of the other boys yelled at him. He stopped for a few seconds, and then moved up a couple more steps. The second tallest boy ran down the pile, stopped in front of the toddler, and scolded him.

JP couldn't hear everything he was saying, but he did hear enough to know he was telling him he couldn't go up there. The little one started to cry, but he stopped climbing. He sat down right where he was and didn't move, still whimpering at his plight.

One of the older boys ran down the pile and grabbed a stick, pointing it at the others as if it were a rifle. The other boys suddenly scattered, grabbing their weapons and ducking for cover.

The heavyset woman returned carrying a baby on her hip. JP grabbed his phone again and took more photos. Then with his binoculars he watched as the woman grabbed the little boy by the arm from the junk pile. The boy suddenly cried even louder as she marched him firmly around the side of the house.

JP had seen enough and was certain he had evidence enough to at least get CPS out to this house. The grounds were reason enough to pull these children from that home, whether or not they belonged there. At the very least, they would be ordered to clean up the yard and make it safe for the children. At worst, they were there illegally, as Tuper suspected.

~~~

JP went back to his car and texted the photos he had taken to his friend Ernie Madrigal, a San Diego County Deputy Sheriff. He had already given him the information he had obtained earlier from Tuper. Shortly after the photos were sent, Ernie called him.

"I've been working on this all morning. Neither Joe nor Grace Waters has a warrant, but I spoke with the detective on the case in San Jacinto where they were suspects. He's real certain they were involved, but he couldn't get enough evidence on them to make an arrest. The cops kept watching them for a long time, but they took off in the night and they never knew where they went. He couldn't really do much since they didn't have a warrant for anything."

"So now what?" JP asked.

"With these photos, we can go out and pick those

kids up. There's no question that they're in danger with all that crap around there. While we have the kids, we can get some DNA and find out if any of them are in the registry."

"How soon will you be picking them up?"

"Today."

JP felt relieved. No matter what, those children needed protection.

~~~

Back at his office, JP started research on Dr. Melinda Richards. He soon discovered that she had no criminal record, but lots of complaints and numerous lawsuits in her past. He ignored those since he knew Tuper was already aware of them. The last known address, according to the DMV, was on Conejo Drive in San Bernardino, which was a two-hour drive. He didn't want to go to someone's house this late. It would have to wait until morning.

JP remembered he had a friend, Apollo, who had recently joined the San Bernardino Police Department. JP and his girlfriend Sabre had attended his graduation from the Police Academy some six months ago. They knew Apollo from a case seven years before when he was a teenage runaway charged with murder. He ended up being cleared of all charges and was now working for the other side.

JP called Apollo and asked him if he could check out the residence and see if she lived there.

"Sure, I'll be able to take care of it in about an hour. You said it was a woman, right?"

"Yes. Her name is Dr. Melinda Richards."

There were a few seconds of silence on the phone then Apollo said, "Just a minute. I need to check something."

JP could hear him typing.

Then Apollo asked, "How are you involved with Dr. Richards?"

"Why? Does it matter?"

"It matters."

"There's nothing illegal going down if that's your concern. But if it's a problem for you to check on her, I'll just drive out there tomorrow."

"You don't need to do that, but can you tell me why you need to see her?"

"I'm helping a friend who's looking for a missing child. We think Dr. Richards performed an in vitro procedure on the surrogate mother about six years ago, and we're hoping she can provide us with some information."

"That isn't going to happen because Dr. Richards is dead. She was murdered a couple of weeks ago. I don't think Homicide has any good leads, so if you have something to offer, I'm sure they'd be grateful."

"I just might. I'll get back to you."

CHAPTER FORTY-EIGHT

"Dr. Melinda Richards is dead," Tuper said when he hung up the phone. "Murdered."

"When?" Lana asked.

"New Year's Eve. In her home."

"Why couldn't I find that?" Lana asked.

"Don't know," Tuper said. "She was in San Bernardino, California, where she had lived for about four months."

"I was actually talking to myself, but thanks, that explains it. I was searching in a different county. You know, that means she was killed shortly before Mason was kidnapped."

"Your point?" Tuper figured she was probably thinking the same thing he was. *It was too coincidental.*

"Don't you think it's strange that all of a sudden Dr. Richards is dead? We know the doctor was involved somehow with Jessica, probably performed the in vitro procedure, and now the child from that procedure is missing. I still think it was Elizabeth Strong. She's mental and wants her kid."

"But we have nothing that connects Elizabeth to either Jessica or Dr. Richards," Tuper said.

"If it's not Elizabeth, it could still be the surrogate mother who wants her child back."

"So she went on a killing spree?"

Clarice entered the room. "What did I miss?"

Lana explained what they had learned. "So, now what?"

"Now, I need to find a connection between Elizabeth Strong and Jessica or the doctor. Or find out who Mason's surrogate mother is."

"How is that going to help find Mason?" Clarice asked.

"If we know who we're looking for, the cops may be able to track her," Tuper said, "and if this storm ever lets up, maybe I can help."

"Let's see what's going on out there." Clarice walked to the television and turned up the volume.

The cameras showed white upon white. The reporter was using phrases like "paralyzed city" and "immobilized region" as he showed cars and buildings that had been destroyed, trees and poles that had fallen, some crashing into houses, and stranded cars along city roads.

"The governor is speaking," the reporter said. The camera switched to the governor in his office, but no sound was heard. The screen split with the reporter on one side and the governor on the other. "We're having some trouble with our sound, but I can tell you the governor has declared an emergency for the state of Montana. He is pleading with the people to stay off the roads and in their homes."

"Strong winds have created blizzard conditions with a whiteout giving us less than ten feet of visibility in some areas," the reporter said. "The wind is causing snow drifts and dangerous wind chills. These intense winds have brought down trees and utility poles, and destroyed buildings across the state." As he spoke, photos of houses and offices that had been hit by falling trees flashed across the screen. One house was torn off its foundation and leaning to one side. Another had the roof smashed by a fallen tree.

He continued, "Emergency vehicles are stuck on highways where the snowplows are attempting to keep ahead of the storm. In some areas, the snowplows are leading ambulances to the hospital. In Helena alone, three deaths have been reported due to accidents on the Interstate, one heart attack in a man who couldn't get to the hospital in time, and one apparently due to hypothermia. Ambulances are trying to get to people who are sick or injured in their homes, but with little success." He paused. "Okay, we have the governor now."

The screen was filled with just the governor as he spoke.

"We are in a state of emergency. Heavy snow accumulations have immobilized our city and much of the state. Motorists are stranded and emergency services have been disrupted. Several buildings have collapsed. Heavy snow and wind have brought down trees and power lines, destroying some homes and businesses. Power has been disrupted in parts of the city.

"All vehicles must stay off the highways and city streets. Please stay in your homes. It's too dangerous to be driving in these conditions and doing so creates more problems for emergency vehicles. We are doing everything we can to take care of the sick and the injured, but every time someone ventures out and gets stranded, it takes away valuable resources. We've asked for help from neighboring states, but most are in a similar situation or may very well be by tomorrow. We have every available ambulance, fire truck, tow truck, and snowplow working around the clock. There are two shelters set up downtown for people who have been stranded."

The addresses and phone numbers of the shelters came on the bottom of the television screen.

"I ask you once again not to go out in this storm," the governor said. "I know many of you have lost contact with loved ones, but please do not add to this disaster by getting yourself stranded."

When the governor stopped speaking, Clarice

muted the television and they all returned to the dining room.

"I need to get out there and find that boy," Tuper said.

Clarice and Lana both looked at him with furrowed brows. "Did you hear anything they just said?" Clarice asked.

"I ain't goin' right now."

The lights flickered but stayed on.

Clarice went to the cupboard in the hallway and retrieved a box with candles. "We might be needing these," she said as she set them on the table. The lights flickered again several times, and then it went black.

CHAPTER FORTY-NINE

Clarice and Lana both turned on the flashlight apps on their cell phones.

"Is there anything that phone can't do?" Tuper asked.

"It won't do my laundry," Lana said. "Do you need help, Clarice?"

"Yes. Start lighting some of those candles. There's matches in the top drawer by the dishwasher in the kitchen."

Lana lit four candles and set them around, one on the counter between the dining room and the kitchen, one on the dining room table, one on the coffee table in the living room, and one in the bathroom.

Clarice used her flashlight and went to the hallway to retrieve the extra blankets she had in the cupboard. "We may be needing these to keep warm if this power stays out." She laid the blankets on an overstuffed chair in the living room.

"Now what?" Tuper asked.

"I'm going to make some sandwiches since I can't make much else for dinner and it's already getting late. I have some ham and cheese. That's right, Lana, you don't eat meat. I can make you a cheese sandwich or peanut butter and jelly. Which would you like?"

"PB & J is fine with me."

"Me too," Tuper said.

"Good, then we can drink up that milk. If that refrigerator is out too long, it'll go bad."

"Got an ice chest?" Tuper asked.

"Yes, it's right back there." She pointed to the laundry room off the rear of the kitchen.

Tuper got the ice chest and went outside. He returned with a chest full of snow. "You can put what you need in here. It'll keep cold. I'll change the snow in the morning if we don't have power."

"That's clever. Thanks," Clarice said.

"Been without power a time or two. Had to do somethin'."

"Clarice, do you need help?" Lana asked.

"No, thanks."

"Then I'll keep working."

"Don't you need electricity?" Tuper asked.

"I have about four hours on this battery and I have a fully charged backup, so I'm good for most of the night."

Tuper walked over to the fireplace and added a log to the fire. Then he paced from one room to the next and back. He hated being cooped up. It felt like jail, an experience he was all too familiar with. It was many years ago, and the most he spent in confinement was five days, but it felt like an eternity. He was in a bar fight that he didn't instigate, but the other guy got the worst of it so it looked bad. When it was all sorted out, he was released without any criminal charges. He had done many things since that could've landed him in jail, but he was smarter and didn't get caught or, in a couple of cases, had a good lawyer who kept him out except for a night or two.

He wanted to get out there and look for Mason, but he had no idea where to start or how soon he could go out. He knew Jerome would be on the snowplow; maybe he would know more about the storm. Tuper sat at the table and called Jerome.

"Toop, you're not out in this mess, are you?"

"No, I'd like to go, but thought I should check with you first."

"You'll have to speak up. It's hard to hear with the

plow and the wind."

Tuper spoke louder. "How soon before you think I can go out?"

Clarice shook her head and scowled at Tuper.

"It's going to be a while unless you have a snowmobile or some other means of snow-ready transportation. The roads fill up with snowdrifts as soon as I plow them. The wind blows it right back."

"How much longer do you think you'll be plowing?"

"What?"

"When is your shift over?" Tuper shouted.

"It's been over for a while, but they don't have any replacements. I expect I'll be here most of the night. Just a minute, there's a call on my radio."

Tuper could hear someone speaking, but he couldn't understand what was said. Then Jerome said, "I'm not close enough, better get someone else."

Jerome was speaking so loud that both Clarice and Lana could hear what he said. Clarice retrieved the milk from the refrigerator and Lana continued to work on her computer.

"You there, Toop?"

"Yup."

"Are you still looking for Randy Jenkins' missing boy?"

"Yes, why?"

Lana looked up from her laptop. Clarice took a seat next to Tuper at the table.

"I saw a kid that sure looked like him. I couldn't be certain because he was all bundled up, but I got a pretty good look at his face once. I couldn't swear to it, but he looked very familiar."

"Where was he?"

"He was with some woman who got stranded on the Lincoln Road off-ramp. I contacted Dispatch but they were a minimum of four hours out."

"Where are they now?"

"I couldn't leave them there so I plowed my way with them to a house on Frontage Road. That's where she said she was staying with a friend."

"What did she look like?"

"I don't know what color her hair was because she had a beanie on so I couldn't really see it. She was fairly tall, her nose a little pointy, but decently attractive. Not a lot of makeup. That's about all I can tell you; she was pretty bundled up too. Oh, she did have a furry white coat with blood on her sleeve. She said she got it from her son's nose bleed."

"Did she tell you her name?"

"What?"

"Her name?"

"She said it was Liz. She seemed a little odd, kind of nervous, but I figured she was just worried about being stranded in this weather. She was driving a car with California license plates."

"You didn't happen to get the plate number, did you?"

"I did. I had to call it in to Dispatch. I wrote it down in my log, but I can't get to it right now. I'll have to call you back with it."

Lana and Clarice were both wide-eyed now, listening to every word.

"But I remember the address of the house if you want that."

"Absolutely."

Jerome gave him the address. Tuper repeated it to make sure it was correct. Lana and Clarice both wrote it down. Tuper didn't bother.

"I was going to call you earlier," Jerome said, "but I didn't get a chance. Besides, I was afraid you'd try to come out in this weather. I know what a stubborn old goat you are."

"Couldn't have done anything earlier anyway."

"And you still can't." Jerome was adamant.

"Did you get the kid's name?"

"His mother, at least she said she was his mother, called him Valentin."

CHAPTER FIFTY

"That has to be Elizabeth Strong," Lana said excitedly. "She's from California. Her name is Liz. And she called the boy Valentin. She must have Mason. And that means Mason is alive. What are we going to do?"

"*We* aren't doing anything. Jerome said he'd call me when the storm lets up and I'll go see him for myself."

"Are you going to call the cops?"

"As soon as I know it's Mason, I'll let them know. We don't know anything for sure yet."

"I'm going with you when you go," Lana said.

"No, you're not."

"If she has Mason, she has killed two people already, and maybe three, if she's the one who killed the doctor."

"And that's exactly why you're not going."

Lana picked up half of a sandwich that Clarice had placed on the table and took a couple of bites. Then she put it down and started typing. Within minutes, she said, "I'm in."

"In what?" Clarice asked.

"I'm in the records for Lewis and Clark County so I can see who owns the house where Mason is."

"You don't know for sure it's Mason."

"Whatever. The house where the kid is."

"It didn't take you long to get into the county records." Clarice was fascinated. "How did you do it?"

"It was pretty simple. I Googled Lewis and Clark County, clicked on 'Search Public Records,' acknowledged the disclaimer, clicked on 'Public Login,' and voila—I'm in. The hard part is sorting through the records, but hopefully, the address will pinpoint it pretty fast." Lana paused. "And there it is."

"Amazing," Clarice said.

"Not really. Anyone can do that. It was a simple Google search into public records."

After a few minutes of silence, Tuper asked, "Well?"

"The owners are a couple named Ed and Brijet Neff. That name sounds familiar, but I've seen so many names in the past few days, it might not mean anything. Does it mean anything to either of you?"

Clarice shook her head.

Without responding, Tuper walked to the window and looked out. With the lights out in the neighborhood, he couldn't see much. He moved to the front door and opened it just enough to peek out. The cold blast hit him in the face and he pushed the door closed.

"I guess that's a 'no,'" Lana said.

She gulped down the rest of her sandwich and returned to her laptop. She still had a few hours left on this battery and then she would have to switch. When that was gone, she would be useless. She started with a Google search of Ed and Brijet Neff and discovered he was a musician who had played bluegrass music for nearly fifty years. He played in a lot of local venues for years but had moved to the San Francisco Bay area a few years back where he was still playing. He seemed to be best known for the mandolin, but also played fiddle, guitar, bass, and a little banjo.

She shook her head and started to say something out loud to herself when she remembered she wasn't alone. This was all very interesting, but it wasn't getting her anywhere. She had to stay on task or she would run out of battery life.

She saw Clarice walk to the back of the house.

Shortly after, Tuper's phone rang and he left the room as well. She was glad the distractions were gone, but it didn't last long. Tuper returned, walked to the door, and briefly opened and closed it again.

Lana shivered, and then went on about her task. She checked Ed's and Brijet's criminal histories but found none. She decided to concentrate on the house itself, which she determined to be their family home where they had raised three children, two girls and a boy. Their son was the youngest and he had been killed in Afghanistan. She started to follow up on more family history but stopped herself. She had to stay on task.

Tuper strolled past her again, around the table, and opened the front door. Lana realized the noise from outside wasn't so loud, though she still felt the cold air.

"That's cold," she said loudly.

"It is," Tuper said. "Can't see anything out the window."

"How's the storm?" Lana asked in a quieter but still irritated voice.

"Winds are dying down," Tuper said. "Still snowin' pretty good."

Lana looked out the window but couldn't see anything.

Clarice returned in her pajamas. "Did I hear you say the storm has let up?"

"Winds ain't howlin' like they were. Still gonna be a while. I just talked to Jerome. He went home to catch up on a little sleep. He'll be back on the plow before dawn. Clarice, Jerome said he'd text you the license plate number on that car."

Lana glanced at Tuper and wondered why he didn't get the number from Jerome. He was supposedly so good remembering numbers, why would he need it texted?

A beep came from a phone on the counter. "That must be Jerome." She picked up the phone and read the text. "B-S-T-R-O-N-G."

"Are you kidding me?" Lana said.

Tuper looked puzzled.

"Be strong," Lana said. "Her plate is her name. That has to be Elizabeth." Lana started typing. "I'll let you know in just a few minutes." No one said anything while she searched. It took her a little longer than she thought and when she got it, she looked up. Clarice had sat down at the table and was nodding off. Tuper was still pacing.

"The car is registered to Calvin Strong."

Clarice stood up. "I'm with Jerome. I'm going to get some sleep. You two should do the same. Neither of you have slept in a while." She turned her head toward Tuper. "You can take Mary Ann's room. She's safe and sound at her boyfriend's house and won't be coming home until the roads are clear."

"Thanks," Tuper said.

"Lana?" Clarice said.

"I'm just going to check a few more things. I want to see if I can find a familial connection between Elizabeth and Calvin."

When Clarice and Tuper left, Lana began her attempt at tracing the Strong family tree. It didn't prove that difficult. She already had Elizabeth's parents' names from other records she had previously hacked. She followed up and discovered the mother was deceased and her obituary stated she was survived by three children: Elizabeth Strong from San Jacinto, Calvin Strong from Riverside, and Helen Strong-Bates from Fontana, California.

She went back to trying to find something else that might help them. The problem was that she had reached a dead end and she was tired. Every time she started to look for something, she got side-tracked; besides, she really didn't know where else to look.

She closed down what she was doing, and checked her email accounts. She found nothing important until she went to the Hotmail account. *He* had sent another email. She rubbed her hands together, then clasped them, and held them in front of her mouth. She knew she was stalling. *Just open it. Get it over with.* She clicked on the email and it opened to the side.

--*Stay out of Bank of America. I know you were in there.*

She hit the "x," closing her email account and immediately sent a message to Ravic.

Lana: *What did you do in B of A?*
Ravic: *Nice 2 hear from you 2.*
Lana: *I got an email. He thinks I was there. What did U do?*
Ravic: *Just poked him a little. Made his life a little more difficult. He can't follow anything.*
Lana: *You ticked him off.*
Ravic: *Good. I meant 2. Do you want 2 know what I did?*
Lana: *No. It's better I don't.*
Ravic: *Everything else okay?*
Lana: *All good. Battery is a little low and I don't know when I'll get a charge.*
Ravic: *Go then.*

She wondered if Ravic knew where she was. It might have been his way of asking about the storm, but he'd never say anything that might give her away. Lana felt secure on their chat line, but you never knew. Ravic had taught her a long time ago not to give anything away about your location.

Lana shut down her computer and went to bed.

CHAPTER FIFTY-ONE

It was four-thirty in the morning when Jerome called Tuper to let him know he was going back to plowing.

"I need to go check on that little boy," Tuper said.

"The worst of the storm is pretty much over, but the roads are still covered. You won't be able to get very far until everything is plowed."

"Any chance you can come get me?"

"And then what?"

"Take me to Donnie's. He's not far from the house where you took the boy."

"And then what?"

"He's boarding my horse Pepper. I'll get around just fine on him."

Jerome paused.

"I got to find that little boy," Tuper said.

"Then call the cops."

"I have to make sure it's Mason."

"Alright, but I'm going out on a limb here. I'm not supposed to carry anyone in my cab."

"Thanks, bud."

"I'll be there in ten minutes. Be ready to go. I can drop you off and still get to work on time; besides, I can plow I-15 up to Lincoln. That's part of my route."

Tuper had slept in his clothes but he put his boots, hat, coat, and gloves on. Then he picked up a flashlight and, without turning it on, walked out to the living room as quietly as he could. He could hear his boots click as he made his way through the dark room toward the door with Ringo swishing along beside him. He didn't turn the flashlight on for fear it would wake Lana. He tried to be even quieter when he passed the sofa where Lana was sleeping, but he bumped into a bag sitting on the floor. She didn't say anything, so he kept going.

He opened the front door and stepped out, turning his flashlight on. Ringo scampered across the snow. In some of the snow hills he all but disappeared, but bounced back and continued his romp.

The wind had ceased, but snowflakes continued to fall, though much lighter than before. The temperature was well below freezing. Tuper flashed his light on his car. It was almost buried. It would take him an hour just to shovel the car out, much less get down the road.

"Ringo, let's go," Tuper said.

Ringo soon appeared and ran up on the deck. Tuper waited for him to shake, and then he opened the door and let him inside. He intended to close the door behind him and go, but he heard Lana say, "Are you leaving?"

"Yeah, but Ringo is staying."

"I want to go with you."

"No, it's too dangerous and you'll drive me nuts. Stay here and let me know if you find anything else that might help."

"I already did. Elizabeth Strong has a brother named Calvin."

"So it *is* her."

"It must be. Are you going to the Neff house?"

"It's all I got to go on."

"Is the storm over?"

"Pretty much."

"But the roads will still be covered, right? You can't drive in this."

"I know a guy," Tuper said, and closed the door.

He tread through the snow to the end of the road and within minutes spotted the big, yellow truck plowing toward him. Jerome stopped and picked him up.

"I think you're crazy, you know," Jerome said.

"You'd be right."

On the way, they mostly talked about the damage from the storm, until Jerome said, "Randy must be going a little crazy with his son missing. I'd be out of my mind by now."

"He's dead. So is his wife. Both of them murdered."

"What?" His big eyes widened. "Does the killer have Mason?"

"I think so."

"And you think it's that woman I saw?"

"It could be."

Jerome turned off on the same off-ramp where he had picked up the woman and child. He pointed to the side of the road. "There's her car. You can barely see the tail of it sticking up. Dispatch already knows about it. They'll be sending a tow truck to take it away if she doesn't take care of it herself."

When they reached the driveway to Donnie's, Tuper said, "I can get out here."

Jerome checked the time. "I can get you to the barn."

Jerome plowed his way right up to Donnie's barn and let Tuper off.

"Be careful," Jerome called from his truck.

Tuper nodded and went inside the barn. He turned on the light and was thankful Donnie still had power. There were four stalls that contained horses. The last one held a pinto Quarter Horse gelding. Tuper reached up and stroked the horse's head. "Hi, Pepper. You ready for a ride?"

Tuper checked his water trough and found it had plenty of water. Then he got a little grain from the barrel and gave it to Pepper who immediately started eating. Tuper was standing there watching him eat when he heard the door crack open. He turned around slowly to see a gray-haired man with a long beard, about Tuper's age or older, standing at the door pointing a rifle at him.

"Good Lord," Donnie said as he lowered his rifle, "I could've shot your ass." He approached Tuper. "What the hell you doing here in the middle of the night?"

"It ain't the middle of the night. The sun'll be sneakin' up in another hour."

"Did you come by here to feed your horse? He'd a been fed soon enough."

"No, I need to take him out for a bit. I just wanted to give him a little food before we left in case I'm not back by breakfast."

"Why didn't you call?"

"Didn't want to wake you up."

"That worked well."

Tuper got his saddle and blanket from the tack room and put them on Pepper while Donnie tried to find out where he was going.

"It's my business, Donnie. Nothin' you need to worry yourself about."

"It must be some pretty important business if you're going out in this storm." Donnie said.

"Storm's over."

"But it's dang cold out there still, and in some spots the snow is as deep as Pepper is tall."

"Best I take some snowshoes with me then."

"That would be good." Donnie strode across the room and took a pair of snowshoes from a hook on the wall and brought them back. "Here you go."

Tuper tied them to the back of his saddlebag, checked the cinch, and then mounted Pepper.

"See you later, Donnie." Tuper rode out of the barn on his way to Ed and Brijet Neff's house.

CHAPTER FIFTY-TWO

Pepper and Tuper galloped along the side of the frontage road where Jerome had plowed, and then cut across a field that Tuper knew was not fenced in. He had ridden in this area a lot because it was close to Donnie's. He had kept one or more of his horses here from time to time over the last thirty years. There wasn't much around here the first time he came. No houses around for miles. Now the city was creeping closer every day. It made him feel old, cramped, and a little displaced.

It was cold, but it felt good to be in the saddle. It had been weeks since he had ridden. This is where Tuper felt the most at home. He knew Pepper liked it too because he held his head high as they moved along across the field.

The ride to the Neff house took only about fifteen minutes even though they had to slow down a lot to maneuver through the snow and the darkness. He did have some light from the moon and the snow had stopped falling. Tuper wore a good, fur-lined wool coat, a vest, a flannel shirt, and long johns. He could still feel the cold, but mostly his face and ears were tingling. He was sorry he hadn't brought earmuffs.

The house was only about fifty yards away when Tuper slowed Pepper to a walk. His plan was to get there before daylight, which would start in another ten or fifteen minutes. He didn't want Elizabeth, or whoever it was, to leave before he got there. Beyond that, he wasn't sure what he was going to do.

Tuper removed his pistol from its holster, approached the house as quietly as he could, and dismounted. He was relieved when he heard no dogs bark, although he knew there could still be one inside. He snuck up to the back side of the house and tried to peer in a window, but all he saw was a closed shade. He listened for noise from inside but didn't hear any. A line of light jutted across the horizon behind a cloud cover. The sky above the clouds went from dark blue to black and then more clouds. Soon it would be daylight.

Tuper thought about parking Pepper outside, knocking on the door, and claiming to be the mounted police checking to see if everything was okay. But he didn't think Elizabeth would answer the door, especially since she had Mason, or some other kid. So, instead, he approached the back door. As he got closer, he saw the snow on the steps had been disturbed and a single set of footprints led to a nearby shed. He followed the prints as he edged his way around the side of the shed to an open door on the east side. The top of the sun had turned the sky to a lighter blue and it gave enough light to see inside. The shed was empty, but a line of fresh tracks from a snowmobile led out of the shed and across the yard.

Still not certain if anyone was in the house, Tuper climbed the three steps to the back door and opened it. It led to a service porch with a freezer on the left and a small two-seater bench on the right. Above the bench was a rack where two hats and a scarf hung. There was enough light from a window to see his way around.

Holding his gun in one hand, he tried the knob on the door that led into the house. It was unlocked. He pushed it open about an inch, then stepped back and used his foot to open it wider. It was darker in the house than on the porch so he pulled his flashlight out of his pocket and shined it around the living room. No sign of life.

If anyone was there, they would have likely heard

him or seen the light from his flashlight by now, so he called out, "Mounted police. Anyone here?"

No answer.

With his flashlight in one hand and his gun in the other, he continued through the house. He searched the kitchen, opening the pantry door and checking under the table, but found nothing. He stalked back to the living room and flashed his light into the hallway. There were three doors off the hallway, all open. He stepped into one bedroom and flashed the light around. He couldn't see behind the bed, so he took a step toward the other side of it. He heard a noise behind him. Tuper turned around just as a woman wielding a knife flew out of the closet and jumped on him, knocking him onto the bed. Her eyes looked wild and she was gritting her teeth.

Tuper dropped his flashlight but held onto his gun. She reached her left arm up and attempted to bring the knife down into Tuper's chest. He threw his left arm forward and thrust her up in the air, preventing the knife from hitting him. He held her there dangling for a split-second as she swung the knife around trying to cut him. As she sliced into his jacket, he grabbed a fistful of her shirt and threw her onto the bed next to him. He scrambled to hold her and get on his feet. As he did, she lunged forward and stabbed him in the leg.

The pain shot through him and his first reaction was to shoot her, but he couldn't shoot a woman. With his free hand, he grabbed her wrist, bent it back, and shook the knife free. Once the knife was gone, he holstered his gun and used both arms to contain her.

Tuper took a deep breath. He was shaking and his adrenaline was at an all-time high.

"Where's Mason?" Tuper asked.

"No, no, Mason!" she screamed as she struggled to get away.

Teresa Burrell

Tuper held on tight. "Where's the boy?"

"Valentin! Valentin!"

"Okay, okay," Tuper said softly. "Where is Valentin?"

She turned her head slowly around to face him. Tuper half-expected it to keep going all the way around like in *The Exorcist*.

"I don't know," she said, one loud word at a time.

"You need to calm down. Let's go into the living room and figure this out."

He gave her a gentle nudge in the direction of the door. She moved along without incident until they reached the living room. When Tuper flipped the light switch on, the woman started screaming again. A lot of nonsensical words came out of her mouth. Every so often she said, "Valentin." Then suddenly she stopped yelling and raised her foot high in the air, exposing her bare foot.

"She took my shoes," she said in a normal voice.

"Who?" Tuper asked.

"She took my shoes. Can't go outside. No shoes."

Tuper still didn't know who this woman was for sure, but he was pretty sure she had had a psychotic break. He guessed she was probably Elizabeth Strong, but then who was on the snowmobile? And where was Mason?

"What's your name?" Tuper asked.

"My name is Pudden Tane. Ask me again, and I'll tell you the same."

Tuper hadn't heard that rhyme since he was a small boy. It reminded him of his mother who always told him it was impolite to just come out and ask someone, "What's your name?" She said you deserved it if they said, "Pudden Tane."

"Are you Elizabeth?"

"Of course I'm Elizabeth. I'm Valentin's Elizabeth.

My Valentine. My Valentine. Where oh where is my Valentin?"

Tuper studied her face. She didn't have a long, thin nose like Jerome had described and she wasn't that tall. Perhaps this wasn't Elizabeth after all. But then, who was this?

Tuper was pretty certain he wasn't going to get anything coherent from this woman and he needed to get on the trail of the snowmobile. But first, he took her with him as he searched the rest of the house to make sure Mason wasn't still there, his leg throbbing with every step and blood dripping on the floor. Then he took her to the sofa and told her to sit down.

She sat without incident. Then she lay down and pulled a blanket from the back of the sofa over her. Tuper started to back away.

"Remember, you can't go outside. You have no shoes."

"No shoes," she mumbled, but didn't move.

Tuper dashed outside into the almost-full morning sun, grabbing the scarf that was hanging in the porch as he raced by.

"Pepper," he called.

Around the house came Pepper. Tuper grabbed the saddle horn as he approached and swung himself up onto the horse's back like a rodeo rider. Then he wrapped the scarf he had heisted around his neck, ears, and the bottom half of his face.

Tuper rode in the direction of the snowmobile trail. About twenty yards from the shed, he spotted what he thought was a scarf. He slowed down and got a closer look. It was a gold-colored teddy bear sitting on top of a mound of snow. It had to have been dropped there after the snowfall as it had no snow on top of it. He wished he had left immediately and not gone in the house. He might have caught the kidnapper already.

Now he feared he would lose sight of the trail along the way.

Once he was about a half mile from the house, he stopped, took out his phone, and called Glen, his friend on the police force in Great Falls. He told him about the woman in the house.

"Why didn't you call 9-1-1?"

"Because they'd expect me to stick around and I'd have to answer a bunch of questions. I need to find the boy. You know what I'm saying is real, and they'll listen to you. Oh, and tell them she's a little off and has a knife."

"Alright, but you should let the cops know so they can help find that boy."

"I just did. They can follow the snowmobile tracks when they get here, and tell them there's a teddy bear about twenty yards from the shed. If I find out anything new, I'll let them know."

He hung up, and rode on.

CHAPTER FIFTY-THREE

Tuper followed the snowmobile tracks along Collins Drive and then across another field where he knew there was a dirt road. He wasn't exactly sure where it was because of the snow cover. The tracks led to a small bridge across the viaduct and continued on to Sierra Road, then turned east for about an eighth of a mile around farms, some fenced, some not, to Helberg Drive. He followed the tracks south on Helberg Drive until he reached York Road, where he stopped.

York Road had been plowed and the tracks were gone. He didn't know whether to go left or right, or to cross over York and see if he could pick them up again. He went with the latter because he was very close to the house Gordon was killed in. It was worth a try.

Tuper crossed York onto Herrin Road, but he didn't see any tracks leading to the mobile home park. The snow was piled high near the entrance to the park. No one had been in or out of there either on foot or driving a snowmobile, or any other vehicle. Frustrated and uncertain where to look next, he chose west and rode alongside of York Road until he reached Prickly Pear Creek, but found no tracks.

He turned and headed east along the other side of York Road, trying to find some sign of the snowmobile.

~~~

The power was still out, so Lana got herself a bowl of cereal, using the milk from the ice chest. *The old man's not so dumb after all,* she thought. She sat at the table with a blanket wrapped around her and ate.

Once back at her computer Lana pondered about what they still needed. Her fingers were so cold it hurt when she typed, so every fifteen minutes or so she would warm them by the fire. She had just done that and she was adamant about finding more clues.

She decided to have another look at Jessica's emails, perhaps find an account she hadn't yet discovered. A trip back through the old accounts didn't reveal anything new, but she did discover an AOL account that Jessica used to communicate with only one person, Mel. Every email was about the in vitro procedure. She could tell from the content that Mel was Dr. Melinda Richards.

The email account went back about two years prior to when Gordon was a part of Jessica's life. Jessica had been going to the clinic to be tested to see if in vitro would work for her. She already knew she couldn't carry a baby to term.

Jessica had numerous tests done at the clinic, including testing of her ovarian reserve, which they do before starting any injections. She had several blood tests done which included Day 3 FSH and AMH blood testing, as well as antral follicle counts. These tests helped to predict how her ovaries would respond to the drugs. The results were positive.

One email contained an attachment of a medical report from Dr. Richards' clinic. Lana rubbed her hands together to keep them warm as she read the report. The bottom line was that Dr. Richards confirmed that Jessica would be a good candidate for in vitro fertilization, but she would need a surrogate to carry the baby.

There was a lot of medical jargon in the emails, because Jessica asked lots of questions in her attempt to understand the process. The rest were mostly about scheduling and appointments. She found one email from Jessica that read:

We can be there tonight and you can meet Beth.

She figured Beth was probably Elizabeth Strong.

There were a couple of other emails that mentioned a person whom Jessica referred to as her friend "J." From what Lana could tell, "J" was willing to help, but Lana could not be certain what she was helping with. Was she another surrogate mother? If so, why would she need two? Or was she helping with the arrangements for Elizabeth, or perhaps caring for Jessica through her ordeal?

Lana stood up and stretched. She was frustrated because none of this was really news, except for "J," who may or may not even be important. She decided to concentrate her efforts elsewhere.

Lana was concerned about what Tuper might find at the Neff house. Other than the owner being a musician who didn't live there any more, they knew nothing. Lana's attempts to find a tenant had proved unsuccessful. It appeared it had never been a rental. *Why is that?*

Clarice, with a blanket wrapped around her, entered the room and interrupted Lana's thoughts. "Where's Tuper?"

"He went looking for the kid."

"In this snow? How did he get out?" Clarice pulled the curtain back, leaving it open, and looked out the window. "His car is still here."

"Someone came and got him, I think. He wouldn't let me go."

"Tuper likes to work alone. I'm surprised he has let you do what you have."

"I noticed he's a little pig-headed."

"No, he's a lot pig-headed, but he's also concerned about that little boy. He tries to cover it, but he's really very sensitive."

Lana looked back at her computer screen. "You know, I found the owner of the house where that woman took the boy, but no one has lived there for years. Or at least, there's no record of a tenant. Do you find that odd?"

"There's lots of reasons for that. Maybe it needs fixing and they don't want to spend the money."

"The utilities are still on in Ed Neff's name," Lana said.

"That's more than we have here. Someone could be living there, paying cash, and the Neffs have included the utilities. That's not unusual. Or they could use it when they travel back here from—where did you say they live?"

"Near San Francisco."

"It could be a summer home for the family or something."

"Or maybe someone was murdered there and they don't want anyone to know. Or there's a lot of money or something valuable hidden there. Or—"

Clarice cut her off. "I think it's more likely one of the other scenarios."

"But what are the chances that Elizabeth Strong found this abandoned home, the only abandoned house with the utilities still on?"

"That's a little odd, but what else do you have to work with?"

"Not much, and I only have a few hours of battery time left." She rubbed her hands together and then flexed her fingers, opening and closing them several times to get them limber before she put them back on the keyboard. "It would take way too long to try to find a credit card for Elizabeth, then hack in and find where she has been. Even then, it might not help." She paused. "I think I need to know more about the Neffs and see if I can figure out who is in that house and how Elizabeth got there."

Lana was quiet for a second, and then she said, "I tried everything I could to see if Elizabeth Strong and the Neffs were somehow connected. I didn't find anything, other than they both live in California but they're 500 miles apart. However, you may be onto something. If the Neffs use the house when they travel back here, maybe they are here now."

Lana went on Ed Neff's website and checked his schedule. "Ed had a two-week gig in Reno, Nevada, that ended the day before yesterday. I doubt if he came here after his performance in this storm."

"He would've never made it across the pass," Clarice said. "What about his wife?"

"She was with him, I think, because she has posted a bunch of photos on social media."

"What about other family members? Does he have kids?"

"They had a son who was killed in Afghanistan, and I think they had two daughters. I'll check."

Lana Googled the son's obituary, which referenced his family members, two sisters, Joyce Neff-Spencer and Janette Neff, an uncle, and two aunts.

"Wait a minute," Lana exclaimed. "I think I remember where I saw the Neff name."

She buried herself in her research while Clarice sat quietly. Every few minutes, she would rub her hands to get them warm. About ten minutes later she said, "That's it. I saw his name on the property on Lonesome Loop Road. I didn't pay much attention to it because we were really interested in the tenants, not the owners. But he owns both the property where Jessica and Gordon first lived and the property behind it where Jan Murray lived."

"He owns a lot of houses," Clarice said.

Lana continued to click around, looking for any other property that Mr. and Mrs. Neff owned. "Here's another one. He owns four houses here in Helena. And this last one was very interesting," she mumbled.

"Why?" Clarice asked.

But Lana was still trying to find one more bit of information, which she quickly discovered.

"OMG!"

"What is it?" Clarice was huddled over Lana now, trying to see what was on the computer.

"He owns the house where Jan Murray lives now. The one where Jessica was staying. And Jan Murray is Neff's youngest daughter, Janette Neff. Murray is a married name."

Clarice scurried around and sat down in front of Lana.

"I don't get it. How is Jan Murray involved with Elizabeth Strong?"

"I don't know. Maybe she found out where Mason was and tried to get Mason back. But then why would they be at a house her parents own? I don't know, but I'm calling Tuper."

CHAPTER FIFTY-FOUR

Tuper kept riding around looking for snowmobile tracks. Just off York Road, near Wiley Drive, he saw some tracks. They were all over the place, like someone had driven one way and then made a loop and come back. He followed them the best he could. After he crossed over two streets, he saw the vehicle. He approached it cautiously, but as he got closer he saw it was two teenagers playing in the snow.

He considered going back to Clarice's house because he didn't know where else to go. Mason and whoever had him could have gone anywhere. Tuper needed to get in front of a warm fire before he got frostbite. Besides, his leg hurt where he had been stabbed. There was a big wet mark where he had bled onto his pants, and it felt even colder as if it was frozen.

He wasn't far from South Country Store just off York. He took a chance that it was open, and rode there to get something warm to drink. His leg hurt when he walked, but he did it anyway. He took a large cup from the bin and drew himself a hot chocolate. He wrapped both hands around the cup, warming them, as he paid for it. Then he stood by the window, watching Pepper and drinking it. His phone rang twice before he realized it was for him.

"Hello."

"Why didn't you answer your phone?" Lana said sternly.

"I just did."

"I've called four times. I thought you had your throat cut or something."

"Throat's fine," he said, looking down at his leg.

"Did you find Mason?"

"No. They got away on a snowmobile. I was tracking them but lost the trail."

Lana told him what she had discovered about Jessica's friend Jan Murray.

"That explains where they might be. Gotta go."

Tuper put his phone back in his pocket and then wrapped both hands around his cup as he went outside. He took a big gulp of the hot drink and then threw it in the trash, mounted his horse, and coaxed him to a full run as he crossed the fields heading south. He slowed down only when he had to as he made his way to the house where Jessica had stayed with her friend, picking up the snowmobile tracks once he crossed Howard.

He slowed Pepper down to a walk when he was about three houses away. A few yards ahead and he spotted a snowmobile parked to the side in the driveway. He wasn't sure what to do. He didn't want to spook Jan, if that's who it was. He was hoping she had taken Mason from the kidnapper and called the police. But he was afraid there was more to it than that. He was still deciding what to do when he approached the house, the garage door opened, and a woman stepped out holding a shovel. A car sat in the garage with a cover over it, so Tuper couldn't tell what kind it was. He wondered if it was the Kia.

"Good mornin', ma'am," Tuper said.

"Good morning," she said, and started to shovel her driveway.

"That ain't gonna help until they get these roads plowed."

"They're working their way here. The guy up the street has a plow and he'll be doing our block soon. He always does. I need to be ready when they get them done."

"In a hurry to get somewhere?"

"Just work." Suddenly her voice sounded less trusting. "What are you doing out riding so early in this cold weather?"

"It's part of a community, volunteer, help-your-neighbor program. We go out when there's been a storm. Some are on snowmobiles and some on horses. There's not many means of transportation useful in this weather."

"What do you do?"

"We look for people in trouble. Sometimes people are stranded in cars, or someone is stuck who needs medical attention. You'd be amazed the things we find."

"I didn't know there was such a group."

"It's been around a couple of years now. The word's getting out and more people are helping."

"That's good," she said, and started to shovel again.

"I saw the tracks from your snowmobile and I thought you might be one of us."

"No, I ran to the store and got some milk for my kid." She glanced at the door to the house.

Tuper got down from his horse. "It's gonna take you awhile to shovel that driveway. Don't you have a snowblower?"

"It's not working."

Her shoveling wasn't either. She had made very little progress.

"Can I give you a hand?"

"I'm okay. You must have other people you can help." She looked toward the door again.

"I'm supposed to help people who are in need. Seems to me you need help. I don't mean to be disrespectful, but you ain't gettin' very far." He reached his hand out for the shovel. "Name is Phil," Tuper said, hoping to get a name from her in return. He assumed she was Jan, but she could be Elizabeth for all he knew. If it was Jan, Jessica may have told her about him, so he used the name Phil instead of his own.

"Thanks, Phil," she said, as she handed him the shovel.

Tuper started shoveling and within a minute had cleared more than she had in the entire time they were talking. He had to work faster than her or there was little need for her to let him do it. But he wanted to stall in hopes he would get a glimpse of Mason.

"How old is your son?"

Her eyes widened and her face lost color. She took a step backwards. "How do you know I have a son?"

"You said you took the snowmobile to get him milk this morning," he said softly.

"That's right. Sorry, it's been a long night." Then she added, "My husband isn't feeling well. That's why he's not out here shoveling. He stayed with our son while I went to the store."

Just then the door opened from the house into the garage and a young boy started out.

The woman ran toward him. "Get back inside," she yelled. Then she lowered her voice and said, "It's too cold out here. I don't want you getting sick."

The boy closed the door. Tuper started shoveling as if he hadn't been watching.

She walked back. "I can finish this."

"Look, you're cold and you have a son to tend to. Why don't you go on in and I'll finish this up?"

"Are you sure?"

"Yes. No need for both of us to be out in the cold. And if you wouldn't mind, I could use a hot cup of whatever you got, coffee, tea, hot chocolate, milk, water. It don't matter much to me as long as it's warm."

"Okay," she said and left.

Tuper took out his cell and called Denis Castro.

"I think I found the missing boy, Mason Jenkins."

"Toop, we're in the middle of a crisis here too. You need to call direct. They'll listen now. You made believers out of them with the last call. I'm giving you the cell number for Detective Tony Ayala. I told him about you."

"What ya tell him?"

"Enough."

Tuper wished his friend Pat was available. He was on the mend but still not well enough. He hung up and called the number Denis had given him, told him the address, and that he had seen the kid. He was pretty certain it was Mason Jenkins.

"Can you see them right now?"

"No, I'm outside shoveling her driveway. They're inside the house."

"I'll be there as quickly as I can."

"Good. She's a little jumpy. She could spook."

CHAPTER FIFTY-FIVE

About five minutes later, the woman came outside carrying a coffee mug in one hand and holding the boy's hand with the other. He was wearing boots, a heavy jacket, a ski mask, and a backpack. She shooed him toward the snowmobile.

She walked over to Tuper, handed him the mug, and stepped away.

"I'm taking my son to his grandma's," she said, as she strode away. "You don't need to stay and finish. But if you choose to, just leave the shovel by the door when you leave." She closed the garage door with a remote and jumped on the snowmobile. Tuper stepped toward it, but she drove across her front lawn and off her property.

"Jan," Tuper yelled as he ran after her, "you don't need to run."

Not sure if she even heard him, he called for Pepper who came running. Tuper mounted and followed her. He was able to keep up as long as she was still in the neighborhood, but he knew that when she reached an open field or a straight shot on a road, he'd lose her. Besides, if he got too close, he was afraid she might take too many chances in her effort to get away, putting Mason in danger.

She turned left two blocks from her home. He followed, trying to stay on the same track so Pepper didn't hit any soft spots. She crossed through an unfenced yard, across the street and through a vacant lot, with Tuper close behind. When she reached Howard, there were more open areas. She went off the road and started across a field. The snow was flying in every direction as she dug a trench through the soft snow.

The snowmobile went part way up on its tail, then turned on its side, and slid across the snow. Both passengers flew through the air. The boy landed about ten feet from the vehicle. The woman rolled through the snow and disappeared in a snowdrift.

Tuper kicked Pepper in the sides and they galloped across the field, only stopping when he got to the boy. He still didn't see the woman but he heard her call "Mason!"

Tuper jumped off and leaned down to the child. "Are you okay?"

The little boy looked up wide-eyed and, with the biggest grin, said, "That was so fun."

Tuper chuckled.

"Where's Aunt Jan?" Mason asked.

So she *was* Jan. "I'm gonna check on her right now. Do you like horses?" Tuper asked.

"Sure."

"Keep an eye on Pepper for me while I check on her, okay?"

Tuper trudged to the snowmobile, pulled out the key, and put it in his pocket, then kept moving in the direction where he heard the woman calling. She was half-buried in snow and trying to get up.

"Is Mason okay?" she asked.

"He's fine. How 'bout you?"

"I'm okay, I think." She scrambled up.

Tuper took hold of her arm, helped her up, and brought her back to Mason, calling Detective Ayala as he walked. He gave him the best description he could for their location.

"Does she have a weapon?"

"Not that I've seen."

"We're not far," Ayala said.

"Roads haven't been plowed here."

"We're on sleds."

"Hurry up," Tuper said. "It's cold."

"Are you a cop?" Jan asked just before they reached Mason who was playing in the snow and talking to Pepper.

"Nope," Tuper said.

"You're the guy Jessica hired to find Mason, aren't you?"

"Where's my mommy?"

"Hey, Mason, want to sit on my horse?"

Mason jumped up. "Yeah."

Tuper let go of Jan and lifted Mason up onto the horse. "Now, you sit still. Don't kick him or anything and he'll just stand there." Tuper took the reins just to be sure, but he kept an eye on Jan. If she ran, so what? He didn't care. She couldn't get far on foot before they caught her. She wasn't taking Mason, he'd see to that.

Tuper turned his back to Pepper and Mason, and said softly, "Who was the woman at your parents' old house?"

Jan didn't answer.

"It was Elizabeth Strong, right?"

"How did you know that?"

Tuper took her by the arm again and led her to the snowmobile. He let go of her and yanked the snowmobile up off its side. "Have a seat." Once she was seated, he asked, "How did you know about Elizabeth?"

"We were surrogate mothers for Jessica and Gordon."

"Both of you?"

"Yes. Elizabeth was injected first. It worked right off, but then she miscarried. So I did it."

"Elizabeth seemed pretty out of it when I saw her. Did she know what she was doing when she agreed to the surrogacy?"

"I'm not sure, but she was much better back then."

"So you knew her in California?"

"I met her a few times; we weren't close."

"But you were close with Jessica?"

"Yes. She asked me to be a surrogate first but I was afraid it would ruin our relationship. Besides, I didn't want to go through all that pain. So she basically tricked Elizabeth into doing it."

"How?"

"Beth, that's what she went by, was a mental patient, but she was very mild and calm. She had no episodes of violence of any kind and she was pliable. I don't think she ever really understood that she was carrying a baby for someone else. When her body started changing and she was having morning sickness, her personality started to change as well. Jessica stayed by her side as much as she could and tried to explain what was going on, but Elizabeth seemed to understand less and less. Then on Valentine's Day she freaked out. She started screaming that she didn't want a baby. Jessica tried to calm her down, but she thrashed around on the floor like she was mad, and then finally collapsed. The doctor came, but Elizabeth had miscarried."

"Dr. Richards?"

Jan gave Tuper an incredulous stare. "Yes. I take it you know about her too."

Tuper nodded.

"Elizabeth kept saying she wanted her Valentine. She even named him Valentin. She became more and more delusional about the baby. She thought Jessica and the doctor were keeping him from her. When she became belligerent, Jessica had to get rid of her. She dropped her off at her parents' house. She figured no one would believe the story if she told it, and she was right."

"Then you stepped up?"

"Yes. Jessica was so distraught. She was running out of time. She and Gordon wanted to leave as soon as they could after his release from jail. And she was determined not to go without a baby. It was a way for me to get back home to Montana without asking my parents for money. I also wanted to be an aunt, which I could never be. My sister didn't want to have children and my brother was killed in Afghanistan. So I made a deal with Jessica. I would give birth, and then we would all move to Helena. I got my dad to rent a house to them, which worked until they couldn't pay their rent and he evicted them. The agreement was that I would live nearby and watch Mason grow up, and be a part of his life."

"That was quite a sacrifice on your part."

"Initially, I was going to get more out of the bargain, but things didn't work out quite like we planned."

"What do you mean?"

"It wasn't important. The situation was great for all of us."

"Until they filed for divorce?"

Jan scoffed. "There was no divorce. There was never a marriage. They said they didn't need a marriage. Nothing could tear them apart. The divorce was all a ruse."

"Why?"

"Because one day Jessica and I saw Elizabeth. She tracked us down. Actually, she tracked Jessica down. She knew her as Denise Jenkins because that's the name Jessica used with her in California. Elizabeth came to the house and she demanded Mason. Since neither Gordon nor Mason were home, Jessica made up an elaborate story. She told Elizabeth that she and

Gordon were going through a divorce and he had Mason."

"Why didn't Jessica just call the cops?"

"Because she had committed so many crimes. She had talked to a lawyer once who said they could get her for kidnapping Elizabeth, forcing a pregnancy on her, and maybe even manslaughter for the death of her baby. And at that time, Elizabeth seemed pretty normal. We weren't afraid of her."

"How did she expect to pull off the divorce angle?" Tuper asked.

"That afternoon, Jessica called a friend of hers who emailed her a copy of someone's divorce papers. She whited out the names and put theirs in and made copies so you couldn't see the Wite-Out. It didn't take her long, and it made her story plausible. Elizabeth was big on paperwork. She was quirky that way."

"Why did Alan kidnap the kid?"

"You know about Alan too?"

Again Tuper nodded.

"Jessica and Gordon planned to fake a kidnapping so Elizabeth would believe Mason was dead or gone. After a little while, they were going to disappear with Mason and start over. But then Elizabeth hit Alan over the head and took Mason."

"How do you know it was Elizabeth?"

"Because I saw her."

"You saw her kidnap Mason?"

"Yes. I drove up to Randy's mobile home in Leisure Village park just in time to see a woman jump out from behind the bushes, hit Alan over the head, grab Mason, and run. She pushed Mason into a gold Honda and sped off."

"Did you know *who* she was?"

"At first I thought it was Jessica, but it wasn't her car. Then I saw the California license plate with

BSTRONG on it, and I figured it must have been Elizabeth." She continued. "I drove after her. I kept calling Gordon as I drove, but got no answer. But I knew that if I could get Mason back for him, everything would be alright."

"For *him*?"

"For them, I mean."

"Did you ever call Jessica?"

"No, because Gordon was close and I thought I might need someone stronger." She paused. "I followed her onto East Custer and then I lost her. After driving back and forth several times, I spotted the car at the end of a dirt road in what looked like a junk yard. It was just starting to get dark when I drove in, but I kept my lights off. I almost ran into some old tires alongside the road. I parked behind some trees before I reached the car. As I snuck up closer, I realized that rather than a junk yard, it was just a junky yard. I started snooping around an old trailer that sat on a foundation but appeared to have been unoccupied for some time. There were no other buildings in sight, so I figured they must be in there."

"Why didn't you call the cops?"

"Because I thought I could just get Mason and take him to Gordon, but when I snuck up to the door and listened, the door flew open smacking me in the head. I felt myself tumble to the ground and I hit my head on something really hard. The next thing I knew, I was inside and tied to a chair. She kept me there for days."

"Where was Mason?"

"In another room. Whenever I would ask about him, she would say he was sleeping. I didn't know whether he was dead or alive for quite a while. She must have been drugging him or something because he was so quiet. She would take him food and I would hear some talking, and then he'd be really quiet again."

She paused. "She was actually pretty good to me. She fed me and took me to the bathroom when I needed. She never would untie me, though."

"How did you get to your parents' home?"

"It was really cold in the trailer. We didn't have any electricity or heat and the storm was coming. It took me quite a while to talk her into moving, but I think it just finally got too cold for her. I gave her the key and she went and checked it out before she took us. I was afraid she would go without me, but she didn't."

"What happened when you got to your old house?"

"She tied me to a bed, but she would sit and talk to me. At first, she was more coherent. She got worse every day, but she definitely had a plan. She kept saying, 'Two things to do before I leave.' Then she started saying, 'One thing to do before I leave.' She never would say what it was. Yesterday, she came back with blood on her jacket and said, 'All done.' I asked her what happened but she wouldn't say. I was so afraid she had done something to Mason. I kept screaming like a madwoman until she finally brought Mason in to see me. He tried to run to me, but she wouldn't let him."

"How did you get away?"

"She wanted to leave and I knew as soon as the storm let up, she would find a way. So I called her in the night to take me to the bathroom. I figured she wouldn't be as alert and I was right. I was able to catch her off guard and I shoved her real hard against the sink. She hit her head and fell to the floor. I didn't check to see if she was alive, I just ran to her room and got Mason. He was groggy, but he was able to cut the ropes from my hands."

"And then you left on the snowmobile?"

"Yes. We always stored it there. My sister and I used it from time to time. Mostly I use it, but it stays there in case she wants it."

"Did you kill Gordon?"

Her cold, pink face turned white. "Gordon's dead?" She buried her face in her hands and sobbed.

Tuper believed her pain to be real or she was a really good actress. Either way, he felt bad that he had blurted it out. If she didn't know about Gordon's death, then she probably didn't know about Jessica's either. He decided to hold off on that bit of information. He waited and let her cry.

Finally, she looked up and sniffed back the tears. "No, I didn't kill him. I loved him." Then she added, "Just like I love Jessica."

Something still didn't set right with Tuper. He believed her story up until the point where Elizabeth took her hostage. He wasn't sure, but he had a few ways of checking it out.

"And once Jessica and Gordon had Mason back, they were going to leave and start over?"

"Yes."

"Only you didn't like that plan, did you?" Tuper was fishing, but it paid off.

Jan jerked her head around. "I haven't done anything wrong. In fact, I saved Mason from Elizabeth. Who knows what she would've done to him? That woman is whacko."

"So why'd you run from me?"

"I had to get away from that crazy woman, and I didn't know who you were. You could've been in on it with her."

Tuper was not buying her reason for running but Jan was done talking. She refused to answer any more of his questions. They waited in silence until the detective showed up.

CHAPTER FIFTY-SIX

The sun was shining and the world glistened as Tuper left the police department and rode Pepper back to Donnie's. The snow was starting to melt, making the ground slushy in some places and icy in others. The storm was over but the resulting accidents and problems had just begun. If too much snow melted and then it got cold again, the streets would be like sheets of ice, causing a multitude of accidents. People, especially the elderly, would be falling and breaking bones. The aftermath was always a mess.

When he was younger, the winter storms brought a certain kind of excitement for Tuper. Now they just seemed destructive, and a lot of work. He was feeling his age and the sharp pain in his leg reminded him that he had been stabbed. He would have gone to Urgent Care, but he knew he'd be waiting for hours because of the storm victims. He wanted to get back to Clarice's and get warm. In spite of all that, he felt good that Mason was alive and safe.

Tuper led Pepper into the barn, removed his saddle, and wiped him down. Then he gave him more food and water before Donnie came out. Donnie had agreed to give Tuper a ride, and since Jerome had plowed his way over there, the drive was easy. Jerome and the other workers had been busy. Interstate 15 was completely clean on both sides and cars were moving at almost full speed. *Life will soon be back to normal*, Tuper thought. *Except for Mason. His life will never be the same.*

Donnie dropped Tuper off at the snow-packed driveway and he limped the twenty yards or so to the house. Tired, cold, and in pain, the warm air welcomed him as he entered Clarice's home.

"Power's on, eh?" Tuper said.

"Yes," Clarice said, "and you look like something the cat drug in. Are you okay?"

"Rough mornin'."

"Tell us what happened, old man," Lana chimed in. "Did you find Mason?"

"Sure did. He must've been pretty terrified for a while, but by the time I found him, he was healthy and happy." He paused. "'Course he don't know yet that his folks are both dead."

Tuper removed his jacket and hat, and then stood by the fire. Clarice brought him a cup of hot tea.

"What's that all over your pants?" Clarice asked. "It looks like grease or something."

"Just blood."

Lana came over to look. "Whose blood is it?"

"Mine."

"Are you hurt?" Clarice asked.

"Don't think it's that bad. It stopped bleedin' a long time ago. It's either not that deep or it froze shut. Guess I'll know if it thaws out."

"What happened?" Clarice demanded.

Tuper told them about the woman at the Neff house with the knife whom he believed to be Elizabeth Strong. "Detective Ayala said they have her in custody and he'd let me know when she was ID'd. She had blood on her coat jacket sleeve, which I expect they'll find belongs to Jessica."

Clarice went to the hallway and returned with a pair of sweat pants and a shirt. "Here. Go take a hot shower. It'll warm up your body. Check your leg and see if we can bandage it or if you need to go to Urgent Care. I'll wash your clothes and you can put them on later after you've had something to eat. Then you can tell us the rest of the story."

Clarice and Lana had just finished making lunch when Tuper came into the kitchen wearing the sweats with one leg rolled up. He was holding a white washcloth that had started turning red over his leg just above the knee.

Clarice pulled out a chair for Tuper. "Come here and sit." She turned to Lana. "Go in the hallway closet and grab a towel and another washcloth from the bottom shelf. And there's a first-aid kit two shelves above that. Bring it. And a bottle of peroxide." Clarice slid another chair in front of Tuper, lifting his foot so he could rest his leg on it.

Clarice removed the washcloth and examined the inch-long cut. She dabbed around it with the washcloth.

"It doesn't look too deep, but you may want to go and see if you need stitches."

When Lana returned with the washcloth and towel, the cut was exposed.

"Eww…" she said and cringed. Clarice frowned at her.

Clarice handed her the bloody washcloth and said, "Here, rinse this out."

"It ain't that bad," Tuper said. "A couple Band-Aids oughta do the trick. Got one of those butterfly Band-Aid things?"

Clarice knew there was no point in arguing with him so when Lana returned with the wet washcloth, she cleaned off the blood around the cut. Tuper tightened his body when she poured peroxide on the open wound, but he didn't make a sound. Clarice cleaned up the foam and poured again. Then she dabbed some ointment on the cut and applied a large square Band-Aid.

Tuper pulled the leg of his sweat pants down over the cut, took his foot off the chair, and proceeded to finish his story. He told everything in his own succinct way, although he had to speak up a few times so he could be heard over the snowblower outside.

"Let me see if I've got this straight," Lana said. "Gordon had his friend Alan Bowman kidnap his own kid so he and Jessica could run away with him. But before Gordon even got his son, someone, probably Elizabeth Strong, hit Alan over the head and took the boy. But Jan Murray saw Elizabeth do it, followed her, got caught, then got away and managed to get Mason back. In the meantime, Elizabeth killed both Gordon and Jessica, and the storm hit, making it impossible for either of them to leave town." She raised her index finger in the air. "Unless someone else killed Jessica and Gordon, but why would they? And Jan's story doesn't quite work for me. I think she had more to do with it. If she wasn't some part of this scheme, she would've taken him to the police or the hospital right away."

"That's what *I* thought," Tuper said.

"Remember that night you saw the black Kia at Gordon's?" Lana asked. "You thought it was Jessica because it was the same car she drove to see you previously. You thought that was her car. Later you discovered she had a Chevy Aveo." She raised both hands palms-up. "That's it! Jan and Gordon were having an affair. Jessica thought he was seeing someone. How convenient for him to pick the woman closest to him. Jan and Gordon must've planned to run off with the boy but everyone's plans halted because Elizabeth took Mason. So who killed Gordon? Was it the jilted wife, the jealous girlfriend, or the crazy surrogate?"

"I think yer onto somethin'," Tuper said.

Lana's eyes widened. "If Jan was tied up in the trailer, who was driving the black Kia you saw at

Gordon's house? It could've been Elizabeth. That way, her car wouldn't be seen, but you saw that car before. Who was driving it when Jessica was dropped off at the Mini Basket?"

"And was that the car that was covered in Jan's garage?"

"The only way that could happen is if Jan was driving another car. Unless—"

Tuper interrupted. "Clarice, do you think my clothes are dry?"

"I'll check," Clarice said, and disappeared into the laundry room.

"Are you thinking what I'm thinking?" Lana asked.

"That's a scary thought," Tuper said.

"What I'm thinking is scary?" Lana asked.

"No, that I might be thinkin' the same thing you are."

CHAPTER FIFTY-SEVEN

Tuper drove along East Custer looking for the trailer where Jan said they had been held hostage. He spotted what looked like the place; at least, there was a trailer and hills of snow that could have been piles of junk. He couldn't see a car parked anywhere near the trailer, but there were lots of spots where there could be one hidden, and mounds of snow that could be covering a car.

East Custer was clean, and the first ten feet of the road were as well, but the road leading up to the trailer was not. He wished he had Pepper but it would take too long to go get him, ride over here, and then take him back.

He parked in the driveway that had been cleared, put on some snowshoes from the back of his car, and trekked the 100 yards or so to the trailer. The snow was untouched except for a few animal tracks, so no one had been here since the storm. Jan had said they had left before it hit. The cops could show up at any minute if Jan had told them about this place. Tuper hoped that didn't happen since he really didn't want to deal with that right now. He was just there looking for the car Jan was driving, which was not in the clearing near the trees as she had stated.

He found a couple of other mounds, but when he brushed back the snow, all he found was an old rusty pickup and a pile of junk. He was convinced there was no drivable car on the lot. He considered going inside the trailer but decided against it. He didn't want to disturb any evidence that might be there and the missing car told him all he needed to know.

Once back at the car, he headed north on Interstate 15. The pavement was so clean that you would never have known it had snowed if it weren't for the mounds of white on either side of the road.

A little over an hour later, he pulled up in front of Alan Bowman's house in Great Falls. He hadn't called ahead for fear Alan would make certain not to be home. It was still early and, since Alan didn't have a job, he guessed he was sleeping. He was right. Tuper had to pound three times on the door to get him to answer.

"What do you want?" Alan asked when he finally opened the door. "I already told you everything I know."

Tuper stepped inside without an invitation, forcing Alan to take a step backwards.

"This'll only take a minute, but it's cold out there."

"What is it?"

"Did you ever meet a woman at Gordon's named Elizabeth?"

"Who's Gordon?"

"I mean Randy."

He shook his head. "No. I don't think so."

"How about Jan Murray?"

He sneered. "I met her a few times."

"I take it you didn't think much of her?"

"I don't know what kind of hold she had on Randy, but whatever it was, he was afraid of her."

"Were Randy and Jan having an affair?"

He laughed. "Far from it. She wanted to, but he loved Denise, and he wanted no part of Jan."

"So you don't think that when he had you take Mason, he was going to run off with Jan?"

"No," he said loudly. "That's why they did it, to get away from Jan."

"That's not what you told me before."

"Because that was the cover story. Since they are

both dead now, I guess it doesn't matter. Jan had something on both of them, and they wanted out. Mason was the only thing that Jan loved more than herself. They thought they could leave and she would stick around trying to find Mason, but then someone took Mason and everything got complicated."

"And they never mentioned anyone named Elizabeth, or Beth, or Liz?"

"Not that I recall."

~~~

Lana could never go without finishing a puzzle or reading a book she had started. This was no different. She was not satisfied that they had all the answers even though Mason was found. She had to know who killed Jessica and Gordon.

She started with a DMV search to see if Jan had another car, but the only vehicle registered to her was the black Kia. If Jan had borrowed another car from a friend, she would have no way of tracing it.

Lana delved into Jan's background, starting with her birth. Janette Marie Neff was involved in several sports through her teen years. She made the papers for being the first girl on the high school ice hockey team in her sophomore year. There was no record of her playing the next two years and she didn't graduate from that high school. She received her high school diploma from Montana Academy, a therapeutic boarding school in Marion, Montana. Lana wondered if Jan had a juvenile record, but that would take too long to hack. She would look later if she had time.

The next few years of Jan's life were easy to follow. Jan attended Helena College University of Montana, where she received a transfer degree in Interior Space Planning & Design, but she never transferred to another college. She was married the following summer to John Murray.

Wondering what happened to Mr. Murray, Lana continued to follow Jan's trail. "Shazam!" she said aloud to the empty room. Clarice and Mary Ann had both gone back to work and Tuper was still out being Tuper. When she shouted, Caspar came over to the table wagging his tail and looking for attention. She reached down and petted him. Then refocused on her task.

A half hour or so later, she yelled, "Yowza!" She became more and more animated as her search went on. By the time Tuper arrived, she was too excited to contain herself. "Wait'll you hear what I found out." She punched some keys. "That's it," she said. "That's it."

"What's it?"

"First of all, Jan doesn't own another car, so if she's telling the truth, she was using someone else's car. But I don't think she was telling the truth."

"Me either," Tuper said.

Lana kept talking. "Jan was in an institution when she was in high school, and her husband, John Murray, got an annulment only a few months after their wedding based on his claim that she was schizophrenic and had not disclosed it to him prior to their marriage."

"And that worked?"

"Apparently, but there was a lot more too. She also told him she was pregnant, but she wasn't, and then he claimed they never consummated the marriage after they were wed."

"So she slept with him before they were married, but not afterward?"

"Exactly, unless he lied, of course. But I think he told the truth. It all makes sense. I think that woman has a bug in her operating system."

"Her what?"

"Never mind. Where did you go anyway?"

"I went to the trailer Jan told me about. There were no cars there that were in running order. So, unless someone stole her car, she lied about being there."

"Now I'm confused again," Lana said. "Gordon knew Jan for a lot of years, so he must've known she was a whack job. Why would he plan to run off with her to mother his child?"

"He didn't. According to Alan Bowman, she had somethin' on Jessica and Gordon. He didn't know what, but I expect it was the whole illegal in vitro thing. He also said that Jan wanted to be with Gordon, but he and Jessica were planning to run away and leave her behind. They wanted her to believe the kid was gone, but then it all went sour when the kid got snatched."

CHAPTER FIFTY-EIGHT

"Hey, JP," Tuper said when he answered his phone.

"I got some information for you about those kids in Bonsall," JP said.

"Any of it good?"

"Some of it is."

"Just a sec. I'll put you on speaker so Agony can hear it." Tuper took the phone from his ear and looked at the face of it, but he couldn't remember which button to push.

"Give it to me," Lana said.

He handed it to her. She pushed a button and laid the phone on the table.

"Go ahead, JP," Tuper said.

"They arrested Joe and Grace Waters and charged them with numerous counts of kidnapping, both felony and misdemeanor child endangerment, child neglect, and one charge of felony murder. There was apparently a baby who died about five years ago because he needed medical attention that they weren't aware of."

"And the other kids?" Lana asked.

"They removed eight children from the home, ranging in age from ten months to eleven years, all boys. Joe Waters hasn't said a word, but when you ask Grace Waters a nickel question, she gives you a fifty-cent answer. She couldn't stop talking. She said that she wanted babies and he agreed as long as they were boys so they could work the farm. When they would reach a year or so old, they would take another one so she always had a baby."

"That's sick," Lana said. "Are the kids okay?"

"They're all pretty thin, but not really malnourished. They ate a lot of vegetables and fruit from the farm. That's probably what saved them. Some of them have broken bones that weren't treated and there's a lot of evidence of physical abuse. According to Grace, Joe beat them a lot. None of them have had an education. Grace did a little home schooling, but they are all seriously behind. They never left the farm except to go to church and they weren't allowed to speak to anyone."

"Have they identified any of them?" Lana asked.

"They're running DNA tests on all of them. Grace knew where each child had been kidnapped and the date. She used the date of the kidnapping as their birthday. So each child is a few days or months older than he thought he was. None of them ever had a birthday party, but on that day they could get away with a lot more and there was a house rule that Joe couldn't beat them on their birthday. If they did anything too bad, they would get it the next day." JP paused. "To answer your question, you were right about Aiden. He went missing the same day as one of the boys and Grace identified the location where he was taken. Also, the boy the Waters took had a crescent-shaped birthmark on his shoulder, just like Aiden. They haven't got the DNA test results back yet, but Aiden's parents are pretty hopeful."

"Thanks."

"Thank you. Without your stellar work, who knows how long those boys would have been imprisoned there."

"Just doing my job." She smiled at Tuper.

"Another thing," JP said. "They made an arrest on Dr. Melinda Richards' murder."

"Really?" Tuper said.

"Yes. Apparently, she had made a lot of enemies, botched a lot of pregnancies, and was using other people's embryos to implant in mothers when their own didn't work."

"So someone else came after her?" Lana asked.

"She had lots of threats, but she survived all that. The suspect raped and killed her. He had raped two others but this was the only one he murdered. The cops think she fought back and he killed her. He raped again after that, but the victim got lucky and was able to escape when her roommate came home. The rapist spooked, climbed out the window, and ran."

"Are they sure they have the right person?" Tuper asked, even though the rape put a new spin on Dr. Richards' murder.

"There's a lot of forensic evidence. They just didn't have anything to compare to until his last victim. They got him dead to rights now. I expect he'll take a plea."

"Thanks, JP," Tuper said. "I truly appreciate your help."

"Anytime you got an ox in the ditch, you let me know."

JP hung up.

"He sure says some strange stuff," Lana said.

"And you don't?" Tuper asked.

Lana ignored him and started searching for something on her laptop. After a few minutes, she looked up.

"Here's what we know. Jessica wanted a baby. She found Dr. Richards and legitimately paid her to run tests, but Jessica couldn't carry a baby to term. She met Gordon, fell in love, and they created a test tube baby, but she needed a surrogate mother. For some reason, she paid the rest under the table to the doctor, probably because they didn't have Elizabeth's consent, though she had somehow convinced Elizabeth to do it.

When she lost the baby, Elizabeth thought Jessica had stolen *her* baby.

"Then Jessica got Jan to be the surrogate, but Jan wanted to stay a part of the baby's life, which seemed okay at first. Jessica probably didn't know Jan was as crazy as she was. Then Jan fell for Gordon and wanted him and the baby. Jessica and Gordon found out but couldn't get rid of Jan, so they decided to fake a kidnapping, run away without Jan, and start over. But Elizabeth showed up and stole the kid from Alan as he was handing him over to Gordon. Jan probably saw Jessica go to Gordon's house and figured out what they were up to. She followed Elizabeth and Mason, but Elizabeth caught her and held her prisoner in the trailer." She paused. "And this is where it doesn't work for me, because you saw her car after that."

"That's right," Tuper said, "and her car would still be at the trailer."

"Jan said she convinced Elizabeth to move to the Neff home and that she didn't get away until this morning, when you caught her. She also said that Elizabeth came back there with blood on her coat."

"What's wrong with that?" Tuper asked.

Lana turned the laptop so Tuper could see the screen. "Look at this post on Jan's Facebook page from a couple of weeks ago. Jan's wearing the white coat."

"So? Elizabeth could have taken Jan's coat and wore it when she went out."

"Maybe," Lana said. "Do you have Jerome's phone number?"

"Yeah. You want me to call him?"

"No." She paused. "Yes, call him and tell him I'm going to text him two pictures. We need to know if Elizabeth was the woman he helped that night."

Lana already had a photo of Elizabeth on her

phone, and she downloaded one of Jan while Tuper was talking to Jerome. When he finished, he gave Lana the phone number. She sent both photos to Jerome, first the one of Elizabeth and then Jan with a text.

Lana: *Was either of these women the one you helped last night?*
Jerome: *Yes, the second one.*
Lana: *Are you certain?*
Jerome: *Absolutely.*

"We assumed it was Elizabeth who did the killing partly because we thought she killed the doctor," Lana said, "but now we know she didn't kill the doctor. Maybe she didn't kill anyone. I think Jan captured Elizabeth when she followed her, instead of the other way around."

"Which would explain why there is no car at the trailer. I wish I knew if it was the car with the cover in the garage."

"The car is probably wherever Jan found Elizabeth, but if that's the case, you wouldn't have seen the Kia at all. Unless Jan followed Elizabeth, took her and Mason hostage, and went straight to her parents' house. She could have driven either her car or Elizabeth's. At some point she had to have retrieved the other car."

"She probably didn't get a friend to take her to the car. That would be too risky."

"She probably took Uber."

"Who's Uber?"

"It's not a *who*. It's like a taxi service, but cheaper."

"Can you find out if she used Uber?"

"Probably."

"And where she took it?"

"Why not? But where are you going?"

"How do you know I'm going anywhere?"

"Because you're getting antsy. You always do that when you're ready to leave."

"I'm going to see Jan's neighbors."

CHAPTER FIFTY-NINE

Tuper knocked on several doors, getting no helpful information until he went to the house almost directly across the street from Jan Murray's house. The house had a big bay window and a good view of Jan's front yard and garage.

When the homeowner, Mrs. Craven, came to the door, Tuper introduced himself as Phil, the neighborhood watch guy checking on things after the storm.

"We're doing fine. Jeff, up the street, always plows the roads, and for a small fee will blow our driveways. Most of the neighbors use him so our street stays pretty clear."

"It's nice to have neighbors like that," Tuper said. "I was by early the morning after the storm and helped the young woman across the street shovel her driveway so she could take her son to his grandma's. She said her husband was ill and couldn't do it."

"You got took, mister, because she doesn't have a son or a husband."

"Well, why do you suppose she told me that?"

"Probably to get you to do the work. She's not a very friendly neighbor. And things have been a little strange over there the past few weeks."

"Really, how's that?"

"She has a female friend staying with her, but they come and go a lot all times of the day and night. Something's not right there."

"I saw she had a snowmobile. Does she use that a lot?"

"It's been sitting in her garage until just before this

storm hit."

"Is that right?"

"Remember, we had a pretty good snow the day before we got the big storm. That's when she came back here with her black car. She parked it in her garage and covered it up. Then she got on the snowmobile and took off. I haven't seen her since."

~~~

When Tuper returned to Clarice's, he shared what he had learned. "She did have her car with her, but she switched it out for the snowmobile when the weather got bad. But how did she get Elizabeth's car?"

"I know that one," Lana said. "She took an Uber from the Neffs' house to a cheap hotel on North Fee Street called the Baymont Inn & Suites in Helena. I called and spoke to the Uber driver and found out she was dropped off right by her car, a gold Honda. She got in it and drove off."

"The driver told you all that?"

"I told him I was his passenger, described what I looked like, and that I was wearing a big, furry, white coat. I took a chance with that one. Then I said I lost my purse and wondered if it was left in his car. When he said that it wasn't, I asked him what exactly I did there so I could retrace my steps. And he told me."

Tuper was impressed with her skills, which, of course he didn't tell her.

"And that means Jan could have killed both Gordon and Jessica," Lana said.

Tuper stroked his mustache. "If she'd a left right away once she had Mason, she would've gotten away clean."

"But she didn't, and I bet it's because she thought she could convince Gordon to go with her. That's why you saw her black Kia there. She probably saw more than that. She may have seen what we saw, Jessica and Gordon together, or at least figured out that they were together."

"Which is why Jan told me they were scheming to get away from Elizabeth."

"Exactly. She probably didn't mean to kill Gordon, but she definitely meant to kill Jessica. Jessica must have caught on because while Jan was gone, Jessica left Jan's house and moved into the Residence Inn. Jan came looking for her, killed her, and started back to her parents' house but got caught in the storm. That's when Jerome helped her. And since she couldn't go anywhere in that weather, she went back to her parents' house and waited until the storm lifted. And the rest is history."

CHAPTER SIXTY

"We need to go get that envelope that Jessica gave you," Lana said.

"*We* don't need to do anything." Tuper stroked his mustache.

"Come on. I know you're dying to see what's in that envelope, and I want to see your cabin. You said it was beautiful there and I'm tired of being cooped up."

"The cabin ain't beautiful. The view is."

Clarice entered the room. "It is a gorgeous view. You should take her along, Tuper. She needs a break from that machine." She nodded toward the laptop. "The sun has been shining for two days now, the roads are probably all clear, and I'd like to know what's in that envelope too."

Tuper put on his hat and grabbed his jacket. "I'm sure I'll live to regret this."

Lana didn't wait for him to change his mind. She had her coat, scarf, and hat on before he got to the door.

"Let's go, Ringo."

Ringo wagged his tail all the way to the door and on outside. He'd run forward about fifteen feet and then come back, and then do it again until they all reached Tuper's car. Tuper let him in the back seat. He pawed at the towel on the seat until he had the towel just like he wanted it, and sat down. Lana sat in the front.

Before they were out of the driveway, Lana started chatting. "What do you think is in the envelope?" She didn't wait for an answer. "Maybe Jessica tells us everything that happened; then we'll know for sure. Although I'm pretty sure it's just the way we figured it out. Besides, your cop friend said she confessed to 'accidentally' killing Gordon and that she doesn't remember killing Jessica. She remembered watching it like it was a movie, but she didn't know it was her doing it. She's going to be in the looney-bin a long time." Without taking a breath, she asked, "So, what do you think is in the envelope?"

"No idea."

"That's it? Not even a guess?"

"I don't guess."

"Well, I think it's going to be something we already know, like she and Gordon were trying to get away from Elizabeth and Jan. Or that she used a surrogate. Wait, Jessica said to make sure Mason ended up with family, but *she* doesn't have any family so she must be talking about Gordon's family." Lana checked her side mirror.

Tuper glanced at her but didn't say anything. Lana remained quiet for about three miles and then started again trying to guess what might be in the envelope. She kept it up until the turnoff at Clancy that led up the mountain.

A soft, white blanket of snow still covered the mountain but the roads had been plowed. "Wow, this is beautiful," Lana said.

"Ain't seen nothin' yet."

As they climbed, the beauty unfolded before their eyes. The tall, gorgeous fir trees lined the road. "Look, a deer," Lana called out. "It's so cute." She pointed ahead. "There's another one."

"Lots of those around. Too bad I don't have my rifle handy."

She ignored him.

Once the paved road ran out, the ruts were filled with snow. It had been plowed, but not professionally, and had been driven on by other cars for at least a day or two. They moved slowly along the bumpy, curvy road until Tuper turned off. After they drove about ten feet and made a slight curve, she could see the cabin.

"There it is. Home sweet home."

"You live *here*?"

"Not in the winter. It's too cold, but it's nice and peaceful in the summer." He stopped the car and stepped out, sinking about six inches into the snow. "Watch your step," he said.

Lana looked around in awe at the creek, the mountain, the valley. She stood there for about a minute just taking it all in. "It's amazing."

Tuper trudged on ahead and pushed the door open. She followed.

"The cabin ain't much, but I'm gonna be fixin' it up come spring." He planned every winter to fix it up in the spring, but spring always took on a life of its own. *Maybe this will be the year*, he thought.

He walked to the table and picked up the envelope and handed it to Lana. "Here you go."

"You want me to read it first?" Lana asked.

"You're more anxious than I am. Let's take it outside where there's more light and you can read it and tell me what it says."

Lana looked at him as if she understood more than he was saying. "Fair enough."

She opened the envelope as she left the cabin. It contained two single sheets of paper folded together, another single sheet folded separately, and another document with four sheets of paper folded together. She opened the large one first. "It's a 'Last Will and Testament' for Trinidad Jessica Andrade." She glanced down the first page. "Her name and state of residence. Here's something. She names Lenore Price Webster as her executor." She looked up from the document. "That's odd. According to Lenore, she never even met

Jessica, or at least she never met Gordon's girlfriend, who we now know was Jessica." She continued to peruse the papers. "She leaves all her possessions to Mason. And she names Lenore as Mason's guardian."

"When was the will written?" Tuper asked.

She looked at the date on the document. "Two days before she was killed."

Lana folded the will and stuck it back in the envelope. She took the two sheets that were folded together and opened them up. Each one was a copy of a birth certificate. "It looks like two birth certificates," Lana said, "but they're not stamped with the state seal, so they may never have been filed with the state. One is for Mason Gordon Price, which would explain why I didn't find it because it was never filed. The parents are Trinidad Jessica Andrade and Gordon Albert Price. The doctor is Dr. Melinda Richards and the birthdate is February 14."

Lana looked at the other birth certificate and furrowed her brow.

"What is it?" Tuper asked.

"This one is for Noah Gordon Price, born the same day to Jessica and Gordon." She looked back at the other certificate, compared the two, and then up at Tuper. "The box is checked for 'twins.'" Again she looked up. "She had twins?"

"What's on the other paper?"

Lana stuck the birth certificates back in the envelope and opened the folded single sheet of paper and read:

Please see that my boys are raised together. I've watched Lenore from afar. She's a good mother and the boys deserve to grow up knowing each other. Denise/Jessica

CHAPTER SIXTY-ONE

JP called Tuper as he pulled up in front of Lenore Price's house. "I'm meeting with Lenore in a few minutes. I have the copies of the birth certificates, the note, and the will you sent. Anything else I need to know before I meet her?"

"According to the detective on the case here," Tuper said, "Jan did give birth to two boys, but she thought one of them died. She knew she was pregnant with twins and she had convinced herself that she would get one of the boys."

"Jessica and Gordon probably thought she was too unstable to raise a kid. The question is, how much did Lenore know?"

"Right on."

JP rang the doorbell of the Price estate where Lenore had agreed to meet him. A tall man with a slightly gray, receding hairline, who appeared to be in his early fifties, answered the door.

"I'm Frank Webster, Lenore's husband. Please come in." JP followed him into the living room where Lenore sat in an armchair next to the sofa. "You know Lenore."

"Hi, ma'am. Nice to see you again."

A half-smile came across a terrified face.

"Please have a seat," Frank said. JP sat down in an empty armchair and Frank stood beside his wife.

"You said you had information about the circumstances of our son's birth and his birthparents," Frank said.

"That's correct."

"You mean Gordon?" Frank asked. Lenore just listened.

"That's right."

"But we already know that he is dead. What else do you know?"

"You may want to run DNA testing again, but we already did that and we know who his mother was."

"Was?"

"I'm afraid she's also dead," JP said. Then he handed them a copy of Noah's birth certificate. "We found this, but we don't believe it was ever recorded."

Frank looked at the document and then handed it to Lenore.

"Where did you get this?" Frank asked.

"His mother left it before she died," JP said.

"But why would Gordon leave Noah with me?" Lenore finally spoke.

"I was hoping you could tell us," JP said.

"He came to me and said he was leaving town and he would probably never return. He said he had a precious gift for me, something I had always wanted. He said he hoped it would make up for some of the distance between us. Then he took the baby out of the car and handed him to me. I tried to question him about whose child it was. He just kept saying it was his, but he couldn't keep him and I would know what to do. I told him I needed papers or something, but he just said there weren't any and that I should file whatever I needed to get legal custody of him."

"And you didn't know anything about how Noah came to be born?"

"I don't know what you mean. I had no idea Gordon had or was having a child."

JP explained about the in vitro and the surrogate mother, and then asked, "So, did you get legal papers?"

"Yes. It took us years, but we finally got guardianship of him. We want to adopt but so far we haven't been able to."

"Maybe that'll be easier now," JP said.

Lenore's eyes widened. "Noah's not the boy you were looking for when you came here before, right?"

"No, he wasn't."

"Did you find him?" Her voice got soft, as if she were afraid to ask.

"We did, and he's doing well."

Lenore sighed. "Thank God."

"That's the other thing I think you should know. It appears that Noah and Mason, the child who was missing, are twins."

Lenore gasped and Frank reached down and took her hand in his. "So Mason is Gordon's son?" Lenore said. "You weren't sure when you were last here."

"He was an in vitro baby as well and was born the same date as Noah by the same surrogate mother."

"Noah has a brother, a twin brother," Lenore said, looking up at Frank.

JP waited for a few seconds to let it sink in and then he said, "Mason is in the custody of the State of Montana and they're looking for relatives. If you're interested in having him, you may want to contact the authorities." JP handed them a piece of paper with the phone number for the social worker on Mason's case.

"Of course," Frank said. Lenore nodded and bit back tears.

JP gave them Jessica's will and the final note she wrote. "His mother wanted you to raise the boys together."

Lenore read the note and began to weep.

"I don't know what kind of a battle you'll have, but it's my understanding that Jessica doesn't have any living family. I'm sure the surrogate mother is going to be locked up for a while, either in a mental hospital or in prison, so CFSD in Montana is looking for family."

"We're not afraid of a fight," Frank said.

CHAPTER SIXTY-TWO

After a great deal of begging, Tuper took Lana to Donnie's to see his horses.

"Can we ride?" Lana asked.

"You know how?"

"You think I'm a city slicker or something?"

"Yup."

"Well, maybe I am, but I still want to ride."

"Have you ever been on a horse, besides the kind in front of Walmart?"

"I had a friend who had horses. We rode a couple of times when we were kids. Come on, let's go for a ride."

Tuper decided to humor her and saddled up Pepper for himself and Flipper, a sorrel gelding, for Lana. Flipper was gentle and easy to control. Tuper hoped he wouldn't be too much for Lana.

"Do you know how to mount?"

"From the rear, right?" She smiled.

"Yeah, you try that."

They brought the horses out of the barn. "Need some help?" Tuper asked, but before he got the question out, Lana had mounted and taken off. She was a natural.

When Tuper caught up to her, he said, "Okay, you know how to ride, but you don't know the terrain, so stick with me." They rode on across the fields that only had spots of snow remaining. The snow-capped mountains lingered in the distance. Tuper watched Lana's face as they rode. She seemed happier and more at peace than he had ever seen her. She wasn't such a bad kid, and she sure knew her stuff on that machine, but that's about all he really knew about her, which was about as much as she knew about him.

~~~

Lana was quieter than usual on her way back to Clarice's. Although he was pretty sure he would regret it, Tuper asked, "What are you going to do now?"

"With my life?"

"Yeah."

She checked the side mirror before she answered. "Clarice said I could stay with her until I can get my own place. She got me a job at Nickels setting up a website for him. She said she knows a few others who might need one as well. She said she could teach me to tend bar, but I'm not sure I'd be very good at it. I don't want to take advantage of her hospitality either, so if I don't get more computer work, I'll probably try the bartender gig."

When Lana checked the mirror again, Tuper said, "I don't know who you're running from or hiding from, and I ain't gonna ask 'cause it's none of my business. But if you ever need my help, let me know."

Lana looked at Tuper. Her mouth opened as if she was going to deny it, but then she just nodded and said, "Thanks, Pops, I will."

About the Author

Teresa Burrell has dedicated her life to helping children and their families. Her first career was spent teaching elementary school in the San Bernardino City School District. As an attorney, Ms. Burrell has spent countless hours working pro bono in the family court system. For twelve years she practiced law in San Diego Superior Court, Juvenile Division. She continues to advocate children's issues and write novels, many of which are inspired by actual legal cases.

If you liked Tuper, you can find him in The Advocate's Felony, book #6 of Teresa Burrell's THE ADVOCATE SERIES. If you liked JP, he is all throughout THE ADVOCATE SERIES.

Teresa Burrell is available at www.teresaburrell.com
Keep in touch with her on Facebook at
www.facebook.com/theadvocateseries

What did you think about
MASON'S MISSING?
Please send an email to Teresa and let her know.
She can be reached at:
teresa@teresaburrell.com

If you like this author's writing, the best way to compliment her is by writing a review and telling your friends.

OTHER BOOKS BY TERESA

THE ADVOCATE SERIES

THE ADVOCATE
(Book 1)

THE ADVOCATE'S BETRAYAL
(Book 2)

THE ADVOCATE'S CONVICTION
(Book 3)

THE ADVOCATE'S DILEMMA
(Book 4)

THE ADVOCATE'S EX PARTE
(Book 5)

THE ADVOCATE'S FELONY
(Book 6)

THE ADVOCATE'S GEOCACHE
(Book 7)

THE ADVOCATE'S HOMICIDES
(Book 8)

Made in the USA
Columbia, SC
17 June 2021